THE PORTAL TRAITOR

WRITTEN AND ILLUSTRATED

BY A.V. WEMBLEY

For Janice

Copyright © 2021 A.V.Wembley

All rights reserved.

ISBN:9798729908608

This book is dedicated to my wonderful friends Tanner Griffin, Torie Griffin, and Alivia Hunter for giving me the support and motivation I needed to finish this project. Also to my editor Stirling Myles, who I am always... grateful... for...

CONTENTS

1	1
2	Pg 16
3	Pg 26
4	Pg 35
5	Pg 48
6	Pg 55
7	Pg 58
8	Pg 63
9	Pg 77
10	Pg 83
11	Pg 91
12	Pg 101
13	Pg 107

14	Pg 114
15	Pg 124
16	Pg 133
17	Pg 146
18	Pg 152
19	Pg 159
20	Pg 166
21	Pg 174
22	Pg 182
23	Pg 188
24	Pg 192
25	Pg 202
Epilogue	Pg 205
Appendix i	Pg 207
Appendix ii	Pg 212

In Ninth sector Dashan, your story is all you have. A person may be unremarkable as a whole, but as long as he has something to teach, he will live on. He will live not only in the portal fluid that binds dimensions together but in lessons and mythos that children of the sand will learn for generations to come. A story is a valuable thing to have, especially for someone like me who has nothing else to their name.

Now I fear that I will lose my story as well. After being stripped of my dignity, my heritage, and maybe even my faith, I'm afraid I have no choice but to try and save what I know I do have at my disposal.

So please, listen. If all goes as I think it will, you won't have to for long.

I would've never guessed that while picking up the week's rations, that Dark was soon to take me. I wasn't stupid not to suspect that, as Dark-related incidents were seemingly on the decline in our sector, and I, nor anyone around me, had suffered any hardship.

When Darkness is present, you can never predict what will happen because that's just Dark's whole thing. It feeds on and revels in pain, suffering, and loss. It's almost the very embodiment of those things. I had never even seen a Dark Supporter up close until the day I became one.

Unwillingly, of course. But no one believes me. No one ever does. You'd believe me even less if I were to say that even if Dark takes you, your heart can still lie with Light; because mine does.

I ought to retell the whole thing. Maybe then someone will understand what I'm trying to get across.

None of this is my fault.

Things just happen for no good reason, whether you want them to or not. Sure, I've made mistakes while trying to regain my footing, but does that make me a monster? Does that mean I no longer deserve to be a child of Light?

I want to show that a person who does something bad and a "bad person" isn't always the same thing. I should know.

If not for Dark, the day all this mess started would have been a day of fairly regular chores, but one I much preferred to others: the day my mother and I cooked and prepared our food for the week.

I took the bushel of fruits in my arms, shifting them to sit comfortably. One of the Farmer's Guild leaders, a ground elf by the name of Yera, spotted me as I did so.

"You got it, Guno?" Her voice was cautious, her wide eyes shifting to me, then back to the load in my arms. "Wouldn't want you spilling your pay on the way home. Do you need a bit of rope or something to tie them together?" I nodded, a bit shallow with the weight I was carrying.

"Alright, just a sec." Yera's small figure disappeared under the shade of the rations shed for a few moments. She returned with a bit of cord and set it over her shoulder as she took the fruits gingerly from my grasp. I wiped some sweat from my brow, taking the moment of rest.

Yera was half my height but extremely strong even at her small Ground Elven stature. She set the fruits in the dirt and fastened them together with a few tight knots. On the ground, the leathery fruits reached up to her neck. She held them out for me.

"Oh, thanks." She was right; the fruits were much easier to carry tied up. "See you tomorrow." She waved goodbye, and I started away toward my cottage. It was unfortunate the farming district and my place were on opposite sides of the village. The amount I walked every day showed, as my skin had grown darker and my feet more calloused since I began to work there. At least, as I was walking, my hood could protect my eyes from the harsh desert sun.

Dashan must be a peculiar place to other dimensions. It's a land with separated cities, protected by rings of mountains which they hid inside, with long stretches of nothing but sand in between. Well, sand and Limbers. The Limbers, they would have to be the strangest of all. They were undeniably unique creatures, with their spindly legs, leathery skin, and beady eyes that shine out from their towering forms like holes poked in a piece of parchment. Terrifying things- yet close to home for all citizens. I was drifting away in my thoughts on the walk, the chatter of sellers, children, and other villagers blurring together into one steady hum by the time I reached my home.

I finally came to the front porch, dropping my fruits with less care than I probably should've. I shook out my arms and opted for dragging the fruit inside instead of carrying it.

"Mama?" The sound of my call fell dead inside the cottage. No answer. She said she'd be home. Had she gone out to buy something?

Maybe. I scanned the house again. For some reason or another, the silence was almost suffocating as I brought my load inside and heaved it onto the little table beside the furnace. My muscles, untrained for heavy lifting, sighed in relief as I leaned over the table to catch my breath.

I set aside my suspicion over the silence to search the cottage. Something about that quiet just wasn't right. I was used to a lot of noise when I came home- the shuffling of my mother painting, repairing clothes, or humming along to music in the square outside.

But there was none of that. Even the bustle outside seemed to have gone mute. My footsteps, even, didn't make as much commotion as they should have. Something was occupying all the space where the sound should've been.

My eyes swept the main room, and that was when I caught my first glimpse of it. A viscous-looking black substance, slowly crawling in from the kitchen. Its traverse across the wood slats of the floor made my stomach curdle. If I didn't see correctly, I might've mistaken the black substance as a simple shadow, a trick of the light. I could've even thought it was some deep chasm opening up in the floor, if not for the slight shine off the top of it. Despite being thick, it was far from stagnant, pooling across the floor at a concerning pace.

"Uh... anyone home?" My voice cut through the silence once again. I crept closer despite my mounting fear, despite the gaps in the floor being filled in with the darkness. I gathered myself enough to look into the kitchen.

I don't know what I had expected. Perhaps some part of me always thought this would happen. It was the sort of thing kids in Dashan were prepped for their entire lives, but seeing my mother dead in person felt a lot different than I could've ever imagined.

There wasn't room for confusion when the wave of shock hit. I stood there for quite a while in the doorway, likely for hours. As I did, the darkness continued to seep around my feet, and I watched how still my mother was. The cavity in her chest, a place where blood or something human should've been, had been completely taken over by this same substance clinging to the soles of my feet. The worst part was how content my mother's face seemed to be as she was left there on the ground with this darkness consuming her. I could only imagine it was the sinister work of someone in His order. A Dark supporter. An evil creature who lived to serve the very embodiment of suffering Himself, the force that strung together every murder and robbery and betrayal and abandonment in Dashan.

* * *

Shaking, my hands came to cup my mother's face, pushing away her grey curls that so closely mirrored mine. All was still but this darkness that I was kneeling in. It burnt my skin worse than a fever. My head fell into the crook of her neck. I let everything blur into one: my sobs into her body, which I could've sworn was still warm, and the Dark water leaking from my mother's wound, threatening to swallow the both of us.

Would it be ironic if I were to wish death upon her attackers, despite what I was taught? If I were to bottle up my sorrow and rage and let it out upon whoever chose to do this? Would I be just as bad as them?

I was being foolish, I audibly told myself.

Just as Light opens paths for us, she can tear them away just as quickly.

I was told to accept it with benevolence. But what if I didn't want to? What if I'd changed my mind?

I gripped onto the front of my mother's tunic, my body aching with fervor as I'd never felt. If I kept crying, would I eventually come apart too? The idea didn't seem so bad. I didn't care that this black stuff seeped between my fingers and covered my face and neck as I clutched desperately at her shirt, feeling for something other than this damned burning.

It was nearly sundown when I felt any change from the awful irritation that never seemed to cease. There was a light tap on my back; I held my mother closer as I tensed, turning my wide eyes upon a figure I didn't even see enter—a woman in a deep cloak.

I could have sworn she was death itself. The woman's face was gracefully hidden by shadow in the dwindling light from the windows. I didn't move. I could only stare like a startled animal, feeling my tears mix with the ichor on my cheeks. If I hadn't already been so filled with sorrowful rage, her presence would've been enough to get me there. She seemed to radiate the same burning feeling already shaking me to my bones. A feeling that kept me on edge, every muscle of mine itching to pounce against its own will.

This wasn't grief, was it? No. It couldn't be.

"What an untimely demise for your poor mother." The woman standing over us cooed, her crimson-gloved hands folding in front of her as she pulled them out from under the cloak. "How old was she?"

I didn't say anything. I wanted to be left alone.

No. I wanted to retaliate. I couldn't decide what I wanted. I felt as if my sorrow and rage were competing for dominance - my brain running rapidly in every direction.

* * *

"You're right. It doesn't matter much, does it." The woman said. I had a suspicion that her soft, caring tone wasn't genuine. "But I know what does matter. Your *freedom*."

I squinted up at her. How would a creature of evil like her know what freedom meant? How would she even have the *right* to know? I gritted my teeth, emitting a low growl.

"Leave me alone," was all I could manage. I could make out a smile creeping across her darkened face. She shook her head in a pitying manner.

"Is that *really* what you want?" She asked in a voice that lilted softly, "To be left alone? You do know that this was bound to happen, right? You're lucky it happened while you were already an adult. What are you, twenty-four?"

That remark had been something I was already beating myself with long before she'd even entered the house. To admit that I was grieving even a little at this age would have taken years of effort on my own. Had it been anyone else here with me, I would have denied it. However, this figure had my best interests in mind. She echoed my thoughts perfectly. That scared me, but it wasn't enough to offset the eerie sense of ease that her presence brought.

I nodded, my lip quivering. She knelt beside me, tenderly pulling a stray curl of hair out of my eyes and tucking it behind my ear.

"You poor thing." She sounded like she meant it that time. "You deserve so much more... you *deserve* that freedom you want so badly." She didn't seem to mind the Dark substance coating the floor beneath our feet. She let her cloak hang in it. I finally let my hands slip away from my mother's body.

"I'll tell you what: I can get you out of here, and I can help you get out all that *anger* you have inside."

"Who are you?" I whispered as her hand came to touch my chest.

"I'm glad you asked." The woman stood up, extending a hand encased in silk. "I am a sort of interdimensional mediator. I sense the woes in others, especially those here in Dashan."

It seemed reasonable at the time. I didn't think about how I'd never heard of those so-called "Mediators" before, ever. I was completely enraptured by how she made me feel welcome in my newfound rage.

Maybe this is how it's supposed to feel, I thought. It certainly felt right, in a way. It at least made more sense than the muddied, confusing mixture of feelings I had before the woman arrived.

"My job is to help them gain the ability to travel and have independence, either through portal devices or other means." The cloaked lady continued, pulling me to my feet and giving me a hearty pat on the back. I was surprised she was a good bit shorter than I was, and being a Dashaner at only six feet tall, I lacked in height myself.

"What do I have to do? To get free." I asked feebly. I swayed on my feet from my weak knees. I would have insisted I were fine if not for the fact that the woman held out her arms to spot me. She would have known I was lying before the words even left my mouth. She lowered her arms slowly back to her sides as I glared into the shadow of her hood. The details became even more obscure the harder I tried- except for her rouged lips curling into a smile. She went to grab my wrist. I ripped my hand away.

"Ah- my apologies- ah... follow me." The woman said curtly, turning on a heel to leave. My gaze moved back down to my mother's body. I knelt one last time, closing her eyes and pressing three fingers to my forehead...

You will be missed; I told her from somewhere deep in my mind. For a moment, it felt as if she listened; acknowledged my respects. It was enough, but something inside me still craved repentance. I could cry as much as I wanted, but in the end, *someone* had to pay for this. Maybe this woman was just the answer I needed.

I met the cloaked lady by the door.

"I know who killed your mother," She said, her back facing me. "And I know how you can right the wrongs that have occurred. Get your peace. Then leave." She turned partially over her shoulder. I could make out a curl of straw-blonde hair peeking from under her hood. "All you need to do is end the life of the man who ended hers. It'll be so simple." She opened the front door. Instinctively, I grabbed my walking stick kept by the cottage's entrance: a memento once kept by my father and had since been passed down to me. My bones shook with anguish and rage. I knew I'd do anything at that point.

"How. How do I do it? And how will you get me out of here?" My question was followed by a low, silky laugh that emitted from the woman. The sound only prodded at me and stoked the fire in my stomach. I clicked with distaste at the sting.

"Here. Just take these." Her glove again extended from her cloak, this time holding out a small cloth pouch. I took it with hesitance. "There are coins inside to give your mother's killer. Coins laced with a powerful poison. If you want to live, open the bag and turn it over onto the table, but do not touch the coins."

"And how does this help me get out of here?"

"Your mother's killer is the baker of this town. He's a vile man. He's been causing disruption all-around your village, your neighbors have told me. Robbings, false promises, murders - He's made a practice of it, I've been informed." She opened the front door and stepped outside, waiting for me to follow. "Not only will you avenge your mother, but you will have done a *great service* to your village. So much so that I'm willing to provide you with a portal device, as is part of my civic duties."

"Wait- really-" I almost slammed the door in my haste to get outside—a portal device... *the stuff of dreams.*

It was a thing every Dashaner wanted and a thing few of us could afford. Portal devices used the power of Light to open portals to any dimension. It was a source of unlimited travel. So, of course, they came at a very lofty price, especially since they were bound to one's own Brightness and were specially fit to conform to that person's energy.

The woman's cloak had put me on edge, but portal devices were exclusively a tool of Light, only made by other Light supporters. The cloaked woman couldn't possibly be a Dark supporter, I reasoned.

"This device can get you out of here, away from Limbers, away from the creatures that hide in the sand, out to get you... away from those dreadful Dark Supporters and horrible people like the baker," Her grin widened. " Am I *wrong about that?*"

I shook my head.

She wasn't wrong, but I didn't say so. I shrugged my shoulder so that I could wipe my tears on the sleeve of my tunic and shook my head. I sniffled and continued past her.

"I'll do it," I said. I started into the street with little regard to anything besides my direction as I stumbled down my front steps, veering past villagers left and right.

I approached a crowded part of town. With a raw throat, I screamed into the crowd with indistinct ramblings and howls that made no sense, even to me. They didn't then, and they wouldn't now. I'd find the cloaked woman back at my doorstep once I was done, and she'd get me out of here. She would be the answer, that I was sure.

My pace began to slow. I ran right into a lady holding a basket of clothes, and she didn't move an inch. I blinked, shivering with another unnerving sob. She was completely still as I tried to shake her with my Dark-covered hands. The stimulating heat was everywhere now - in the air, humming beneath my feet and ringing in my ears.

• • •

Chest heaving, I looked around. To my immediate dread, everyone else stood dead in place. I noticed just now how the stifling silence in my cottage had now rolled out throughout the entirety of the town. Even at the most distant point I could see on this street; there wasn't a movement or sound. Even the creatures for sale down the lane had stopped their thrashing in little cages with their beady eyes and dangerously sharp tails. I turned further and was tossed to the ground. I cried out and shifted wildly in the sand. I could just make out the woman standing above me. *How did she catch up?*

"Whoa there, boy, don't be so eager," She laughed. My hands dug into the sand, and as they flexed, I could've sworn there was more Dark substance on them. The sand clung to wherever it coated my skin. Nevertheless, I reached for my staff that I'd tossed to the ground, trying to rouse that frozen lady. It was just out of my reach. I stood to get it, but I was thrown right back to the ground again.

"*-Uff!*" I couldn't tell if it was from the sheer rage in me, or all the crying or the breath getting knocked out from it, but the sharp ache in my chest was only encouraging this heat.
A heel dug into my back, pushing me further into the sand. I squirmed beneath it. After the last push, she let me go, and I scrambled to look up at her. Still, somehow, even outside, I couldn't see her face.

"You can't be so quick to carry this out. What about the patrollers? You're going to have to plan your escape. How fast can you run?" I didn't consider that all of the civilians around us had been frozen in place, likely due to *her* doings. I was too baffled by the act alone to make any moves, but the patrollers were a concern of mine for sure.

"T-they- they're..."

"Frozen. Yes." The woman pulled her hood further over her face. "It's a power we have, and one you can easily gain. A power that can grant you freedom without a cost, without the need for money like a portal device would and without the need for maintenance."

Her voice was one of honeyed grandeur, even as she kicked me into the ground. "All you need to do is a bit of training. And I know just the thing to get you started- but now, you need to carry out your duty. Then you need to *run*. Do you hear me?"
There was nothing I could do from that point but listen to her. I nodded rapidly, feeling my heartbeat against the sand, my stomach and bare forearms beginning to sting against the heat of it.

• • •

I sat there on the ground as I watched her walk away, feeling more tears slide over my nose and down my cheeks. At least they eased the burning in my face.

Decisively, I stood, trying to use my staff to support me. As I did, the town quickly returned to motion. I stumbled backward before catching my footing. I hadn't noticed someone approaching me until I heard a voice speak up. I had to blink and rub my eyes before I could tell who it was.

"Guno! Did ya drop this?" It was Cypress. He was a half-ground elf, which gave his features the signature pointedness, and his body its spindly but spry nature. He would often knock on my door until my mother would answer, only to chicken out and bolt away half the time. The other times, he would call upon me to race across town. Cypress usually won.

My eyes trailed down to the thing he was holding: a bag of coins. I felt my blood run cold. "Oh- thanks, yeah, I did." I took the pouch from him and pocketed it, stealing a glance behind me. The woman had vanished. I furiously wiped my eyes with a sniffle, attempting to hide my hands.

"Hey, did you hear the announcements recently? The Light and Portal Ball is coming up. Imagine if we got a ride and went to the capital! I wouldn't be against a dance with the prince, that's for sure. You alright, buddy?"

I blinked and returned my attention to him. "Prince. Yes. What's his name again?"

"Ha! You're too much, Guno."

"I'm not joking-" I make a purring, clicking intonation at the back of my throat. This was a habit I'd picked up at a young age trying to impersonate calls in the pet market and a noise I made instinctively ever since.

"In that case, I definitely won't remind you." He began to jog away, still chattering. "..Figure it out on your own. It'll be an adventure! A quest! I believe in you! The power of Light will bring it fresh into your mind." I watched him bounce along for a moment before turning away to start toward the bakery. Cypress would often regale me with wild fantasies of what he imagined castle life to be like. More often than not those dreams included the prince. I was always glad to listen and indulge him, but I myself was never one for dreaming. The capital was far away, atop a cluster of mountains. There was no way to leave the city limits and travel there without hiring a sand drifter, which was only used for taking criminals to the sector's prison, or on the rare occasion, how the guards from the capital searched the cities.

We barely hear from the capital, especially if there's a problem. Sometimes I wonder what the Capital folks even do. They're not obligated to attend to any problems that matter, so do they just relax? Play chess? Mess about with the imports from other dimensions so advanced we have no clue what to do with them?

I knew the prince's name; I just didn't feel like encouraging Cypress. My good friend, along with countless others around my age, would relentlessly go on about him- Prince Rengas Averell, Son of Light, heir to the sector. He was the one kicking up his feet with a cup of exotic Earth tea while all of us writhed under Dark's relentless grip. It didn't do any good to fawn over him. The fact he was considered painfully attractive wouldn't fix that I'm being followed around by a Dark supporter.

But I can't judge. I've never felt an attraction toward anyone. Maybe the prince made a compelling argument to those who do feel that type of way.

All I wanted to do was turn around and see my mother.

Everyone seemed much too calm. Undisturbed. Had they not seen? Had they never heard me cry? I continued to walk in the direction of the bakery, though my pace slowed. I would have thought any exclamation I made could have caused a ruckus... people like to say I'm reserved. I don't see any use projecting my problems on others, is all. We've all had our hardships. I'm not gonna put mine above anyone else's. *But this.* I believe it's fair to say this counted for something.

I arrived at the bakery. It was the only one in our small village. The family running it had been doing so for many generations without a change in location, so the structure, though cozy, needed some repair. I let myself inside, and I could almost feel the warmth of that woman's presence. It made the hair on the back of my neck stand on end.

"Ah, it's Lamplight's boy! Nice to see you again," The baker, a father of six, greeted me full-heartedly, addressing me by my surname. "Just doing weekly errands, I presume?"

"Yes. I wish I had a more exciting occasion, but I'm afraid it'll just be some bread."

"What kind? How many?"

"Er, two loaves. Standard. Thank you." I went for my usual order if I were to buy bread for the week. It was deeply upsetting to think that if all went according to plan, the order itself wouldn't matter anyway. I feigned ignorance for a long moment, shifting my weight back and forth. I hoped he didn't notice the black slime on my hands that I attempted to wipe off my pants.

The baker took the loaves from the back shelf, wrapped them, and set them down on the counter. I faltered after my hand grabbed the satchel in my pocket, but I quickly shoved down my worries to open the bag, overturning and emptying it onto the counter just as I had been told. I looked them over and counted them in my head. It was just enough for what I had ordered, and the coins didn't look out of place or foreign in the slightest; just thin copper discs an inch across, with the Dashan emblem and the number nine engraved in each. He took the coins, and I took my bread. Everything was going smoothly until I pushed the front door open.

The isolated sound of weight hitting the floor. I knew what it meant immediately but somehow couldn't believe it was true.

I whirled around to see the baker no longer standing behind the counter. I dropped the bread, rushed back to the counter, and peered over it with a heavy feeling in my stomach. I ought to help, right? I couldn't have done this. *Not me.* It couldn't have been me who stopped his heart so suddenly. This was that woman's doing. I didn't have that sort of power, I told myself.

Her plan was working smoothly in all of the worst ways.
I had let the woman take another life. She wasn't a mediator at all, was she? *She was a monster*, just like all the rest of Dark's army. I was stupid to have gone soft. Once I heard footsteps from behind the counter, I took the opportunity to flee the scene, throwing the door open just as I heard the baker's wife cry out.

I did as I was told and ran, maneuvering down the crowded streets. My heart was racing so fast that if it went any faster, I was sure I'd get overstimulated and keel over like a startled rodent.

I could still feel the Dark lady near me. What was she doing standing around? The droning sirens began, and I assumed the person who had seen me in the bakery must have called the patrollers. If they caught me, I was dead immediately. I started to scream. I called to nothing, and my hands started to heat again. That Dark feeling.

"What are you doing! I'm gonna die like this! Can't you freeze time again or whatever in Light's name you do!" Something in me activated as I heard patrollers shouting commands in the distance. The shifting Dark feeling crept up my arms along with all my anger, my grief, my regrets. It was pushing down into my feet, too. Now I

seemed to travel at some miraculously accelerated pace despite my own capacity for such. People blurred by, and eventually, I could only concentrate on this Darkness inside me and the steady beat of my bare feet on the earth.

There was something jet black racing through the crowd. It wasn't natural. It was too clean and much too shiny. It imitated life but had none of the heavy sounds or rusted metallic qualities that came with being a machine.

Civilians screamed and scattered in its wake, but the patrollers were still advancing. Both were closing in from either side.

The machine's wheels stirred a cloud of dust from the earth as the machine screeched to a stop only ten feet or so in front of me. The side of it opened to reveal a similarly clean interior.

"Come on, boy!" It's the Dark supporter woman. She was sitting inside, along with someone else. There was an open spot, so I dove inside before I could think of anything else. The door slammed behind me almost miraculously. The vehicle -or whatever it is I was inside- started to move. It was dizzying in the way it moved, going much too smoothly for something that went so fast. As it began to accelerate, I watched my town disappear out the back window: patrollers, who had previously been pursuing me, continued to pour from seemingly every crevice between buildings, running helplessly at our vehicle like a swarm of flighty birds. When we passed the city limit, they completely stopped.

Even patrollers are afraid of what waits in the Farlands. Even patrollers are wise enough to be afraid. I hoped the machine structure we were in would be sturdy enough not to give in if a Limber or another creature were to attack.

I eventually turned around in the leather seat I was in to face forward. By now, all I could see in all directions was deep amber sand: gentle hills, a mountain here and there, and maybe a town in the distance- recognizable only by a ring of mountains that would protect it from any desert creatures.

I wondered, leaning against the window, if these Dark supporters were going to take me to another dimension. With my mother gone, I had nothing but my staff and the clothes and bandages on me. I did have something new, though: it was this strange rage that began to brew inside me with the hooded woman's appearance. That, and hope. The hope that wherever I was going would be better than home.

It was every young Dashaner's dream to leave. To travel to some other distant dimension, a place where you could take a trip out of town without getting eaten alive or even dying from the heat before something could come to eat you.

As a child, stories about other dimensions were ridiculously popular. Stories of lavish places with cool temperatures, shining pools of water, and even shinier clothing. All the dimensions in folk tales were safe and full of luxury, providing hope to a child that felt all was inevitable as soon as they came into existence.

To be truthful, at that young age, some things *can* be inevitable- but it's good to let a child dream. My friends and I used to pick our favorite dimensions. We would design our ideal lives there; what our professions would be, perhaps what our alien hybrid children, husbands, or wives would look like. We'd discuss our portal devices, what they would look like if we were to get one, and how they'd work. I always said my portal device would be my father's staff.

Some children were insistent on their allegiance to Dashan and the 9th sector as a nation. When Cypress and his wild soul, when we were only thirteen, said, "When I leave, good riddance to the Limbers! I never want to see their shining eyes ever again." It was met with a few gasps of incredulousness. I remember an adult nearby scolding him, telling the boy it was "Disrespectful to speak like that." and to "Keep in mind the balance, even including the Dark of limbers."

And I understood at the time. Limbers are sacred. But even if they are, that doesn't change the fact they pose a threat to everyone's safety.

I hadn't taken into account that there could be *worse* dimensions than ours. That wherever we were going could well be more dangerous than Dashan ever was.

I didn't know whether my wildest dreams were coming true or if this was the end for me.

We drove for long enough to where even the capital was nowhere to be seen. Though every minute stuffed inside the shell of this machine with these two women heightened my senses and made every inch of my skin crawl, I had to lay low. It would be safest to keep my head. If I lashed out, it would only get me killed quicker. My hands reached for my hair, pulling it out of its pigtails and into my face in chunks.

"What's your name, kid?" One of their voices piped up, making me jump. It seemed to be coming from the one operating the machine we were in. I could see her hands turning a sort of wheel, but they were mostly obscured by the back of her head, with its sleek hair that hung nearly to her waist. She and the dark supporter woman both had a sort of calmness and professionalism in their movements that could only suggest they'd done this many times before.

"Uh, It's-" My hands had returned to holding the staff in my lap, and at this point, they'd gone slick with sweat. "Cypress. Cypress Cadler." My voice was course and timid. It must've been so obvious this wasn't the truth because both of the figures in the seats in front of me erupted into laughter. The driver's was carefree to the point where it was obnoxious, and the hooded one's was unsurprisingly haughty.

"Cypress! You could at least pick a more *flattering* name." The hooded Dark supporter leaned back in her seat and finally let down the hood of her cloak to reveal herself. "Cypress. Pathetically Dashan. You'd never hear a name like Cypress anywhere else, would you?"

She turned her head slightly, smirking with the brightest red lipstick I'd ever seen. She was nice to look at in some twisted way. She was certainly paler than anyone I'd seen, and her hair shined a light yellow. It was in perfect ringlets that framed her face, and her bangs making a thick curtain covering both of her eyes.

The woman with black hair had large, dark-tinted glasses that reached past her eyebrows. Maybe I was just paranoid, but something told me this wasn't a simple coincidence. It was probably a Dark supporter thing unless it was some un-Dashanly custom.

The woman with black hair scowled, baring her fangs at me and scrunching up her pointy nose while still looking at the desert ahead of her. "Ya gonna answer her? It isn't polite to ignore people while they're speaking."

I pull my staff closer to me with unease. There was nothing to say. I'd made a terrible lie, and she'd detected it right away. No way in the Afterdull was I going to be obedient when they'd just killed my mother. I didn't know what she'd expected.

I needed to find a way out. Maybe if I jumped out of the machine and landed well enough, I wouldn't be too hurt. Maybe I'd sprain or break something, but that was honestly worth it.
I couldn't decide what to do. Leave and return to my old life, with the possibility of getting ripped limb from limb on the walk there, or stay in this odd machine with two strange witches- one my mother's killer- and spend my days on the roam in possibly a safer dimension?

I spent what felt like hours seething in the backseat, my heart slamming against the outside of my chest, tempting to break out completely. I hated this. I hated the witches before me. I felt more hate than I had ever experienced at once, more hate than when my

⁎ ⁎ ⁎

childhood best friend left me to rot, more hate than when my father did the same, more than every loss and embarrassment I could gather. This was hate that craved violence like its very life depended on it. You would think after all the trauma I had just experienced, violence was the very last thing I would want. And still, something left me wanting more.

The two witches were muttering things to one another under their breaths, glancing back at me now and again. I didn't know what they were searching for, since they certainly weren't concerned for my well-being.

Fortunately, the uncomfortable silence didn't last much longer. The two women looked at one another and lowered their heads. The driver with the glasses turned forward and tensed. The golden-haired one gently placed her hand on the other's arm and the other on the machine's wall. I could feel my eyes go wide as the windows were overtaken with darkness... Darkness so deep that it blocked out everything, and once the windows were obscured, I could sense it had swallowed us whole. The shadows and intricacies of it curled around my middle, pulling me into a warm embrace. Like the feeling I had previously, it held all this buzzing energy and an insatiable hunger for action. For a while, I could see and feel nothing but this. Then I, along with the machine and the women, was in another place altogether. I could tell only because now I could feel again and make out shapes beyond the darkness. It had gone brighter, but only by comparison. I knew only one thing for certain: It wasn't Dashan.

We came to a quick stop. I let out a hiss as my head slammed into the seat in front of me.

"Watch it!" I was thumped on the head by the blonde witch. I slumped back to clutch at my head while it throbbed. As my eyes came back into focus, I could start to make out more shapes, big and small, skulking outside my window. Most of them moved at an unsettlingly slow pace. I hardly noticed that the two witches were moving much quicker. They'd already left the car. I started to fumble with buttons and things on the door of the vehicle. I found a handle that worked and jerked the door open. As I did, I was immediately seized by the two, who came around the back of the car and snapped metal bindings around my wrists.

"Where are we?" I managed, feeling if I said too much I would regret it. Best to follow along until I found an opening to escape.

The blonde witch took me by the shoulders and started leading me away from the car and toward the middle of a wide road only occupied by people and other creatures. I squirmed as things brushed against my legs and recoiled every time I stepped in something slimy with my exposed feet, which only made her grip on me tighten. When I cast a panicked glance to my right, I could see the witch with the dark glasses trailing behind us, a cigarette between her teeth and my staff in her hands... I felt my stomach turn. Hopefully, she would return it to me.

"When exactly will I get my portal device?"

"Once you defeat an opponent I have set out for you." The woman holding me said.

"But, you promised!"

"I promised nothing. I'm doing you a favor by training you. Don't you wish to avenge your mother?"

Did I want to avenge my mother?

I wasn't entirely sure, or at least I hadn't been before, but the more I thought about it and let the familiar warmth of Dark regain a hold on my limbs, on my heart... I knew for certain my answer.

● ● ●

"Yes," I muttered, "More than anything." I didn't consider that the witch who restrained me was the cause - she was the target, the one I should take it all out on. I didn't care who would pay for her death. It could be anyone, for Light's sake.

"Of course, you do. Now come along boy, we're almost there. What a fine fighter you'll be."

Fighter? I never fought seriously. Of course there were playful brawls with Cypress and the other kids in the ring we carved into the sand. It was a place where the ground had been packed down solid, perfect for play or practice. I was reluctant to join because the fights were often too fast-paced and intricate for me to follow. Like a carefully choreographed dance, the kids made moves and dodged blows, maneuvering around one another with such grace. The intent was never to harm, only to disarm the other. Sometimes not even that.

When I joined, I would be almost immediately pinned to the floor or beaten too hard in an accident so the other kid would feel guilty for not going easier on me. The only times I ever won were with Cypress when he let me win. It was a sort of rare kindness that only he would give. He wouldn't tell the other kids either, so it made me look impressive. Cypress wasn't the strongest, but he was definitely up there. He'd utter to me that he'd go easy right before we started, too quiet for the others to hear.

But why? What use was it to her if I fought?

I pulled at the metal rings around my wrists. It could've just been my imagination, but they felt tighter after that. I made a sound of frustration at feeling the Dark sensation again. It seemed to grow every time I got fired up. My hands were so hot I felt if I got any angrier, the cuffs would melt. I heard the blonde witch chuckle behind me. I bared my teeth at her. She was holding my shoulders so tightly I could feel her nails stabbing me through her clothes. She didn't even bat an eye at my effort to scare her; she only gripped me tighter and kept walking.

We were weaving through the crowd, making turns quite often, but now I could generally track where we were headed: an incredibly large and imposing building with the word "Fliondesso's" across the front. The sign might have had lights in it once upon a time, but by the looks of it, they had been busted out a long time ago. That's how people liked things around here - dim and broken. There was a sort of freedom about the chaos, though. I could see how someone could get used to it. As we neared the building, the horrible reek of death and musk only intensified. I was led into an entrance room with some sort of reception desk, behind which sat a wide and stout man. He wasn't a Dashaner and certainly not a Ground Elf. I'd never seen anything like him, which is probably why I was given an even harder thump on the head by the blonde witch for staring.

I peeled my eyes away toward another part of the room. I saw posters on the walls with foreign writing, but others were written in Standard Speech, which I could read. Most dimensions who recognized Dark and Light as commonplace forces in their lives used the same or similar dialects because regular dimension travelers would need to get in and out of different universes and be able to communicate quickly. As Light technology like portal devices became more widely available, the language barriers became less and less of a problem. This language we usually called Standard Speech- but there were variations on it, of course. For instance, the type of Standard Speech the two witches used was often too clean and thought out. It gave me the impression that they weren't originally from a Light and Dark favoring dimension.

Standing behind me was also the witch with dark glasses. She still held my staff, if rather impatiently.

"Another one, eh Alice? You're on a roll," the creature behind the desk grumbled out. The blonde witch tensed. He'd clearly struck a nerve by using that name. The woman behind me threw out her hand, and the creature behind the desk was immediately sent into a violent fit of coughing and sputtering. I jumped back, pulling my cuffed hands to my chest.

"Yes. The last one, she- never-mind about her. Are you going to admit him into the group?" The man didn't respond. The witch, Alice, glanced behind her.

"Go easy, dear. That's enough." The other woman lowered her hand. The large beast was given back his breath and spoke with all the strength he could manage.

"Yes. He's in. Turn him around, pull down his tunic-"

She followed his orders. Something was being drawn on me in a sticky ink, I could feel, right below the base of my neck.
A symbol? No, a number.

"He'll be number sixteen. Bring him in. They'll be starting the selection in ten minutes."

"Thank you," Alice said lowly, and grabbed me by the collar, leading me around a wall that separated the reception from the rest of the place. A massive arena greeted us with incredible amounts of seating. Even so, people were struggling and squabbling with one another to get a seat, and more creatures were still arriving. I was in

※ ※ ※

awe at the magnitude of it all. In the center of this room was a stage, and around that, a cobbled cage made of different types and sizes of chain link and mesh. Above that was a catwalk system hanging from the high ceiling, looking like it was about to fall apart. In the center was a box, probably for an announcer.

I was shown to a low bench, where I was crammed between the two women. Alice took a key from a pocket in her robe and stuck it into the keyhole in my handcuffs. They clicked open.

I could run for it, I thought. But I doubt I'd live very long if I did. That was when an awful chill went up to my spine. I was being watched. Everywhere. Something in this feeling spoke to me- it said:

"You'd be right to think that, boy." I turned to my left where Alice sat and was pocketing the handcuffs while still making direct eye contact with me, or at least I assumed. Her eyes were still obscured beneath her bangs. I shivered and kept my eyes trained on the ground until the witch to my left with the glasses grabbed my chin and moved my face in her direction. She took the cigarette from her mouth and stomped it out on the murky floor with her boot. It went out immediately.

"So cute, you are. C'mon boy, we only have a few minutes until the show starts. You'll need some things to give you an edge." She rummaged around in her pockets, too, pulling out some miscellaneous things: a jar with a bright green substance inside, a blunt-edged spreading knife, and another container filled with a black gel. It resembled the dark liquid present at my mother's death and stuck with me in both a figurative and literal sense.

This stuff was all over this dimension, smeared across the walls and drenching the cage we were seated in front of.

It had attached itself to me and fit like a glove.

The bespectacled witch grinned fiendishly as she began to unscrew the cap on one container.

"My name is Prudence. I deal with the physical realm of Dark's work," She chimed, opening the green stuff and scooping a portion of it with the knife. She held my chin firmly and started spreading the stuff on my face. "Wait a second-, can you take off your top? I think they need to see your number."

I didn't think that was actually a question because I definitely would have answered no; I could still feel Alice's eyes on me. Too many eyes.

I listened, untying my over layer and then pulling off the shirt underneath. My frame was less than impressive, I knew for sure, especially compared to the hulking figures all around me that also had numbers drawn onto their backs. I balled up the clothes in my lap, then removed the bandages that had been protecting my forearms. Prudence watched me intently. It wasn't necessarily a sinister look, but I was shaken nonetheless.

She nudged my shoulder to get me to stop staring off at all the patrons so she could continue her work on my face. This cream burned too, but much less than the Dark ichor itself.

Prudence took a pair of thin gloves from her pockets, which she pulled on. She took a good amount of the green cream between her palms and rubbed them together to coat her hands. When she grasped my shoulders firmly, I felt a surge of energy coarse through my veins. It was similar to the angry feeling but not identical. It was like this substance was trying its best to mimic another: to mimic Dark, which had powers and a level of pain that far outpaced its own. This was more refreshing, at least. I heard Alice pipe up from behind us.

"I'm surprised you have the reservation to protect yourself when spreading those creams of yours, Prue, considering you don't take the same care in anything else." I glanced behind me to see that Alice's eyes were trained on the burnt cigarette buried in the muck. Prue turned my attention back to her. She tutted and ignored Alice's comment crossly before beginning to trace her finger along my shoulder and across my collarbones, connecting to the handprint on my other shoulder. She drew a line in green up from the center of that line to my chin. The sharp pain from her pressing on my throat caused the cream's effects to flare up again.

"This will improve your stamina for the fight." She told me, "I've been working to make creams out of Dark's power for a while, but I haven't experimented much with this one. Tell me how it works out, eh?" She let out a barking laugh that echoed taka mice, the little rodents that assaulted the fruit carts back in my village.

Prudence looked like a taka mouse, too, with that pointy nose of hers. I squinted at it while she took some of the black stuff out of its jar. The smell alone took me back to the scene back in my cottage. There was no doubt in my mind that this was the real deal as pure, unfiltered Dark was rubbed into my temples. I gripped my legs hard to stop bolting out of my seat. Oh, Light. It had done something, that was for sure. I heard her chuckle a bit more as she pulled off her gloves. She tossed them aside, and I was sure I saw the things vanish as soon as they left her hands. She was scrutinizing me again like I was some science project.

● ● ●

"Wow! Stronger than I thought. Maybe I should water it down? What do you think?"

Whatever this stuff was, it was giving me tunnel vision. I found my eyes going from person to person, locking onto them like they were targets. I could hear individual conversations from fifty meters away on the other side of the arena. My hand fumbled upward to clutch at my chest. I could feel my heart beating without touching it. *"Maybe, that would be good,"* I breathed, trying my best to steady myself.

"Your eyes have become so dilated." She leaned closer to my face, and I nearly lashed out at her. A low growling noise sounded from the back of my throat.

If she didn't back off, I swear-

"Oh, of course. Dark makes you hostile. It's just a side effect, kid. Totally normal." She leaned back and gave me as much space as she could manage, given our seating arrangement. "Speaking of side effects: do either of your eyes hurt, by any chance?"

Her tone was strangely hopeful.

"Yes," I growled. I was beginning to find myself being apprehensive. It would be such a release to take out all this tension on someone; let loose everything I've got. I had told the truth. My right eye had started to ache, deep in its base, that only sharpened by the second.

Prudence looked to Alice. Alice's head tipped slowly to the side as she spoke.

"You're gaining power, boy. Power so much more potent than anything Light could provide, and maybe eventually, you will have the power of dimension travel inside of you. A power that doesn't rely on some portal device."

She was cut off by red lights and noise coming from the ceiling. A voice boomed from above. She sounded like she'd swallowed the Dark stuff and let it ferment in her throat. I wouldn't be surprised if that were the truth.

"Welcome, welcome! Creatures of all sizes! The crawly filth of Escuro's core!" The crowd around us went insane, roaring and stomping. I was afraid the floor would cave in. "The votes are in, folks! Our first fighter, with a grand total of five thousand, four hundred and seventy-two creds, is..." The crowd calmed for a moment. "Number sixteen! Come on up here!"

Before I could protest, I felt a few dozen disgusting hands on me, guiding me toward the cage. I tripped, unable to see with all of the hulking figures closing in, and one picked me up by my middle. I saw him open the door to the cage, and I was tossed in like a doll. I hit

● ● ●

the floor of the stage hard. I could feel how cold and slick with grime my back was as I pulled myself back to standing. I took a deep breath as the fire in my veins roared once again, glancing to see if the witches were insight. The crowd had closed around them. I watched the audience shift and drone in one amorphous form, having no clear beginning or end. Any pain I was in was swallowed immediately by the warm reassurance of my rage. I squinted up into the spotlight.

"Oh! We've got a newling! Zero levels. Oh, poor child." The announcer cooed over the speakers to the uproarious delight of the patrons around me. Their laughter was insufferable. I wanted to burn this place to the ground- it was on its last legs anyway.

"Shut up." I hissed. The roar of the crowd overpowered the noise. I cracked my knuckles and stretched out my burning fingers.

"He speaks! What was that, newling?"

"*I SAID, SHUT UP AND LET ME FIGHT!*" I was surprised by my own volume. The crowd quieted once more, and from the corner of my eye, I saw a blonde figure pushing her way through the crowd to press against the side of the cage.

"*Yes, yes! That's the spirit!*" She egged me on. The muttering and subdued laughter turned into a surge of cheers. I rolled my shoulders and lowered my head. My hair fell over my eyes. I couldn't remember the last time my hair had been this loose and wild. The announcer went on, and I tuned it all out. I stumbled to the edge of the cage and gripping onto it for support as I felt this Dark feeling surge up and down my body, melting up my chest and across my neck, up through my hair, spreading hot and vibrant through my fingertips. It was absolutely liberating. Or it was until its grip on my eye tightened.

Like a bright crack of lightning through my skull, the pain shocked straight through my eye and deeper. I whined in a raspy slur, gripping the chain link so hard it bent. When I opened my eyes again, I couldn't see in the one that was stinging. Even with my senses obscured, I could still tell what was going on behind me when another number was called, and the entire cage shook with a new addition.

I turned slowly, keeping my head low as I surveyed the other contestant. He wasn't broad, only dizzyingly tall. His cloaked figure stretched far above mine. Where he should've had feet, there were only rigid, bony spikes that threatened to crack the floor we were standing on. As I looked up to his face- well, I didn't see a face either. Only a thick curtain of hair swayed as he shifted his weight. His damned spike legs dragged across the floor, making a horrible grinding sound. I was practically foaming at the mouth now, growling animalistically just to contest the noise with a worse one. I similarly dragged my feet to him, advancing in a sort of crouching skulk. I slowly allowed the sounds and stimulus to filter in.

"Sticks! Are you ready, old boy?" The voice boomed, and the shape stomped his spike of a foot into the ground. I jumped as it shook the ground beneath us, a small crack left in the floor beneath the strike. I could sense commotion behind me: movement and an exchange of conversation that went in a wave through the crowd. I barely noticed the low rattling noise my opponent was making; Sticks, I assumed, was his name.

Something struck my heel. I jumped out of the way, thinking it was an early offhand attack. I looked down to the sight of my staff partially covered in grime, tossed in with us. I supposed it would be better to have a weapon, after all.

It's not a Light weapon?

I heard. In reality, the noise I received was more of a thought than noise. It rang clear despite all the racket surrounding us. It was the witch again, Alice, speaking to me without speech itself. A mere prickle over the blanket of Dark sensations I already had.

No. Only an heirloom,

I told her.

It should do fine then,

She responded and bid me good luck as she returned me to the task at hand. I felt in tune, and most of all, ready. If I wasn't in this odd state, I wouldn't be able to even walk this close to Sticks as I was now, let alone fight him.

The Dark is already inside you, boy. Let go. Let it take hold. Let it flourish from your very soul.

At first I wasn't sure what to make of it, but I gave it a shot. I felt around and explored my surroundings, as I always have. I thought of what it must mean to be Dark, staring up into Sticks' hidden eyes. Taking a wide stance, I imagined how this could connect me to a community. Someplace where everyone had this common feeling, something at the very origin: this material. Slick and rank and horrid, but clearly of use. A material clung to me so readily and craved to sink into my skin.

Perhaps, I could use that craving to my advantage.

The roaring around us grew. The match had begun. I watched as Sticks got into a starting position, hunching over and spreading out his weight. I tried to copy him.

"Newling, are you ready?" The voice from above called to me. The pain was gripping further and further back every second. I stifled a scream to speak, wiping my face that had already become slick with sweat. I turned my face up into the light.

"Ready!" I roared into the sky, over the crowd, and they roared right back. My voice was dripping with all of the remorse I held. The remorse I would use to get ahead. I discreetly lowered myself and grabbed the staff. Sticks was asked as well, and he responded with a noise that was more grinding than speech. Somewhere in there, another "Ready" could be heard.

"First to fall unconscious loses! Let the tournament begin!"

Everything swung into motion much too quickly. Sticks reached at me with an enormous claw that appeared from under his cloak, catching me on the back of the leg. I lost my footing like I weighed nothing and managed to scramble away before he could get another swipe at me. I tried to strike him with my staff, but he caught it and tore it out of my hands, tossing it away. Now I was really screwed- no weapon, no claws, no fangs, no venom.

The only way I could think of winning was if I was faster than Sticks. It was the only thing I was that he was not.

I scrambled helplessly, closely evading blow after blow until I was backed against a corner of the cage. He raised a spike and struck, and as I tried to roll away, the razor-sharp edges of it cut me clean across the side. I screamed as it tore through my skin, intentionally pushing my voice over the top. Clutching my side, I reached up for his mop of hair and pulled down as hard as I could. Sticks was shaking, trying to get at me, and looking down, I understood why: I was trapped in the corner, but Sticks' foot spike was tangled in the cage's mesh and chain link. It was then that I saw my opportunity.

He managed to scratch me badly once more as I used his spike leg as a boost, vaulting myself up the chain link. I didn't think about the fact that the sides of the spike were still as sharp as they had been before. They cut into my foot, slowing my climb as I made my way up the chain-link and eventually out of his reach. I could see the entire crowd from up here. All of their eyes were turned toward me. My wounds that once throbbed agonizingly began to numb under the general swell of Dark. This substance had covered up my wounds, shifting curiously to cover them like some nefarious bandage. I watched the Dark stuff creep over the cuts in my foot before my sights locked back on my target.

Now, more than ever, I wanted that wretched creature dead. The structure creaked with my weight as I made my way up onto the roof of the cage. I hung loosely from the different pieces of mesh that had been so haphazardly tied and soldered together. I looked down.

* * *

Sticks was pacing in circles, evading any chance of me tackling him from above. Maybe if I went back down the other side and leaped from high enough, it would give me enough momentum. I made my way over with gaining ease and determination.

With a sickening snap, one of my arms dropped and a large panel with it. Now I only held on with one arm. Not only was there less room to climb, but it also wouldn't be long until the other panels caved in too. Though there were no rules against hanging onto the cage, I could tell the structure wasn't meant for it.

As I stared downward again, a small wave of uneasiness that broke through Dark's lull briefly went over me. I must have been three stories up in the air. The image was enough to shake off some of the numbing anger in exchange for a moment of clarity and panic. I swung and tossed the piece of metal down at Sticks as hard as I could. It hit him, but only enough to make his attempts more aggravated as he paced and clawed at the cage wall. He stuck his claws into the side of the cage, trying to meet me halfway, but only managed to get tangled again in the chain link.

He was going to fall right into my trap if he kept lingering next to the edge right below me. The cage gave many more complaints while I scaled down it but thankfully didn't give out again. I stared down at his shifty figure, aiming for it as I prepared to leap.

I jumped, ready to land right on his skull- but before I could, I was swiped right out of the air. There was a moment of vibrant, angry exhilaration when I was swung over the crowd, a moment of hope with his single hand wrapping all the way around my middle, but all of that crashed down as I slammed into the floor.

There was very little left, then. It was as if Dark saw how my will faltered and grew bored, deciding to leave too as Sticks raised a spike to my hand.

I could manage very little, my breaths coming slow and labored. There was no sight in my eyes but a vague outline of Sticks over me. I expected more hits to come. My body tensed despite it all as I prepared for Sticks to end my misery, but nothing happened for the next few moments that passed. My opponent only loomed as a warm, fuzzy shape over me as my consciousness dwindled. He made some noise, up at the sky. He didn't look at me anymore. He wasn't readying his claws. Was it over? But I wasn't out yet. That made no sense.

I watched as Sticks deceived me once more and raised his claw above my head, closing it into a fist.

Then, I really *was* out.

I awoke to the ache of my injuries returning to me. Immediately I regretted waking up at all, not that it was my choice. I was curled up in something warm, moving with a soft up-and-down sort of motion. When I managed to peel my eyes open, it was apparent someone was carrying me. They took good care to keep me close. It was a great shock when blinking dazedly upward; I saw a familiar curtain of hair.

"Ssstigs?" I tried to move, but flexing any of my muscles just made the agony so much worse. All I could do was lay low.
He made a series of coos and clucks. They didn't feel intimidating. If anything, they rang soothing against the dwindling bustle around us. I could tell we were still in the arena; only it was starting to clear out.

"I called. It." His voice sounded quite similar to his spikes along the ground: deep, convoluted, and very drawn out. I blinked up at him in confusion. Surprisingly, I didn't have the urge to hurt him anymore. Bright Saint Parkeyre, what had Dark done to me? It hadn't actually been me in that ring. It was a different creature entirely that fought so dirty that it nearly tore this place apart.

"What?" I creaked, rolling over closer to his chest as he carried me through a scrappy curtain into a smaller, even dingier chamber.

"I had to beat you. To end the battle." I was lowered gently onto a little rickety cot. Squinting past him, I could see Alice and Prudence slipping into this chamber as well. Odd containers filled with all sorts of unpleasant-looking things and rolls of bandages adorned shelves on the walls. There were no weapons in sight and no signs of this room being a torture chamber or a ritual circle. Even so, all three of them looming over me set something off. It caused me to bolt upright on the cot, only to be gently guided back to my spot by Sticks. He set his large hands on my shoulders and pushed down, making me sit. His posture was rigid and pained as he addressed the two witches.

● ● ●

"You talk. Talk. Make him understand." He released me and went to sit on another little bed on the far side of the room. The witches obliged and turned to me fluidly and in sync.

"Sticks saw something when he was about to knock you out, boy." Alice hummed proudly, sinking beside me. I glared at her hard and scooted away. "You've already let Darkness take hold within you," She continued, " You're a first-level Dark supporter now." She tilted her head to the side, her crimson lips curling upward into a twisted smile. "Welcome to the club, Lamplight."

Whatever they were trying to do, it wasn't gonna work. I was just going along with the ride before I got my chance to make a break for it. *I wasn't a Dark supporter.*

"Oh, but you are. In the most technical sense. Here. Allow me to show you what you're here for. What I see in you," She took my hand, gently turning it over so she could examine my palm. I was too tense to move. She'd reached into my thoughts again without permission. "Dark chooses only the most capable to work for him. Those who have faced horrible hardships and through it all have managed to survive." She gestured at me with a finger. "When I came to you, I found Dark had already settled in your soul. I could see the potential you had to become someone truly great."

She was making some strong claims, but I'd already made up my mind. I pulled my hand back quickly, bracing myself on the cot as I tried to stand.

"But I *lost*. You said I'd get a portal device once I won a fight." Alice chuckled guiltily, if she could even feel guilt, smiling as she clasped her gloved hands to her chest.

"Well-*yes,* that is what I said, isn't it. But hey, there are always other cycles! Another round will be up in an hour if you're up for another go." She reached for me, and I stumbled back so readily I bumped into Prue. She didn't even bat an eye.

"No-! No. That's it. I'm not a part of your team, or whatever, and I don't want to 'have another go.'" Though my head was light and my vision remained cloudy, I figured I had enough energy to get out the door. "I'm gonna go get help somewhere else. I don't need you holding my hand." I backed out of the room, past Sticks and Prue. Alice had gone quiet, hands in her lap. "You made it so I'm alone, and so now that's what I am. Alone. Don't try and clean me up when this is all *your* fault, okay-! You're the reason I'm in this dump, with all these cuts." I feverishly gripped for my side. The Dark substance was waning. Perhaps Dark felt my hatred for him and was planning to leave me to die. Or maybe I was just too weak for him.

• • •

Alice had appeared surprised at my outburst but quickly regained composure.

"You may want to be more careful what you say in Escuro." She leaned back, eyeing me from under her golden bangs. "If you go out, hide that eye. You're easy pickings. I'd like to see how long you last."

"Wait- excuse me?" I spat, growling as I felt my knees buckle. I could feel my wounds were still opening back up. I leaned over heaving and roaring with all my might at nothing in particular just to stop the Dark from leaving. I'd bleed out if He weren't there to keep me sealed up. "*My eye?* What about it?"

"You gain a special pupil and iris for each level you gain. And with each level, your power only grows." She noted, taking something from Prudence and flipping it open. She held it out for me to see: a pocket mirror. I crawled closer and pushed the hair in my face out of my eyes, tucking some of the curls behind my ears. Tentatively, I stared into my reflection. My right iris had become colorless, just a pinpoint of white with a thin ring on the very edge. It stared deep into me. Something about it didn't seem all mine, even when nestled into my skull. It wanted to belong, that was for sure. But there was something about how its vibrant fervor contrasted against my own heavy eyes, soft grey hair, and gentle features that suggested it was trying much too hard to fit. My hand lifted to it, trying to inspect its curiosities further, but the mirror was pulled away.

"Do you see now how this will get you killed? Other Dark supporters see you as an easy target at just level one, and Light supporters, well..."

"I *am* a Light Supporter. My faith lies with Her."

"Quit that nonsense! Do you see yourself? You'd be crazy to think that classist charlatan in the sky would ever take you back."

I stared fiercely at her even as I began to shake, and my throat began to sting. Sniffling and heaving, I stood once more, roughly moving my hair to lay over my eyes.

"Where's my staff? I'm leaving." I told her. She stood then and reared up as if she was about to make a move but ultimately thought against it.

"Fine. See for yourself how long you last. I'll always be here to guide you back to the right path. Your staff should be right outside."

If she said anything after that, I didn't hear it. I was too busy balling up my rage, letting it build and wrap around itself, and silencing any sadness left from Alice's words. I took my staff and used it as a crutch as I pulled myself out of that cesspool of a building, feet dragging through the Dark sludge that clung to every surface. I scrubbed at my face to try and get any of Prudence's cream off it. It was horribly offensive that she chose to put it on my face in particular. Only royals in Dashan decorated their faces to denote their status close to Light. To make the same sort of designs with a substance made of pure Dark was blatant sacrilege. I wasn't even close to royal, which practically just rubbed it in my face how much of a joke they thought I was.

I didn't know what I thought I was doing by leaving in my state, but everything about the two witches screamed a trap that would force me into coerced labor, or worse.

I eventually found my way outside. I struggled to see through my hair in the dim light of Escuro, with its shifting figures and crawly things that left you struggling to stand even on a good day. Creatures slithered around my legs. I was going mad! Didn't any of them know a thing about personal space?

"Back off!" I barked at a creature with an exoskeleton I wasn't even certain had a consciousness of its own, and it split into three with a displeased rattle. I screamed at it until it scurried off. After that, I was given a bit of a birth navigating through the streets, making irrational noises and clutching at myself like a mangy quadruped.

Something deep red snaked through the living traffic. A two-legged being, similar to me, weaving through the throng in confusing patterns. They didn't match the rest of the crowd at all. Unlike me and this figure, the crowd was quiet besides a few pained grumbles.

This other person really had some nerve. I could only make out frantic mumbles until they came within range. "Have you seen- oh gods, sorry- my apologies, sir- ma'am? I was just-"

Even then, I could only make out pieces. They were approaching quickly, being pushed with the current of organisms, until the currents had us collide. And make no exception, I growled at this biped too as I was slammed into their chest. I held my staff in front of me, and the figure went still, stretching out their arms so no one would bump into us. They grabbed me and pulled me off toward a secluded side street. I clawed and pushed at them the whole way.

"Hey! What do you think you're doing! Get off me, I'll-"

"Oh, I bet you will." The red-cloaked figure purred. They were only a bit taller than me, a bit broader too. I abandoned Alice's advice and parted my hair away from my eyes to see their -*his* face.

"So sorry to bother you. Are you Guno Lamplight?" It was a warm, soothing voice like milk with honey. A voice like that didn't belong here. I couldn't believe what I saw when I squinted through the dark up at him. His hood couldn't possibly hide the neatly done face paint going in a stripe over his nose. Ninth Sector's lovely prince Rengas, Son of Light, heir to the throne, stared curiously down at me. It was worse than how Prudence stared. With Prudence, I was an experiment. With him, I was an attraction. An exotic animal. A pretty item in a shop window.

Well, at least I *thought* it was Rengas. Looked an awful lot like him. In this place of Darkness and trickery, there wasn't any way to be certain, was there? If he was an imposter, whoever this was was doing a very good job at playing the part.

And if it was Rengas, what in Light's name would he be doing here, knowing my name?

When I recovered from my initial shock, I backed toward the crowd- but he had already cut in front of me. I tried to dodge out of his way, and he blocked me with his towering figure and agile moves every time.

"Please tell me if you're Guno! If you're not, I'll leave you alone!" He stood still. "But you look *exactly* like in the papers. You must be him." He reached for me, and I smacked his hand away immediately.

"Yeah, people tell me that a lot," I muttered and attempted to duck under his outstretched arm, which was dripping with jewelry. He ran in front of me again. My nose bumped right into his chest. I reeled back, rubbing it with a scowl.

"Hey, you're hurt!" The prince noted, pointing at my side. At this point, the Dark substance on my wounds had receded enough to show fresh blood. The familiar shock and ache of the injuries opening back up made it difficult to breathe, and I leaned more onto my staff for support.

"Oh, I didn't see that. Thanks." I growled, sarcasm thick in my voice. I didn't have time for this. I stopped trying to struggle past him, letting my head hang. "Alright, who are you, and what do you want from me? I don't have all day."

Any remaining Dark in my system had given my voice a bite. Now that Darkness was dwindling, I couldn't make as much of an impact. That was one good thing about Him, I guessed. He made people listen to you.

"You don't know who I am? Really?" Now I was *sure* it was Rengas. An impostor would never say it with such genuine disappointment. It made my blood boil. My lip curled as I spoke.

"I had my doubts. But I guess I do know, now that you mention it."

"Good. Now we have to go."

"*Go?*" I cocked my head at him. "I'm not going anywhere with you."

"I'll heal you! I want to help. I saw you in the paper as I said. *You fascinate me.*"
He was folding his hands together, shuffling from foot to foot with impatience.

"Yeah, 's that supposed to make me feel better?" My voice, along with my body, weakened by the second. Dark was almost all worn out.

"I mean, maybe? It doesn't matter. All that matters is getting you back to Dashan."

This whole fiasco had me beginning to believe that wasn't such a bad idea. Were all other dimensions like this? If so, maybe I should've fought to stay home after all. Maybe the rest of the multiverse was just this. All the fables about glittering cities of metal and glass, dreams of industry, lands of endless green and foliage were all just that-myths.

But I'd already screwed up back at home. If all dimensions were even more desolate than Dashan, it didn't even matter because I couldn't return to where I came from. I was a murderer, as far as Dashan was concerned. The prince had probably come to arrest me personally. I'd be locked up, then inevitably be proven guilty at trial, then be thrown in-

It made me feel sick to my stomach even tempting the thought. My knees, already weak from my multiple injuries, gave out. The prince caught me before I could fall and let me use him to try and get to my feet again.

"Oh- oh my. We better get going soon. You don't look so good." It was either the kindness of his voice, the desperate state I was in, or perhaps both that caused me to agree to it. His hands fidgeted behind my back. I was about to bark at him when I felt a cool wind on my face.

I watched in shock as a tear opened up in front of us, suspended in thin air. It was a rift filled with miraculous swirling light that pushed a strong breeze through into the street. I couldn't take my eyes off it. It echoed stories I had heard throughout my childhood and adolescence, and I knew what it was instantly. A portal. A physical manifestation of Light's energy: flighty, delicate, cold... and *beautiful.* The prince set one of my arms over his shoulders to support me.

"Ready? We're gonna walk right through, and we'll be at the capital immediately. It can feel a little odd at first. Hold onto me."

He must have known I'd never stepped through a portal before. Why would I have, at my status? How pretentious, not to even consider it.

Pretentious, but not incorrect.

My irritation was cut off as we entered the portal's embrace. I was submerged in a feeling like jumping into cold water, except much lighter.

The next thing I knew, Rengas had picked me up and was gently lowering me into a bed. I clung frantically to the prince and my staff as he set me down, the pain in my body reinvigorating. Any Dark I had on me was now gone... strange. The portal must have wiped me clean of any Dark. It certainly felt like it. If Dark had been patching up my wounds, Light just opened them up again.

At least it hadn't been a trap. Looking out the large windows, I could see nothing but distant specks of light, smudged out against the rest of the landscape. I could only assume those were the floating lights of villages, which could only mean one thing: he really had taken me to the capital. The capital was a building so high up and out of reach it disconnected completely with the rest of society, not that it had to connect. It just had to rule.

"It's late. None of the palace staff will be awake. Perhaps I can get Ginger." The prince murmured to himself, undoing the clasp on his cloak. He folded it and placed the bundle of cloth to the side. "Here, I can set your staff down for you." He held out his hands. Too shocked to resist, I handed it over. He propped it up at the bedside. Thank Light. If he'd tried to steal it, I would've brought Dark back just to knock him out. I didn't care if he was the prince. I wouldn't care if he was an elder. With a deep exhale, I settled my nerves, sinking back against the pillow.

Now I could see this was the prince's element. This room, with its tall windows, delicate cloth decorating the room, and lush plant life in every corner. His getup, in all its complex glory. My eyes went over him as he sat down at the foot of the bed.

This was the poster boy Cypress always spoke of. Who everyone spoke of—the angelic figure of Light herself.

His clothes were adorned with all sorts of precious metal fastenings and bright crimson sashes wrapped around his shoulders. Something around his waist similar to a corset was made entirely of Limber leather, as well as his boots. It would have cost more credits than I'd ever seen in one place.

His skin was a warm shade of brown, going pink around his cheeks. Everything about him had this sort of rosiness to that the pictures in the paper could never do justice.

The prince gazed down at me solemnly.

"May I see your injuries?" He scooted a bit closer, and I tried to sit up, moving a violently shaking hand away from my ribs to show him. "You must've had a long day."

This was all such an odd change of pace. His soft expression was just so well-meaning. *Was I still being arrested?* It didn't seem like it anymore.

He took a cloth from the bedside and lightly touched it to the cut by my rib. He held out his other hand for me to take while he dabbed at it gently. I clutched onto the hand I was given, tears welling up in my eyes.

"Kevik!" I cursed, bending over and gritting my teeth. The prince uttered several apologies as he sped up to finish.

"It'll be over soon." He soothed.

Rengas rose from his spot to get some more supplies for my side and returned to dress it. As he wiped at it with antiseptic, he actually appeared *worried*. His eyebrows were pushed together, and his heavy-lidded eyes were gentle but focused. His concentration didn't falter even as I was wrenching a hard grip into his shoulder with my other hand. "If you don't mind me asking, what's your eye about? I've never seen one like that."

My chest heaved as I tried to keep still. "It's personal."

"I won't hurt you. I'd never. I'm not that sort of ruler. He said as he spread a cream on my injuries. My grip on his hand and shoulder loosened. The cream cooled the burning and allowed me to breathe.

"No. I won't tell you."

The prince looked away from me, exhaling impatiently at the bed.

"Fair enough. You've probably been through a lot. I won't push you just yet." By his tone, I could tell he meant it jokingly- but I hadn't found the remark funny in the slightest.

Then, he began cleaning the gash on my jaw, one I'd almost forgotten about. There was a long period of silence where I had to sit still and take it, feeling the soft brushing of cloth against my skin. I didn't know why he was going so easy on me. He had no reason to besides being "fascinating," as he put it. As the prince continued to care for me, I found my eyes growing heavy. His figure shifted in and out of focus, but I fought to stay awake despite my exhaustion.

• • •

Alice was still out there looking for me. I had to stay alert. But maybe it would be pointless to fight sleep. If Alice wanted to enter the Capital and tear it to shreds, she would have done so long ago. It would be reasonable to say I was safe here. Maybe the castle acted as some sort of Light base—a sanctuary of Her divine energy. Keeping my wits about me was all I could do until I found a way out.

The prince had long finished dressing my wounds and hesitantly reached out to shake me by my shoulder. My eyes blinked open.

"Come get me or the General if you need anything. I'll see you in the morning. Safe-night, Guno."

He sounded like my mother, the way he said that. The recollection of it all made my fingertips sting.

"Safe-night." I creaked, pulling my arms close to myself and away from him. He seemed to get the hint. The prince stood and wandered back to the healing room door, where another figure was standing. They raised their hand to me in greeting. I did nothing in return, my thoughts too convoluted to allow me to give an appropriate response.

And so I drifted to sleep there on the healer's bed, with hopes that in the morning this mess would all be over-and hopes that if it weren't, Light would spare me.

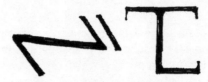

I awoke to two large eyes staring into mine. I leaped out of bed, nearly tripping over the sheets in my haste, and was ready to fight for my life once again when I saw the person who had woken me.

He stood at a little over four feet, with large, blade-sharp ears that pivoted down guiltily and a wild mess of dark hair framing his face. The ground elf worried his scaly hands, his beady stare trained on me. "You're up, thank goodness, I thought you were, well, I thought you-"

His lip trembled as he raised his hands, reaching over the bed feebly.

"You thought I'd be dead." I pressed my hand to the bandaging around my middle. It ached, yet not nearly as much as I would've expected. That cream Rengas gave me was really doing the trick. "Well, to be honest, I thought so too."

The ground elf visibly shook, so I limped around the bed, trying not to put weight on my cut foot. I held out my hand.

"I'm Guno. Guno Lamplight." I was at least competent enough to know this man didn't mean any harm.

"Yes, I know- ah, I'm Rocky Thistlet. I work here in the news and announcements department," He chuckled, his hand hesitating over my hand but not touching it. "I read out your crime in yesterday's announcements. You- you should probably get cleaned up." He grimaced sheepishly, pulling back his hand.

There came the noise of large, clanging footsteps from outside— several of them.

"But not now! We've gotta go, come on, come on!"

"Where are we going?"

"The guards are coming! Ginger or Rioh might get ya' in trouble, and I don't want to stay and find out! Come on!"

He squeaked and grabbed my hand, bolting with me out the door and down a hallway. Rocky opened a random door, a little parlor room, and pushed me inside. After I scanned the room, I pressed my ear against the door. I could faintly pick up the sound of Rocky on the other side.

• • •

First, the footsteps became louder. Then, Rocky, probably shaking out of his wits:

"Bright-morning, General!"

"I heard noises all night. What's going on? Who's in there?" There was a pause, and the General sighed. "Is it your brother? I told him not to visit, especially not so close to the Portal Ball, and-"

"No, no. It's not him. It's not anyone."

"There's someone in there; I can hear them making noises. Are they- hey, are they in pain?"

Kev. I'd tried to hold it down, but I must've not been quiet enough.

I stumbled back just in time for the General to open the door. She stood only a little bit shorter than me but was much broader, wearing a wide-shouldered coat that swept around her valiantly and a Light shortsword strapped to her belt. She kept Rocky back from me with one hand. Her sleek, flame-red hair hung barely past her shoulders, and a gleaming monocle could be seen over one of her fierce eyes. They widened, flickering over me.

"What in Light's name?" She muttered breathlessly, pushing the door all the way open. A pack of three guards were the source of the noise, positioned at the ready behind her. "You're Guno Lamplight. I just saw you in the paper just yesterday. How did you get in here?"

I hesitated in front of her, taking a few more clumsy steps backward. "The prince, he sort of brought me in." My volume didn't nearly match hers. I swallowed thickly.

She groaned, running a hand through her hair. Rocky had stopped struggling to get past the General by then and peered cautiously from behind her. A moment passed in silence. I could see the calculation in the General's narrowed eyes.

"We'll see about that." She reached out and grabbed my wrist. Her grip was much stronger than Rocky's. I struggled to keep up, whining when I stepped harshly on the wound across my foot as she rounded a corner.

She ended up dragging me up to a large, empty room. I was led down a beautiful long rug that extended all the way down the expanse up to a low-lying plush lounge that could fit probably five or so people- but that was only occupied by the prince. He had been lounging on his back, seemingly drifting to sleep, but he bolted upright when we entered.

"General! Bright-morning!" He chimed in greeting, chuckling awkwardly as he shifted to perch at the front of the circular cushion. This morning he wore an entirely different outfit which was equally as captivating. The only accessory that remained the same was, of course, the paint decorating his cheeks.

"Is this the boy from yesterday's news? You brought him into the capital?" She released my wrist and pushed me by my shoulders up a short set of stairs to be at Rengas's level. He cleared his throat and stood.

"Yes, I have my reasons; just allow me to-"

"He's already a *Dark supporter*, Your Highness! Did you not notice in your haste to bring him into our place of Light?" She grabbed a large part of the front of my hair, lifting it out of my eyes. "He is already one of them." There was a pause. A finger jabbed into my back. "What is this? Sixteen? This mark. What does it mean, Lamplight?"

"Ginger, please, slow down." He reached over my shoulder to touch the General's. His gaze lowered to me. "I brought him here as an experiment. I want to prove to myself there is enough Light in me and in this capital to turn someone back to Her." His head tilted softly to the side as he scrutinized my eye. "I want to know how He behaves." Ginger raised an eyebrow at that. The prince continued.

"Maybe if we start to understand Him, we will have better relations with Darker sectors and maybe regulate the dimension as a whole. It will keep us out of further chaos." He looked to Ginger again to see if she understood his intent.

"That's not a bad plan, actually. It could even bring you closer to Beaconism."

Beaconism is the highest point a Light supporter can achieve. Becoming part of Her fold even before you die and join her permanently was an honor few could enjoy. I'd never met a Beacon personally. My mother used to tell me about an elder who lived in our village who reached Beaconism after a lifetime of secret practice. They said a piece of Her had floated right down and lodged itself within the old woman. Wherever she went, she took Light's energy with her, holding it right in her arms.

My mother said she possessed a certain attractive quality after reaching Beaconism, which drew people to her as a source of sanctuary. She passed and joined Light when I was a baby. I never got to know her.

"Though the captain is going to be quite displeased having a Dark supporter around," She felt me jolt at being called that and corrected herself, "Or someone who *appears* to support Dark. We saw the whole story in the paper." How much did that news story say? I doubted any of it was completely accurate. "A motorized vehicle came to retrieve you. We don't have those here and never have, but Dark kidnappings have occurred. We will take your word for it this time."

The prince chimed in as he pushed up his sleeves and looked up toward the enormous stained glass window behind him. "If you find you can't control yourself, Lamplight, We may be forced to move you to containment in the sector's facility. I'd hate to do that to you, though. You have so much potential within Light." He spoke like a preacher, gazing longingly out that tall window. He spoke like Alice. It didn't ease me in the slightest. "You were raised with Light, yes?" Rengas looked over his shoulder, his haughty eyes only giving me a passing glance. He stood tall over the two of us, the colored light from the window creating a halo around his figure.

"Yes. My mother told me all of Her stories."

"Your mother, she was mentioned yesterday as well. I am truly sorry. May She keep her well." He bowed his head slightly and pressed three fingers to his forehead- a sign of respect to the deceased. He turned back to us. "What is your favorite myth she told you?"

I pondered that, trying to keep still even with my injuries inhibiting my ability to stand straight. "That would probably be either tales from Afferas or the one where- that child got lost in the portal fluid? I've heard several titles that it has gone by."

"Oh! I heard it as the Ballad of Tallah. It's a wonderful tale." He appeared pleased with that answer, so I tried not to worry so much when Rengas told Ginger to take me on a tour of the capital.

"Show him to a room. Oh, and show him how to get to the library. I'm sure we have the sorts of things he'd like."

As Ginger started to lead me away, I took a last glance behind me at the prince. His lovely eyes were still lowered to me, watching as I went. It was as if the look he gave me was a precious secret shared between us that he'd never tell. He blinked slowly, ringed by that radiant light, in quiet affirmation of something unsaid. What that look meant only Rengas knew, and I'd be left to find out.

I was escorted to a room halfway up a castle spire. It was big and round with yellowish windows that made the natural light tinted during the day. My bed was positioned toward the back. It reminded me of a nest, with all of the pillows and cushions piled onto it. A swinging bench was suspended from the high ceiling. I tried to contain my surprise as I surveyed it. I had brought my staff up here so it wouldn't stay in the healer's room. I held the thing to my chest protectively.

Rocky, who had been trailing along behind us at nearly a jog, caught his breath before handing me a piece of parchment folded neatly.

"Are you sure this is the right place?" I took it cautiously, with an uneasy glance in Ginger's direction.

"Yes. Rocky insisted on giving you a nicer place to stay. It wasn't our original plan, however-"

"-You're our guest! It's the least we can do. Open that. It's a map of the Capital. I made it." Rocky interjected, poking the paper in my hand. I obliged. I admired the handiwork of his drawing. Seemingly completely to scale, the map had tiny neatly-written labels of nearly every room. It had an aerial view of each floor, including all the towers. Another feature, probably added on afterward, was rushed "staff only" labels in several areas.

"It's very nice. Thank you."

"Now come on, let's see the library."

Rocky dragged me the whole way there. I could've used the map and figured it out on my own, I thought. Or I could just use the map to find the way back.

The library loomed three stories tall. A narrow staircase snaked all the way up in a spiral, leading to the upper levels that had little reading nooks and alcoves in each. Crystal pendants hung from beneath the stairwell and walkways. All of them together created a vibrant shower of light against the otherwise drab bookshelves. There was a certain humble kitschiness to this room not shared by the rest of the capital.

"This is... *incredible*." I worded breathlessly, holding out my hand to catch some of the light on my skin. Ginger smiled. It was a weak one that barely dimpled her cheeks.

"I'd rather you be reading than getting into more trouble, that's for sure." She remarked as I took and flipped through a leather-bound booklet. "You're awfully kind for a murderer. You sure that article wasn't just a misunderstanding?" I couldn't tell if she was joking. I looked at her over my shoulder.

"What was that, my General?"

"I won't throw you into 9th Penitentiary regardless. We know it was the work of a Dark supporter. They lure in kids like you to join the cause."

My eyebrows pushed together as my gaze fell from the book to the wood paneling below my feet. The shame was too great. If I lied, I'd only have one more thing to feel guilty about.

"I did it. The article wasn't a mistake." Though I'd never seen the article, the records of the crime itself, I could only imagine how it

had depicted the scene from yesterday. How *I* had been depicted in the paper, and who had read that depiction. I covered my face with my sleeve as my shoulders began to shake. I didn't want to think about it anymore. I'd been forced to grow up within a day and a half's time and facing that was difficult. It always would be, I expected. Families were tight-knit in Dashan for the sole reason that they were hard to come by. A lot of kids envied me because I had a supportive parental figure in the first place. Now I'd joined those kids in being alone. I was on this journey for and by myself, now. "I'm sorry," I told her.
This was so unfair.

"Don't be." Ginger and Rocky said nearly at once. I lowered my arm to see them.

"Can a Dark supporter be brought back to Her? I'm a Light supporter at heart; I know that. The Dark witch who took me said," The panic only made it harder to speak, harder to see through the tears that I blinked and rubbed away with my hand. "She said Light will never take me back. That this is permanent."

"That can't possibly be true! You can't trust anything she says, Guno." Rocky reassured me; Ginger was staring off. She seemed less certain.

They let me find the way back myself, for which I was glad. I wanted to meander around before heading back to my room. Looking at expensive tapestries and calm scenery would surely clear my mind. Every room and hallway was expansive and tastefully decorated. It almost felt as if everything was scaled up, made for a larger creature than a Dashaner or Ground Elf.

I missed the turn to the hall that led to my tower and was soon lured in by the distant sound of music. It was a stringed instrument, perhaps a lyre, accompanied by a soft voice. The panic that lined my consciousness soon ebbed away with my curiosity. I followed the sound to an entrance closed in with a curtain. Slowly, I pushed it open.

Inside I was greeted with a grand music room. Instruments lined each wall, some small ones displayed in clear cases, while others that stood taller than me were propped up on stands. In the center of it all was the music source, who gently fell silent when I entered. The prince looked to the door to see who had interrupted his song. His expression softened upon me.

He began plucking the instrument again, singing in a language I didn't recognize. His song conveyed plenty, even if I didn't know the lyrics. The singing nearly urged me to sit beside him, but I didn't go that far. I continued to stand in the doorway, still holding the curtain.

* * *

The prince was a little hard to take your eyes off of, especially like this. The glossy silks on his belt flowed down around his legs. His pale hair framed his face, falling around it and somewhat over the back of the lounge in lazy strands. His cheeks were still flushed like yesterday, if not more. His head turned from the ceiling to me; his eyelids lowered. That look again. I still couldn't tell what it meant. Perhaps it was "You wish you were me," or "I know your secret."

What secret, Rengas? What secret? I have none. But the way he gazed at me sure made me feel like I did. His song was coming to an end. Before he could say anything else, I clenched my fists, turning and leaving him to his music.

This all felt like some bizarre dream. I would have been completely convinced, except if not for the remaining ache in my step. Something about Rengas also felt too real to be something I'd made up. Maybe that's what Rengas had meant to say with his staring:

It's time to wake up now. Go back home. You've seen enough here.

Or,

You really think you're still dreaming? This is how it has always been.

Once I was out of that room and out of the prince's trance, my aches reminded me that I needed to rest. Reminded me that the torment from yesterday wasn't over.

Oh Light, I'd fallen so low. It didn't matter if Ginger and Rocky weren't mad at me. It didn't even matter if I was forced into it and would have died if I hadn't killed the baker. I should've let her kill me instead and died in honor alongside my mother. My soul was tainted now. Dirtied.

I returned to my room drained and immediately crawled into bed. I shut off the lights, trying to ignore the complaints from my muscles. After a long while, Rocky knocked on my door and told me to come to dinner, and I dismissed him.

I can't recall what I said. It had probably been some groggy, primitive thing that my half-awake brain thought made sense at the time. Then Rocky probably went to dinner confused and frightened because it made no sense, but he didn't care to intrude.

After his call woke me up, I chose to lie there with my eyes open. I rolled over to face the outside window, watching the sunset. With dusk, something peculiar started.

The darker it got, the more my body became on edge. I groaned and shifted to lift my arm from under the covers. Sure enough, I had goosebumps. The hair on the back of my neck stood on end too. My heart rate quickened, preparing for a threat that I couldn't even see. There wasn't anything to fight, surely. The castle was safe; no one Dark could get in unless let in.

Yet there was something there. Not really in my room, or the castle, even. It stood at the very edges of my mind, waiting for its chance to strike. A sinister presence with a confident air. *"I'm not going anywhere,"* it seemed to say, *"Just let me in."*
The scariest part of it, I think, was not being able to tell where it ended, and I began. It was too close. It could be Alice weaseling into my mind like she did before, or it could just be me. A part of myself I'm suppressing without my knowledge. *Which is so, so much worse.*

That would mean Dark was really a part of me. It would mean that rank meanness had already infiltrated my heart, and part of me genuinely wanted to hurt others for no good reason. It hadn't even been that long since I'd officially been "Initiated" into their fold.

I felt my mind opening. Reaching out into the hall, I could almost perfectly picture walking out, down corridors.
A book. It had to be, because what this skulking mind gremlin or brain-infesting witch wanted me to do was go to the library. It repeated the thought over and over like a mantra. I blocked it out. I needed sleep. Covering my head with a pillow, I managed to drown out the thoughts of twisting hallways, crystal clear, and of a certain shabby volume swathed in Darkness like I couldn't even comprehend.

I woke up the next morning in a cold sweat. I whipped my head toward the window and saw that the sun was already a good bit into the sky, and neither moon was in sight. It had to be the afternoon, at least. Usually, sleep resets your mind. It clears most of the feelings from the night prior. But not now. *What did I expect, really?* I had been at the edge of my seat the entire night as I fought myself to get to sleep. The Dark feeling had retreated from the forefront drastically and was now merely a distant recollection, like deja vu: someone has the book.

I pushed aside my covers and found the map, which I'd carelessly thrown onto the desk in my room without bothering to fold the thing back up. As I was about to leave, I spotted a bundle by the door. I crouched beside it: a stack of simple clothes, tied up with a cord.

Changing was a major relief. Even if I had not bathed yet, taking off my old pants and bandages that I wore on my calves and forearms, all of which were filled with sand and grime, felt like a

* * *

luxury. The new clothes were a good bit too big for me, but I didn't mind at all.

I bunched up my new tunic sleeves and went to find the place from my vision last night. This time, I avoided the "music room" marked down on the map and took a shorter route.

With the entity in my head pushing me where it desired, I was certain I wouldn't get lost this time around. The heavy doors were open a crack when I arrived. With effort, I got one open enough to slip inside.

There was the prince again. He sat on a cushion in the seating area in the center of the floor, a book open in his lap. I could tell the cover was once very gaudy and since had become muddied and battered with extensive use. Now it was only a dirty, faded pink. That was the book I needed, all right.

Rengas gave me a hidden smile as we made eye contact.

"So you've gotten your new clothes, I see. Don't worry about the size. We can tailor some better fitting ones later." He hummed, patting the cushion next to him. My eyes, however, were locked on the book. It felt like Rengas was always there when it was least convenient. I eventually decided there would be no harm in sitting by him, especially if I wanted to get the thing in his hands. I growled and clucked under my breath with my hesitation, sitting down cross-legged. The prince's eyes widened slightly. I think he heard me.

"Yeah, I appreciate it. I'm still surprised how I'm not in the dungeon or something."

"Well, *I'm* willing to be forgiving. Rocky is too. As for the rest of the staff, well," He gritted his teeth and rubbed the back of his neck. "I'm trying to keep them away from you. They don't have a reason to be gentle with you like I do. It's simple." He put it plainly, turning to me and raising a hand to my face. I shied away, making more standoffish clicks.

He lowered the offending hand away from me at my wordless request, his gaze falling back to the book in his lap. "Your eye. I wanted to see it."

Just cause he was royalty didn't mean he was entitled to things like that. I clucked some more, changing the subject.

"What is this book about? Looks old." Maybe even older than the other books in here. This place appeared to be more of an archive than a regular library.

"It's a diary. Got it a few years ago as a birthday present from a relic trader friend of mine. He can get into dimensions where they don't even know portals exist, slipping in and out completely unnoticed. Snagged this from an antique shop and brought it to me with little effort at all." His face alight with wonder at the mere thought of his buddy's profession, he handed it over to me. Thank Light. Something inside me breathed a sigh of relief as soon as the pinkish, lacey cover made contact with my hands. "It has a ton of firsthand information on Dark, straight from a personal account. Unfortunately, it's not very scientific. It's mostly," He made vague motions with one hand, "Emotional responses. The person who wrote it was clearly quite young. But it's a diary, not a research project. I didn't expect much more from it." He bit the corner of his lip, leaning closer to me to open the front cover. The close proximity made me squeamish. Even now, I believed he was going to turn on me any moment. I was ready to fight back, though I knew that was completely irrational for the prince to do.

Fortunately, something else grabbed my attention before I could give in to my instinct to flee. The writing on the front page that had been translated into Standard Speech in graphite notes in the margins:

Property of Alice Walker. Do not touch.

Well, Light knew those instructions weren't followed. My grip on the book tightened as soon as I saw the name. This was *hers?* It had to be. Why else would I be so drawn to it? At least that came as a relief, knowing that Alice was probably pushing me toward the book, and not another facet of myself. Pieces of scrap paper had been tucked in between almost every page.

"Are these translations?" I skimmed through but couldn't bring myself to read any of the words yet. It was too heavy to handle. On top of that, just imagine. Alice. Emotional.

"Yes. I did them myself. It became a passion project of mine a few years ago." He ran a hand through his hair and looked away, a hand on one of his reddening cheeks. I wish he would stop doing that: showing himself off as a nervous habit. It was starting to get on my nerves.

"It's impressive." I didn't wish to feed into his ego, but it was the truth. "And you just finished recently?"

"Yes. It was last night, actually. I stayed up to finish. I wanted to have it for you to reference. It's unlikely, but have you heard of this person? Did your Dark mentor say anything about them?"

I froze. Was there really a reason to lie? It was my first impulse, but was it the smart thing to do? What could Rengas possibly do with Alice's name?

The more I thought about it, the more I returned to my gut instinct.

"No. Never heard of her. There's a lot of Dark Supporters in the multiverse, Your Highness."

"I know, I know. I only- I got my hopes up. There's a slim chance. Maybe there's a hierarchy within Dark like there is with us. Who knows if this Alice lady is now some mighty recruiter of-"

"Or she could be dead. Who knows how old this thing is."

"Yeah. That's true," I regretted putting it so harshly, with the slightly downtrodden look dawning on the prince's face, "Anyway. I don't own very many books on Dark. Primary sources like this are my saving grace, however stuffed with filler they may be. That's why you, too, are a blessing from Light!" He clutched his hand to his chest, bowing his head slightly. He shot another clever look at me, which I couldn't deflect. Who could, after being called a "blessing."

"A blessing? Why?" I squinted slightly at him, tucking some hair away from my eyes.

"You're a walking, talking primary source! Why else?" He shook his head incredulously, smacking the book with the top of his hand, "An unlimited supply of *this!* Except you're less dramatic, or at least so I'd hope."

I closed the book in my lap, still holding it tightly. I couldn't help but chuckle a bit, giving him a brief once-over. His ensemble today consisted of much simpler and more modest clothing: a sleek robe-type thing that wrapped around his middle and some loose trousers. He didn't wear any shoes. I suppose there wasn't a need to when you remained indoors most of the time. He had applied a fresh coat of paint to his cheeks, and I could see where he missed in a certain spot near his nose. Perhaps he'd been feeling jumpy this morning.

"Can I borrow this?" I asked, and with too much haste. Oops. Rengas's face showed some suspicion as he took in how tight I was holding the thing.

"I don't know if that's the best idea. You're supposed to be returning to Light, not, you know." I didn't know.
What was his problem? There was nothing wrong with borrowing it for a few days. Besides, I needed it. I ignored how my fingers began to warm and prickle as they pressed into the plush book cover.

"I only mean that you should be careful. I believe your intentions are in the right place, but I think we should keep the book here," He set a hand on my shoulder, the other on top of my hand that was holding the book. It pressed on top of mine, extinguishing the fire of Dark from my skin. "I don't want you to get in any more trouble," I looked up to see his nose scrunching up. Then he pointed it away, shaking his head, "And you should really bathe. I can come to re-dress your wounds after." With regard to my expression, he added: "Or you can do it on your own if you think that would be better."

I chose the latter option. After returning the book to him, Rengas shelved it higher up. The prince showed me to the bath. It was luxurious, much bigger and cleaner than the ones they had down in my village. He told me to wait while fetching the wound dressings, soap, and a new change of clothes.

He presented them to me in a basket. This, too, proved to be so excessive and much different from what I was accustomed to. Rengas lingered for a moment near the exit.

"Come get us if you need anything else. There's a towel in there too. If you will, please report to the throne room when you're all finished. Ginger wants to talk over a few things with you."

I nodded and backed up as he closed the curtain behind him. I stepped to the edge of the sparkling, clear water, looking down at my reflection.

Rengas hadn't been lying. I did need a bath. I would probably have to keep the bandages on until I got out of the water and then change them out after I got mostly dry. Dipping my toes in the water, I could feel that the bathing pool was heated- barely warmer than body temperature. I got to undressing and slipped in.

After doing a few laps back and forth, I began actually washing myself. I thought of how my fingers had Darkened before. Perhaps it was because of my proximity to that book. After Rengas touched me, I didn't feel the same strong need for the book like I did before. What did he do to me? Can higher-up Light supporters cast spells? I didn't think so. I would've heard something about it by now if that was the case.

As much as I hated to admit it, Rengas's touch had felt nice. It felt nice even when I was hurt, and he pressed my wounds. He really must have a lot of Light in him for all that to be true, I thought. He had the calming, stilling effect of Light at his fingertips, and he wasn't even a Beacon yet.

I didn't want to think about the book anymore. That was probably what Alice wanted. I couldn't give her the satisfaction and thinking alone seemed too risky.

A bottle of oil had been placed at the edge of the bathing pool. I poured some into my hand and smoothed it into my hair to tame my curls and make them easier to brush. When wet, I found my hair reached halfway down my chest instead of barely past my shoulders as it would usually rest. It was fun to imagine how cool it would be if I grew my hair out so it would rest that long. The thought distracted me from the

◦ ◦ ◦

pain in my ribs that soon became too much and forced me to get out earlier than I would've liked.

After dressing my own wounds the best I could manage, I took out the change of clothes. Now I had layers: a belt, a thin, gossamer-like undershirt, a top that went over it. The package also included a random piece of patterned cloth. Was this supposed to be a scarf? I ended up tying it in a knot around my waist as well, letting it sit like a looser belt that went over my first one. The whole ensemble didn't look half bad. The pants' cuffs had ribbons on them, presumably so you could bunch them up and tie them at your preferred length. I did so. Looking back at my reflection then, I looked like somebody completely different than the boy from a day or two ago. I didn't know how to feel about it. Though I didn't look like the *same* me, I still looked like myself.

I dried out my hair a little more, packed up my laundry in the basket, took my map, and departed for my room. I had to unload before Ginger wanted me in the throne room.

Light, it felt *so nice* to be clean. I no longer felt the sweaty grit with every step, and the dampness in my hair cooled the back of my neck quite nicely. I could get used to feeling like this, I thought.

    Two guards stood at the entrance to the throne room. When they saw me, they stepped up to the double doors and pulled them open.

    "Many thanks," I noted with a slight bow of my head, passing between them. Rengas and Ginger could be seen on the throne platform; Rengas sprawled out on the throne just as I had seen him before, Ginger standing stiffly with her arms behind her back. She eased up once I came up the steps to meet them while Rengas sat up.

    "You called me, Your Highness? General?" I glanced between them. Did I appear presentable enough?

    "I see you've cleaned up. You look lovely," Ginger said, professionally but kindly, "We'd like to discuss with you our future course of action regarding your place here."

    Rengas nodded, "I think it will be beneficial for all of us. Sit down, sit down." He patted the ground in front of him as he'd done in the library. I sat not quite as close as he requested, instead sitting myself down right at the base of the steps where I had been standing.

    Ginger sat on the arm of the big round throne, crossing her arms. "You may be wondering how long you'll be staying here. After all, guests aren't common in the Capital, even if used for research. There's also the concern of your Dark mentor, who may come back for you if you're taken out of a place of Light such as this." She tapped her fingers on the sleeve of her coat.

    "So I'll tell you this. We will keep you until you are fully competent in your Light abilities, and then we will set you free. This way, even if you do meet up with this mentor again, you will easily be able to defeat them either in wise words or in combat." The prince nodded a little as she spoke but didn't interfere. "Dark and Light are opposite forces. If you are skilled enough in the nullifying presence of Light, Dark's fervor will be extinguished." She paused, taking in a deep breath- "Or at least, so we hope."

Rengas tried and failed to pull his robe closed, which had been slipping off his shoulder on one side. "That's why we're training you with Light. Not only will you rehabilitate and allow me a step closer to true Beaconism, but you will also be prepared to face the world once we aren't here to protect you anymore."

Them, protecting *me?* It felt as if I was protecting them from myself a lot of the time, fighting off my mean-spirited instincts and battling urges that Alice prodded me with. Somehow, I believed that battle would only become harder with time.

"Right. After a few lessons in *meditation*, I'll be right enough to throw punches at a Limber-"

"Guno, I'm serious. Light can be fiercer than you think. You just haven't implemented it in that way yet." Rengas crossed one leg over the other shifting his weight and regarding me with that stare of his.

I tried to avoid it as much as possible.

"Just remember, boy. Like Rengas said. If you ever misstep and hurt any one of us or show your allegiance to Dark, we won't hesitate to remove you from the Capital. Understood?" Ginger adjusted her monocle, her gaze on me being much sterner in nature.

"Yes, General." I bowed my head, looking at my hands.

There came the sound of tromping footsteps behind me. I jolted in alarm, and when I met Ginger's eyes again, she appeared less disciplinary and more alert. The corner of her mouth twitched in a half-sneer. "Captain-" She began but was promptly cut off by a voice, originating from someplace behind me:

"What is all this? I had my suspicions, *but conspiring against me?* No, conspiring against the *law.*" The voice rang weathered and dry- perhaps someone older.

"Captain, we're conspiring against no one. We came to be in private to-" Again; Ginger was interrupted.

"To bring a stranger into this place of Light? What even is his purpose here? I'll take him back down to ground level right this instant."

"There will be none of that, Captain. The boy Lamplight is here to be taught in the ways of higher Light combat, and in turn to allow our prince into Beaconism."

I couldn't turn around. If I did, the Captain would surely notice my Dark eye. All in all, too much to risk. I kept my pleading eyes on Rengas, who seemed to be just as uncertain as I was. He kept twisting the rings on his fingers, but never one in particular: gold, with a thin white band in the center. That must be his portal device, I thought, and it would activate if he were to mess around with it like that. His eyes met mine, and this time letting him watch me didn't feel so invasive. His regard was an assurance that it would be okay.

"Is that right, Rengas? Did you drag this kid in?"
His gaze broke away from me. I let myself remain still. Dark stirred at my fingertips.

"Yes, and you just heard the reason for it."

"Who gave you permission to sneak out like that? Where did you even get him from?" There were more footsteps, getting closer. Rengas threw his hand out, standing. His grand stature cast a shadow over me. The prince stepped down to me -to the Captain, behind me-

"Don't *touch him, Rioh.* It doesn't concern you where he came from."
The captain's voice came in a whisper then. Even at such a low volume, I could pick it all up, clear as day:

"He's a Dark supporter, isn't he," He growled, and I had to hold back a growl myself, "You brought a filthy, sniveling Dark supporter into our-"

"That's *quite enough, Captain!* You are dismissed."

"You think you have the authority to question me? What have you done for Ninth Sector that makes you think you have *any* influence-"

"You are *dismissed.*" He reached over me, probably about to strike out at Rioh. I scampered out of the way just before he could, and Ginger grabbed Rengas's shoulders to pull him back from the captain. I caught a glimpse of him once I could manage to do so.

Rioh had a thin frame, made only slightly less unimpressive by his armor. His fine light gray hair was slicked back from an aged face marked by a deep scar that went across his cheek. One of his arms was outfitted with a heavy bracer that shifted and extended over his hand, its panels rotating menacingly. This was a Light cannon, I was certain. A bionic attachment. It didn't reassure me to know that this man was going to be constantly armed. He thought about pointing it at me- but then decided against it, lowering the cannon and letting the thing deactivate.

"You heard him, Rioh. Go on." She ordered. He obliged when she requested he go, but wouldn't take a single word from the prince. I wondered why. I cowered off to the side, covering my head with my arms. I couldn't be certain if any of them would come to take me away or if Dark would act up. My breaths came short.

"Oh, Light, I'm sorry." I sobbed, gripping at my hair. I muttered so many apologies to Her, Rengas, and Ginger, to my mother, to the man I'd killed just a few days ago. They became lost and dampened beneath the curtain of my own hair I'd surrounded myself in until I felt a light tap on my shoulder. I yelped and shied away only to see Rengas crouched beside me, his robe once again falling off his shoulder. He held out his hand. I took it.

The prince pulled me back to my feet, peering over his shoulder at the General before speaking.

"I'm very sorry you had to see that. Rioh really needs to learn his place around here," He pinched the bridge of his nose, "It wasn't okay for him to treat you like that." Rengas glared fiercely toward the direction where the captain left the room. "He answers to the both of us, yet he just can't seem to get past his thick skull." His lip curled as he tucked his hands into previously hidden pockets inside his trousers. When he traipsed over to meet Ginger once more, I followed along.

Ginger, too, seemed to be fixed on the door at the end of the hall, a small point in the distance from where we stood. She tried averting her gaze to the tapestries instead.

"I apologize as well. Now, where were we?"

"The training schedule?"

"The training schedule. Of course," Ginger pressed her fingertips together in a steeple position, holding them up to her chin as she began to pace. "You will start training with me and Ren. We will condition your body and make you agile so you will be able to plan out moves quicker and with less violence." My head followed her back and forth, back and forth. "Rengas will handle most of the fine-tuning: research on Dark and smaller refinements. Anything more technical he will be in charge of." Ren again began to nod as she spoke.

"We will share the load of training, and if either one of us is busy on one of our set meeting days, the other can come in. But it's good to set a consistent routine for yourself. Light favors order."

Rengas chimed in. His cheeks and ears had gone pinker in his giddy state. "We will do research on how *both* Dark and Light behave. Who knows, maybe there's some helpful tips some Light supporters and Beacons of old are willing to share with us."

"Is it settled, then? Are you up to start, say, next week?" Ginger asked gently, pushing some of her sleek orange hair over her shoulder.

I wasn't certain I'd be strong enough next week, even with this Light-made antiseptic that seemed to patch me up a bit more with each application.

"Yes. That sounds good."

● ● ●

Maybe this would turn out all right, I thought. Maybe, if I ignored Dark long enough, He and Alice would become bored and leave me be. But could I afford to leave Dark for good? I still needed a portal device. Though they were dangerous, Alice and her group held my only chance at true freedom.

Training with Light wouldn't get me a way out of here. Once they trained me, I'd be back on the street. An outcast at best if I was sent back to my village, or worse, an exile if they deposited me in some random city of their choosing. I wouldn't be dead, but my life wouldn't be much better than it.

Rengas's sessions with me started first, only two days after our meeting. They weren't the sort I expected from him at all: instead of rigorous exercise, we began with research. He took me back to the library again, which led me to a door below the stairwell. It was one that I didn't even seem to notice until he pointed it out.
"I have something to show you," He spoke slowly as he leaned against the door handle, his ridiculous flowy sleeves covering his hands. "If you promise not to tell *anyone* what you see."

I raised an eyebrow at him curiously. Who else was there to tell? Anyone in the capital already knew about this little nook, except for maybe the maids, I thought. It isn't like it was completely hidden. It was only the same deep red color as the walls. It didn't even seem to have a locking mechanism. Rengas caught my questioning look, and his shoulders began to shake with laughter.

"I'm joking! I'm joking. Come on in." It took him some manhandling to get the door open, and when he did, he stepped aside.

I was greeted with a stretch of the hallway, oddly slanted at the ceiling to accommodate the stairs above. The hall led into another small space; a study with warm lighting and kitschy decorations, stuffed with books and scrolls on both desks left no extra room. There were cubbies and cabinets to store documents in, too, all of which seemed to be nearly full. On one wall was an enormous map of first through fifteenth sector Dashan with topographical lines and what looked like rivers and lakes. My eyes were locked there for a while in disbelief. Of course, I'd been *told* there were bodies of water, but so close? In our region? It was odd to see the sectors in perspective. Ninth looked disproportionately large compared to the others. Maybe that's why it was so poorly policed, I thought, as I turned back to the prince. He'd settled himself on one of the industrial stools in front of the research desks, where he had a large tome open to a particular page where he'd made quite a few notes.

"Come sit, Lamplight." He patted the seat beside his. I did as I was told, albeit slowly with my remaining aches.

"What's this?" I asked, propping my elbows up on the table to see. There were even crudely drawn *diagrams* among the scraps of paper tucked into this book; models of hands and hearts and skulls with labels to denote Light or Dark-related inner workings.

"Have you ever heard of Edvin's theory?" The prince turned toward me, resituating his sitting position to cross one leg atop the other.

"I haven't," I admitted. It had never occurred to me that people tried to apply Dark and Light to anything concretely biological, though it would make sense why.

"It's the idea that there are Light and Dark centers in everyone's body, no matter where you lie. The key is knowing how to activate the right parts." He slid a drawing over to me that looked relatively fresh. I could imagine the prince had copied it down rather than clipping it straight from the source. The stomach was a "center" of Dark, and the picture showed arrows that connected it to the heart and hands.

"Edvin was someone in the grey just like you. He observed that Dark was fueled by gut instinct most of the time, while Light took more time and thought to develop and put to use." He pointed at the diagram, then tucked it back into the book, "I think the whole concreteness of it lacks truth, but he had the right idea. What do you think? I'm not of mixed-faith myself, so I wouldn't be able to tell." I squinted at the book between Ren's hands. I'd never used "grey" or "mixed-faith" to describe myself, let alone seen it represented in such a scientific context.

"I guess it makes sense. I don't really analyze it that much when Dark comes on, but the gut instinct thing I get."

"Well, maybe you ought to think about it more while fighting and such! Maybe we can conduct our own research!" He suggested brightly, pressing his hands together. "At least, we should compare your feelings to studies already done. Some of them are- unsettling, yes, but I think they will help. Here." The prince stood, pushing up his ornate tunic sleeves to go to a bookshelf and retrieve a thinner, even more worn-down book. The pages themselves were thick, and it became apparent why Ren opened it and revealed paintings and even *photographs* of people with the Dark substance just like mine. I shuddered, lowering my eyes. Some of them were graphic- people bleeding, or in cages, or chains; all seeming to have the alarming monster eyes.

"I'm sorry, Lamplight. I should have warned you." He closed the book again. I bit hard on my lip, keeping my head low, and he set a hand on my back as he turned away from the book and leaned on it with an elbow. "These are the Eclipse Experiments. They were conducted in Elscarade, a sister dimension to ours with slightly more advanced technology. They have a far larger supply of raw materials than we do." He explained as I lifted my face from my hands. His eyes were locked on the front of the book, which was engraved with the same name. I knew vaguely of Elscarade. The shipments of seeds and saplings that the Farmer's Guild received were engraved with the same name.

"They are controversial now that officials realize how inhumane the experiments were, even if the test subject were, you know. Dark." He looked tempted to open the book again. The thought alone made me sick. "Even so, what we found because of these experiments is fascinating. There not only seems to be a physical link to Dark behavior but an emotional one, too." He must have caught the uncomfortable look on my face because he pushed the book away, rubbing my back a little. I silently wished he'd stop but continued to listen.

"Yes. I noticed." I clicked, watching him. Rengas nodded.

"I expected as much. This is probably common knowledge for anyone with a lick of His influence in their body. Succinctly put, Dark has a clear correlation with negative emotions, *especially* anger. The more a subject's anger was stimulated, their Dark power would be too. Then, they concluded, the opposite would be true of Light. Feelings of peace, which is the opposite of that, uh-"

"Feeling of chaos? I could feel the same thing. You're right." I interjected politely. He blinked with surprise.

"Really?" He smiled a little but was quick to flatten it back out. "Fascinating. Well, it makes sense, doesn't it?"

I nodded. *Never visit Elscarade,* I made a mental note to myself. That place sounded worse than the Afterdull. Worse than Dashan.

I didn't know if I would look forward to more of his sessions. It relieved me to know that my feelings were grounded in some common truth, but was it really worth feeling so ostracized in the only place I was safe?

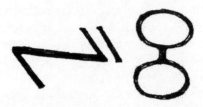

I could remember days when anger was only a passing phase. When grief was a tale told just as myths were around the elders' story circle.

Rocky had handed me a leather-bound notebook as he found me in the hallway after evening tea. His demeanor had been the usual level of skittish when he admitted to making the volume himself. I once again admired the elf's detailed craftsmanship, taken aback by yet another act of generosity by capital staff.

I had been instructed to keep track of my progress in it. Of course, Rocky had said, I could write other things too. It was mine. Now, besides my staff, it was the only possession I could truly call my own. Any other traces of my life in the village could have well been wiped clean by now, depending on who found my house first. Light knows if I'd even see it again. If that life would be waiting for me when I got back, or if this was the new normal.

The first thing I decided to do was chronicle my house. If there wouldn't be any remnants, the least I could manage was to keep a record of it to the best of my memory. I sat down at the desk fashioned for me in the guest room and opened up the book, grabbing an ink pen. I began to sketch in ink, filling in every plant in the front yard. Once I ran out of room, I started to list those items most important.

Kitchen. The soul of the house, with a generously large furnace over which is hung sprigs of herbs and thistle to dry.

Back sunroom. A place of quiet prayer within sight of our garden, blessing it with each morning's light. Where mama and I would pretend our evening teas were held in gold-laden porcelain like the underwhelming tea I had indulged in earlier that day. It was never as satisfying as I'd hoped. Maybe the sunlight from the capital wasn't all that Nezria Lamplight chalked it up to be.

Sitting room. A warm place filled with well-loved cushions and fraying quilts. A place that housed the occasional book club or story circle when mama had been feeling particularly adventurous. Where

Cypress would crash for the night after our late-night antics about town.

The place I loved most of all was the back garden. It was cared for and tended for so dearly that even in bitter seasons that bore little fruit, mama and I would give our plants the same patience as any other month. The sense of pride when we pulled up a particularly large root was unrivaled by anything else.

Would I ever have time to write it all down? I could feel sweat break at my palms as I moved onto the second page, then the third. If the prince's plan failed and I too were erased, what would be left? Sure, Cypress or Yera could tell my story, but would it be enough? I wasn't anyone noteworthy. It would all fall apart. I would become a memory too soon.

Again I yearned for a time when this wouldn't be a concern. As a child, I had faith in the story circles that would recount tales of locals past, whose stories, even in the world of the mundane, could provide helpful or even humorous lessons for future generations. Like stories of the limbers, Cypress and I and a handful of the other children used to be quick to disregard the lessons taught to us through oral tradition. I now regretted the times we would laugh at the kids younger than us for listening so intently to the elders. I'd give anything to be one of them now.

Dark Supporters, too, seemed so distant. The concept was foreign but tempting. Not even a year ago, there were rumors that a Farmer's Guild member I worked with named Fenshae had joined His side. It started at the Scarcends festival, celebrated at the end of the cold and barren months in which villagers scared off creatures from the Farlands with flashy and loud performances and games. Rumors spread like wildfire in villages as small as ours. I recalled sitting among dozens of other youth in the final round of the spear throwing competition. The targets, fitted with hay set ablaze, frightened the crowd just as it excited us. Cypress and his teammates wore costumes that clacked when they ran up to the throwing line, and just as he did, I was tugged by the collar of my shirt.

A new member of the farmer's guild told me in a panic that Fenshae was seen loading sparkthorn seeds into the targets to sabotage the contest. It made sense at the time. I didn't even think about the longstanding feud between the new member and Fenshae, and any doubt was quickly ruled out in my mind when one of the targets accidentally tipped on its side, catching a pet stand.

The screams of hundreds of pet creatures engulfed the village. Cypress thought he was responsible and sulked for weeks. I later found out that the rumor was fabricated to do wrong to Fenshae's family. Their sister, like Cypress, had been one of the contenders. Yet even as I began to find the truth, many others believed the tale. Any accusation of Dark activity was believed without a shred of evidence. It was easy to accuse someone but much harder to get out of said accusation since none of us were more knowledgeable on the behaviors of Dark than the last. Even if someone were educated on the subject, that would only be more cause for that person to be condemned.

I'd never been pinned as one myself, as ironic as that seemed now. Children of Dashan were competitive and ruthless. They were taught to fight tooth and nail to survive and to use their cunning to evade consequence. I usually liked to think I was different from them, but seeing how capital people treat one another was starting to make me feel like that wasn't true.

I missed Cypress. He was brash and foolish, but he really did his best with that kind soul of his. I almost even missed Fenshae. I didn't talk to them all that much, but they were an admirable visionary. They shared my belief in the unfairness of capital society as a whole. They were a real people's person, and I could definitely see them leading a sector of their own one day if given a chance.

My writing became less rushed as I got down any pressing details that I was particularly afraid to forget, including a few more anecdotes from my time with Cypress before forcing myself to close the notebook. My script had been at least legible, I hoped, and having some of it on record would surely provide me some much-needed comfort in my time here. I stood from my desk and stared out the tall windows, from which a familiar Dashan sun was nearing the horizon. It lost all of its wonder and infamy when so high up. With no one to celebrate it with. With no one to cling to and giddily fear the night with. It was practically drab in the way it allowed the two moons to overtake its place, like Dark driving Her away. Light just let it happen in all her practical everyday earthliness.

Acceptance of changes like this was the hardest of all. Just like the moons taking the place of the sun, I was being told to believe that all of this was just the way it was meant to be. That come morning, the sun would be out, and as drab as it may be, things would be normal again.

    Just like we had arranged, Ginger called upon me one morning in the following week with a gentle knock at the door of my quarters. I hurried to finish dressing before letting her in.

    "Guno- ready to go? I have everything set up upstairs once you're ready."

    I'd never been to the castle's training center before. I knew nothing about it except that the prince disappeared up there a few times a week and would not return until late into the night. Once he passed me on the way to bed, bandages tightly wound around his forearms, shimmering with sweat which he wiped away with a cloth draped over his shoulder. His elbows, knees, and paint were tarnished with dirt. It had taken me a while to process how out of place that whole scene had been. He had silently given me one of his gazes before continuing past me and leaving me alone to my late-night tea.

    Where that dirt could have come from, I had no idea- until the General led me up a side staircase off the castle's wing where I, along with the castle staff, had our rooms. At the top was a small holding chamber with a heavy steel door at the end, which Ginger unlocked. She held it open for me.

Inside was an exceptionally large room, a courtyard, with a tall glass ceiling. Light filtered softly through the gigantic plants that lined the perimeter- plants bigger than I could have ever fathomed. The floor was made of soft earth that cooled my feet, which must have been how Rengas managed to get dirtied indoors.

    At the side of this room to the left of the entrance was another side chamber, which Ginger went to while I strode at a calm pace toward the middle of the arena. I could make out a faint line drawn into the dirt that had been mostly scuffed up and covered over. I could imagine how much time the prince must spend here training relentlessly for a threat that may not even arrive. Working night upon night against something he had so little control over.

How could he do it? How could he waste so much time on a cause that wasn't even his to begin with? The training sessions may shape his body for battle, may trim it to Light's lofty standards of a warrior,

• • •

but at the end of the day, the only thing of importance the prince would do with it was arranged social gatherings and write public announcements.

The General returned with a roll of clean bandages for me and a wooden staff similar to my own, but thinner and lighter. It elegantly flared outward on both ends. It wasn't sharp. I don't think it was supposed to be. She tucked both under her arm and motioned for me to move to the benches at the edge of the room. I sat, and she stood before me, obscuring my view of the rest of the courtyard arena. She started to tug on the end of the bandage roll and grabbed my arm. She had a firm grip, and I could feel the warmth of her hand through her glove. It wasn't a burning heat like Dark, though, merely a gentle one. She set aside the staff and pressed the end of the bandage into my palm.

"Hold this down with your other hand," She ordered, and I did so. She wrapped my hand tightly, using a technique I'd never seen before. My arms felt secure once she was finished. She had me bunch up the bottoms of my pants as well and wrapped my knees. I was thankful I'd chosen something simpler to wear that day. Apprehensively I stood and took the staff when Ginger pointed to it.

Once we reached the center of the courtyard, she spoke. "So, Lamplight. What do you usually feel when you fight? Not on the outside, like pain and such; inside. Tell me about what you feel inside. Does anything come to mind?"

I mulled over this. "As in my faith? I always feel a connection to Light, my General. Even when I am seething with rage, I can still feel Her graciousness."

"That must be confusing for you."

"It is, General. Very much so. A bit tiring, too. I can tell She is disappointed in me. She must be. I have betrayed her and the will of portal travel." I bowed my head, away from her gaze. Suddeny I was less certain about starting my training.

"No one can really be certain how Light views them, but I choose to believe She is a forgiving entity. If your heart lies with Her, I'm sure She won't be disappointed." Ginger assured me, though her demeanor remained stern. "If you train in a place of Light such as this, using Light-bound tools, hopefully that will return you fully to Her." She left me alone for a moment to dwell on this before she came back with a simple staff of her own. She held it out in front of her, hands gripping it firmly shoulder-width apart.

"Start with a neutral stance. Ground yourself. Call upon Her will to aid you."

● ● ●

"Okay," I said.

"Whatever you may need at the moment, ask for her guidance in that area. You may ask out loud or in private." Her head lowered slightly, sending a glare flashing across her monocle. With the way she stood like that, planted to the ground, humbly presenting herself even in her obvious strength, it was no wonder she was chosen to lead the law throughout the sector.

"Light, don't let Ginger kill me-" I wheezed out.

"Guno." She bared her teeth in annoyance.

"Sorry! Uh, I'll call to her silently, then."

"Tell me when you're ready."

I drew in a breath, closing my eyes. I thought of what I wanted most of all. I wanted to get rid of this Dark mark that's been printed into my eye, into my heart. I wanted to get back in control. I didn't want Dark to pull me around anymore. I wanted to use my strength for good, somehow.

"Okay, ready."

Ginger led me through a few warm-up steps. The way we trained was like a carefully planned dance. She showed me how to dodge blows, disarm, and how to weave around an opponent to cause as little unnecessary damage as possible. Ginger demonstrated each skill in slow motion first to get down the basics, but over the following weeks, she gradually increased our maneuvers' speed and difficulty.

A few weeks later, it started to feel like real fighting, like the simple tussles back in my village with other kids. The difference was now I knew what I was doing. I could now predict an opponent's actions, and from there, know what paths to take.

I barely blocked one of Ginger's hits with my staff but winced under the force of the blow. I gritted my teeth, prickling with heat. Ginger pressed more of her weight onto me.

"Come on, don't get angry. Dark will surely take you over. Use Light to defeat me with pacifism and justice."

It was easy for her to say. Nothing with Dark was ever that simple.

"I can't," I muttered, struggling to drive the grit and malevolence from my tone. Ginger put more pressure on the staff I was using to block her attack. It was growing ever more difficult to stay on my feet. Any move I took would result in my defeat.

She gave me a shove which sent me tumbling to the ground. From my position crouching on the floor, I rolled to the side to quickly retrieve my staff. Ginger spun her own staff in a gloating manner before thrusting it into the sand. It stuck there.

"Have you given up?" She raised her eyebrows at me. My hand muscles flexed in an attempt to grip my staff harder before I used it as a crutch to pull myself back up. When I held it up in a ready position, Ginger stalled. She stood there useless with eyes wide and mouth partially agape. She took a cautious step toward me.

"Come on now, Lamplight. Remember what I said. Concentrate on cooling down."

Now I realized what she had been staring at. When I looked down, I could see a familiar black substance beginning to crawl up and over my fingers. It started to spread onto the staff I held. I yelped and dropped the thing. I shook out my hands, taking deep, trembling breaths. Ginger cautiously approached the staff and stamped out any Dark ichor on it in the sand with the tip of her boot.

"Alright, that's enough for today. Take it easy. We'll try again tomorrow."

I couldn't bring myself to look up from my hands. Even in a sacred place such as this, my soul was something so fragile that only a few hits had been enough to sway it toward the Darkness. Maybe Ginger had been right about Light's nature. It only seems weak if you believe it to be and don't implement it well. I just needed to think of Light as a weapon the same way Dark is.

A weapon of pacifism? The whole idea seemed hard to wrap my head around, but I guessed that was the point of training. Practice would condition not only my body but my mind as well.

That night arrived just as the ones before. They were nights accompanied with rushed thoughts too foggy to make any sense of. They were the sort of late-night wonderings that only left me with a heavy feeling of regret. A few times my thoughts were so suffocating I thought the blanket had been accidentally pulled over my head.

I cried with little effort at all, lying on my back to face the heavens. I looked upon them each night in a silent confession of my sins.

I'm sure Light heard me. She felt my tears as they streaked hot across my cheeks. She heard my pleas.

I've betrayed you. I've betrayed you and the nature of portal travel. You, and my mother, and everyone whom I shared a connection with back on the ground, in that little circle of mountains, nestled safely away...

My confessions rambled on endlessly. They continued until they lost their meaning and rendered themselves useless.

I slept very little that night in particular. And even when I only managed to catch a glimpse of rest, Alice saw her opportunity in it.

I dreamt I stood in a shallow pool of water. Floating lights illuminated the surface and a tree that swayed in a nonexistent breeze. Beyond this, there was only darkness. I looked down into my reflection.

My monster eye was visible even here, even in my dreams. As I tried to cover it up, my hand became transparent. It still stared back at me from the water. It seemed comfortable there—a constant reminder of what I'd done.

You really think Dark is villainous, don't you? Something thought to me. I squinted up toward the sky.

Well, yes. Of course, I do, I thought back.

I think it is quite beautiful. He is a generous force. He gives those who serve him so much. Gifts, endless life. It thought.

Endless? I reached up and caught one of the floating lights. It burnt out in my clutch.

Endless. You may cause an end, but you'll never face it yourself. You will live on. You will be able to traverse dimensions only through the will of your core and the strength of your faith.

I could feel this presence grinning. When I opened my hand, all that remained of the former light speck was charred dust that trailed down my arm and into the water.

I began to feel my tears again. The presence was scolding me, but I couldn't hear over the sound of my own thoughts.

This was all so heavy.

In the morning, I awoke to the distant sound of a band playing. It stirred me gently awake. After getting up, I stalled for time scribbling nothings into my journal. I felt hesitant to intrude on any festivities given my dream last night. I was fairly certain it was Alice who put that dream and those thoughts in my head. Luckily, my hands remained clear of Dark as I got ready. She didn't dare to make any moves while the sun was up.

I dressed and took time to tend to myself in front of the mirror. In these past weeks, Light training had changed me. The definition of my body had become more pronounced. It was only to the point where if you paid close enough attention, you could see extra dimensions where there used to be none, like in my forearms and shoulders. In the tight shirt I wore, this development was noticeable.

In the time I had not shaved, the sides of my face grew a bit of grey scruff coming down from where my hairline would normally end above my ears. The sideburns, In addition to my new scars, had given me a more mature look than I was used to. I wasn't opposed to it. I could ask for something to shave with if the facial hair ever became too bothersome.

After brushing and pulling up my hair, there was a knock at the door. When I opened it, Rocky greeted me with a small box. "I'm sorry no one told you earlier, but- uh..." He pushed the box toward my chest. "It's the prince's birthday. He just has a few people over, that's all. You may want to put this on."

I took the box and pulled off its lid. A silky, deep blue eyepatch lay inside, packed in with fluff. I took it out carefully.
"Is this for my-"
"Your Dark eye, yes," Rocky stammered, letting himself inside. He closed the door behind him. "We can tell the guests you're his

apprentice, but I'm afraid there isn't much else we can tell since it all kinda relates to..." He swallowed, adjusting the little uniform hat that struggled to sit atop his fluff of hair. "Dark. A lot of it relates to Dark. They wouldn't like that very much."

"Yeah, I would suspect. Is Rioh out there?" I set the box down on my bed and slipped the eyepatch on, adjusting it to fit. I leaned to the side to see it in my reflection. Not bad, actually. I had no depth perception, but this was better than getting caught.

"Yep, he's still kinda mad about you stayin' in the castle and all. Just steer clear of him. You should be fine," He assured me with a small nod. "I gotta get out there. Come on out when you're ready."

"I can go with you. I'd feel safer anyways."

"Aww, that's so sweet, Mister Lamplight."

Since Rocky escorted me, I didn't need to bring my map as we made our way to the throne room. I wondered if I would've needed it even if I'd walked alone. Had I traveled that route enough in the past weeks to do it without assistance? The music helped too, serving as a homing device to guide us, like when I walked in on Rengas during his music practice.

We entered the scene just as the first song ended. The whole room of thirty or so party guests erupted into applause, and luckily only a few of them saw us enter.

The band we had heard outside could now be seen in two sections to the left and the right of the entrance. The music dwindled to a calmer pace, merely providing an atmospheric noise for the guests in attendance.

I wasn't a good liar, but I was a compulsive one. It was probably best to just stay out of the conversation.

The prince was probably on his throne, I thought, because guests were crowding around that area. I couldn't see Rengas himself.

The party attendants were of an unusual assortment. The different species, heights, and sizes of guests showcased Rengas Averell's inter-dimensional connections in full. For Light's sake, there was even a bipedal feline person with a peg leg conversing with Ginger. They both sipped on their drinks while they side-eyed Rengas and his gang.

We passed the two, and Ginger gave us both a wave. I could hear bits and pieces of the prince's voice from someplace in the room yet couldn't spot him no matter how hard I tried. "Salutations, General! Sorry I had to come late, I was getting Lamplight. Rough mornings come to all of us." Rocky patted me on the back, making me bristle and tense despite my obvious fatigue. So clear that, apparently,

* * *

Rocky felt the need to bring it up. Ginger pouted sympathetically and attempted to reassure me as well.

"It's okay, the party hasn't been going long! Ren is getting his birthday presents. If you didn't know, Guno, a nice gesture is just half of the gift exchange for nobles. The other half is diplomacy."

"Diplomacy?" A birthday party seemed like the least appropriate place for something of that sort.

"If other dimensions offer him cool things, he'll be kinder to them and their kind in the future. It's basic Dashaner nature, and Rengas is as basic as it gets."

I chuckled to myself at her comment, looking to Rocky. His eyes were fixed on the prince in question. When he caught me looking, he jumped slightly with a shudder. "Ah! We should see what all the commotion is about." He laughed too, but in an unfunny, skittish manner.

"I agree. See you later, General." I bid her goodbye and followed Rocky toward the group that was now emitting various gasps, "oohs" and "aahs'" at a party guest with a fin of bright green hair held out of his face with a pair of clunky goggles. He stood on the side of the large throne cushion. Now that we had come close enough, we could see the other end of this throne, with the prince of the hour lounged against its backrest.

Rengas wore a makeshift crown of vines and flowers that was likely a present from another person in this cluster. The crown was only one offering of many that were keeping him company.

The man with the tall green hair held up a small rectangular device attached to a thin string that split into two. A section of this rectangular device emitted a strong glow. "Not only does this M-P-Three player glow, ladies and gentlemen- it also emits an audio signal through these here 'buds.' You simply insert both ends into your ears, and you will soon be enjoying audio pleasures from the far-off land of Earth!" The man boasted, wiggling the thing around. A woman beside him with short curly ginger hair tugged on the side of his jacket, whispering something in his ear as he leaned down to her. He stood again.

Rocky and I fought to get closer to Rengas, pushing past a few people. Rocky, being castle staff, helped us cut through without much hassle. Now that there were no obstructions, I could clearly see the other objects that had been presented. A beautiful woven blanket sitting in his lap. A golden comb. A jade dagger. Every gift I laid my eyes upon became more luxurious than the last, but this MP3 player, as the man called it, seemed to be the obvious winner of this petty competition. If a person in the crowd was not astonished by the foreigner's device, they were frustrated that their offering had been overshadowed.

Someone in the group raised their hand, a ground elf woman, likely from another sector. I didn't recognize her. She giggled sheepishly when called on, her large yellow rounded ears pitching downward. "Ah, yes. Um, is this M-Z-Three thing alive? Do you need to feed it?" She peeped, and the green-haired fellow gave a questioning look to his ginger friend. After he got some more whispers from her, he answered:

"No! It does not need food. Only love?" He grimaced—a few individuals awwed. Rengas only smirked, impressed. His arm rested on the back of the throne as he gazed up at the man in goggles with a smug, half-amused regard. He lifted his hand but couldn't reach to take it directly from him. The throne was too large.

The man stepped down from his perch and paced to the other end of the throne to hand it to him.

"You never fail to impress me, Phoenix." He commented slyly, turning the thing over in his hands. Even though Phoenix had said the thing wasn't alive, he was still treating it like some mechanical, glowing newborn pup.

"What do you expect from the biggest portal hub in the multiverse? I know my way around."

Phoenix must have been from Afferas. It was a dimension only the size of a large city, used for the transport of goods. Afferas was the largest portal device manufacturing dimension, too. People who chose to *live* there had to be fearless beyond belief.

"Still, it's impressive- how'd you get into Earth? They're on portal lockdown; how didn't you get caught?"

"I have someone on the inside," Phoenix remarked with a clever tone, gesturing to his ginger friend. She was stout in stature and quite pale. She struggled to introduce herself in Common Speech, her words choppy and imprecise.

"Hello, uh- Me, Jupiter."

"An Earthling! by Light, I'm honored." He shook her hand enthusiastically with both of his. Rengas caught my gaze. "Guno! I didn't think you'd come, ah-" He flushed slightly, letting go of Jupiter. She went back to conversing with Phoenix, tapping his shoulder and motioning for them to step aside, away from the congregation.

Rengas waved politely at Rocky before speaking to me. "I'm glad you decided to join us. I'm sorry it's so crowded; I didn't want to force you to be here if you'd get overwhelmed."

● ● ●

"No, It's okay. I just didn't know this was all going on."

"I really should have told you ahead of time. I try not to make it a big deal, but," He shrugged. That plan clearly didn't work out. "Just wait until the Light and Portal Ball rolls around. Now *that's* a crowd. You'll probably still be at the Capital with us at the time of the ball, shouldn't he?" He asked Rocky, who nodded, his rough crimson scales already beginning to shimmer with sweat.

"Who's hosting this year?" Rocky managed, wringing his hands.

"I believe Tenth, but I'm not certain." Tenth was a smaller sector, yet far denser in population than Ninth. All contained within an enormous cavern, cities were packed, almost touching one another. This made it so some sections between cities were technically Farlands that you could travel through without risk of a creature attack. The sheer number of mountains and hills allowed people to fit into little nooks and crannies and for predators to be none the wiser. Its climate was also a good bit cooler than ours.

A festival there sounded wonderful. They probably wouldn't take me with them, I thought, as exciting as it sounded.

Rengas's eyes fell to the floor. He looked to be deep in thought for a few moments. When his head tilted up again, he was glaring at a point behind us. Turning, I saw Rioh standing with a cluster of what were likely other military leaders. His cold eyes moved from Rengas' to mine. I shivered and quickly averted my gaze.

"Don't worry about the captain. If he knows what's best for him, he'll keep his distance from you," He reached out to pat me on the shoulder. "I already gave him a warning." At least that much was true- nearly throwing his fist into Rioh's face made for a warning and a half. The worrying thing was that Rioh didn't seem phased then, and neither did he now. I was willing to bet the captain would do whatever it took for the "betterment and safety" of the Ninth sector.

"Oh, I had something to ask you," He added, turning to tuck the MP3 player into the blanket he'd gotten for his other present to keep the little machine safe, "I know it's Ginger's turn this afternoon; but can I train with you? I'd be interested in trying to level up from the basic steps we've been practicing." I glanced at Rocky, to whom Rengas was giving very little attention. The elf was already gone, off attending to other guests.

"Of course, your highness."

To my surprise, the prince scoffed. "Don't call me that anymore. Please, call me Rengas."

"Alright, Rengas. I'd love to." I corrected, receiving a jubilant grin from the prince, which faltered as he tried and failed to hide it. Several people were clearly waiting to speak to him, so I stepped back and let them talk.

I wandered back over to Ginger, who was serving herself a drink in a tall glass. It was deep bluish green in color with foam at the top.

"Care for some pommerac wine?" She offered, taking a sip from her glass. Pommeracs, little potent fruits that stained your tongue blue in an instant, must've been the source of the color. I'd never seen one made into wine before.

"Sure. I don't drink very much, so go easy." She snickered, pouring it from a pitcher until the little glass was half full. She handed it over carefully.

"Go easy indeed. This stuff is powerful." Ginger said, yet she took another long sip without batting an eye. I swirled it around, pretending I knew what I was doing, buying time by watching the bubbles in it float to the top.

I took a deep breath before slowly lifting the glass to my lips.

Not terrible. The flavor was a little bitter, but nothing I wasn't used to. There was an extra kick of aftertaste that hit at the back of your tongue. I sputtered and coughed into my fist.

"Ugh, wow, you weren't joking about that." After collecting myself, we stepped away from the drink table. Ginger shrugged.

"So, how is Rengas doing? Please tell me he hasn't gone on another flirting streak again. Those never end well for anyone involved." She raised an eyebrow in his direction. I squinted.

"No! Well, at least not when I was over there. Don't know what he's up to now." Is that what he'd been doing with all those party guests? With Phoenix too? No, that couldn't be true. At least I didn't think so. Bright Saint Parkeyre, I cursed at myself; I didn't want to think about it anymore.

Ginger raised her eyebrows at my expression. "Anyways, he's said he wants to train with me this time, although he's not scheduled for today. I'm guessing he means tonight."

Ginger smiled off in his direction. She appeared way too pleased, especially considering she didn't emote all that often. Not *this* much.

"Tonight?" She quirked an eyebrow, pursing her lips and taking another sip of the pommerac wine.

"Yeah. What of it?" I responded with a small displeased growl.

"Nothing, nothing." She hid another smile behind her glass.

The guests all had an early dinner together in the grand dining hall, where we all sat around a long table that extended from one end of the enormous room to the other. My eyes raked over the vast expanse of fine china and golden ware, causing me to accidentally spill few drops of the oddly shiny soup I was serving myself.

I'd never seen food so closely attended to. Things were evenly portioned and arranged out on large plates to look like flowers. Napkins looked like they were cut from portions of the tapestry. The point of our meal almost felt lost among all its gallantry.

Rocky sat beside me on one side, Ginger on the other. Rengas was at the head of the table, making quite a racket but not picking up much food. Every once and a while, he'd take something small in his mouth, but not often enough to constitute a whole meal. He sat in his chair sideways as if he were still on his throne.

Ginger and Rocky showed perfect table manners, which I tried to emulate. The whole "elbows stay below the table" rule proved to be particularly difficult in the two hours or so we were there. Luckily for me, the captain decided not to join us for that part of the party. I didn't want his eyes on me any more than I'd gotten that day.

Rengas found me right as he was saying goodbye to the last of the guests. His eagerness was nearly alarming, I thought.

He turned to me with another one of his confusing looks. Then he walked right up to me, grabbed my hand, and led me out of the entrance hall. We walked past where Ginger oversaw the guards near the door and down a hallway before he stopped in his tracks. Rengas's hand slipped clumsily away from mine.

"I'm getting carried away. We need training clothes and an extra change, and a towel too for afterward. Do you want me to see to that, or do you want to-"

"I can get my clothes myself, Rengas. It's a nice thought, though." I gave him an encouraging pat on the shoulder. "I'll meet you up there." I turned and started to my room to get them. It was hard to imagine this bumbling fool was the same Rengas Averell that Cypress spoke so highly of just a few months ago. He still had this haughty mystery about him, sure, but I had a feeling that there was more to him than the rumors exchanged back on the ground level. There had already been plenty of evidence to suggest it—for instance, his childish eagerness for something as routine as training.

I packed all my things into my little basket after changing and started up to the courtyard. I took my map with me just in case but ended up not needing to look at it after all.

* * *

Pulling the door open, I wasn't surprised to find that Rengas had already arrived. He was sitting on the floor, wrapping his hands in bandages.
His face was completely bare of paint.
I felt myself prickle with embarrassment as I fell back to shield my eyes.
"Sorry! I didn't know you were- *I hadn't meant to-*" I stammered and tried to back toward the door blindly. I couldn't get the image of it out of my mind. He did know I was going to be here, right?
I heard the prince laugh a little. "No, I should be the one apologizing. I didn't ask if this was okay." There was a small pause. I didn't remove my hand from my eyes. "*Is* it okay if I train without paint? It doesn't really mix with sweat."
"Uh-yeah. Yeah. Sure, that's fine." I cleared my throat rigidly, then lowered my hands, letting the prince come back into view.
He grinned, tipping his head to the side to indicate to the floor beside him. I shook off my nerves to approach him. I set my basket down on one of the benches beside the weapons holding room. From the basket I took some cloth scraps that I'd torn from the pants I came to the capital in.
A week or so ago, I started experimenting with further padding besides mere cloth. I'd tried packing first aid gauze and fluff underneath the bandaging so that if I hit the ground, it would provide a little more protection. I settled down beside him, watching him work, and set the little bundle of cloth scraps in my lap.
I noticed as he wrapped his palms that his fingertips were discolored: reddened in streaks, great scars that had once scoured his hands completely. Yet no skin was terribly disturbed now, leaving only a whisper of whatever caused it. Rengas must've noticed my staring. I opened my mouth to speak when he interrupted, his attention on the cloth in my lap.
"What are those?" He asked, tucking in the bandage on his hand.
"Cloth scraps. I'm going to try using them for padding on my elbows and knees." I took a good amount from the top. "Do you want some?"
"Yes, please." I moved to assist him, holding the bandage and cloth in place as he wrapped. He helped me do the same with my padding.

"Have you tried using your staff to train with? If it means something to you, it may be a more effective Light tool." He said as I brought my hands back to myself.

"I think that's why Ginger hasn't let me try it yet. Maybe she thinks the familial tie it has will be *too* powerful? I can't see the harm in trying it, though."

This staff had been my father's. He set off on a work trip when I was ten to the mining province in Fourth Sector. It was a long way's walk, but it guaranteed a large payout for my family if he ever returned. He made us promise on the day he left not to go looking for him if he didn't make it back. *When* he didn't make it back. It was at that point I already knew what would become of his trip. My mother and I kept our promise. We didn't try. I still regret that.

Before the staff was my father's, it had been my grandmother's and my great-grandfather's before her. My lineage, similarly to a lot of others in Ninth Sector, suffered from a lot of early deaths and missing persons. That kind of thing happened so often that it was almost an expected occurrence. At least I was fortunate enough to have a family completely composed of dedicated Light Supporters.

I thought there was no use in trying to explain that to him. Villagers were used to things that would be unthinkable here in the capital. I'd just make him uncomfortable. In any case, we're nothing alike, I told myself. Whining about things that should be left to the past would do no good.

He looked at me in a way that suggested he was deciding what to say. We were sitting on the floor, all ready to go. If this were Ginger training with me, she'd certainly have me on my feet by now.

"I wouldn't want to disobey Ginger's wishes." He muttered finally, smoothing back his hair, which was just long enough to be bothersome, yet too short of tying the top bit out of his eyes if it went out of order. "We can just use the staves they have here, or we can practice hand-to-hand. What do you think?"

"How about both? Once one disarms the other, we can do hand-to-hand for the rest until the other is completely disarmed?" He agreed. Getting my staff and squaring up to all six and a half or so feet of him was daunting, to say the least, but I tried to keep a tough exterior. I'd proved I could do it before and now was no different. I kept up for a while, ducking beneath his coordinated attacks as they came and jumping over others.

"You're quite fast, Lamplight!" He grinned at me while blocking my hit and using the leverage to toss my staff away from him. As I recoiled and regained my grip, he caught me behind the ankle and sent me stumbling backward. I was able to catch myself without falling, thank Light, but by then; I'd been thrown off my rhythm. I went for a risky high shot that aimed for his head, which he easily dodged. He caught my staff against his and twisted it out of my arms, launching it away. It kicked up the earth as it landed an impressive distance away.

"Well done!" He said, spinning his own staff. His sweat merely added an extra gleam to his skin. I could only imagine what mine looked like as I wiped a good amount of it from my brow.

"Thanks." I clucked in annoyance. Why'd he have to congratulate me? It almost felt mocking.

The prince only frowned slightly and put down his staff. Rengas approached me with that swingy gait of his, raising both hands in front of him. "Well, are you ready?"

I narrowed my eyes at Rengas, raising my hands too - and I sprung myself on him before he could declare the fight's start. It might not have been fair to the prince, but he had a leg up already. It wouldn't do any harm.

    I wound my leg around him, trying to push him back so he would fall, but he only grabbed me around the middle. He tried to push me over, too, and we struggled around for a little while before I opted for a different approach. Wiggling around, I tried to slip out of his arms. I set my foot on his hip, using it as a step as I wrapped my arms around his head and swung forward to knock him off balance. He didn't figure out how to pull me off him in time, and we both came toppling to the ground.

 Lucky thing the prince knew how to fall, and he didn't injure himself. My last thought as I shifted our weight off-balance was, "Oh Light, what if I accidentally kill him." Good thing none of that came to be.

    I struggled to pin him down, and I realized quite quickly the prince's strength as he simply rolled over and pinned me instead, pressing my arms into the ground. I could hear him muttering under his breath: "*Five, four, three, two, one.*"

At that point, I had given up completely on trying to get out of the pin. He was incredibly heavy in height *and* muscle mass, not to mention he had experience.

As he lingered there, I saw him go a deep red. This was the first time I'd seen him without paint. Royalty wasn't supposed to let anyone but their most trusted family see them with an exposed face. The intimacy of that alone had made me nervous throughout our brawl. That was why I lost, I thought. I was put off—no other reason. I'd bet the color his face has now matched the color of his paint quite closely. His eyes were growing hazy and uncertain.

I growled. I couldn't stand that look, especially while he was bare faced. It left too many of my questions unanswered.

"Get offa' me." I gritted my teeth at him, and he obliged.

"Ugh, oh my. I'm deeply sorry." He stood, dusted off his knees, and held out a hand to help me up. "Uh- did the padding help any?"

"I think so," I said stiffly, checking for any damage. There was none that I could see, although I was a bit sore from being held to the ground so roughly. "How about you?" He *looked* fine. More than fine, I would say.

"Yeah, it was a good idea." I glanced at him up and down. It was odd seeing him in exercise clothing too, which was much simpler and more masculine than the things he typically wore around the capital.

He awkwardly offered that we continue. We went through the last few phases of Light training without looking at one another much at all: fighting endurance exercises, where we repeated moves over and over until we got them down. I found these to be much easier with another person practicing alongside you, keeping each movement's beat. First, we pretended our staves were just normal Light spears, then imitated sword movements. After that came muscle building, some weights were brought out from the weapons chamber, and I dragged out the pull-up bar from the arena's sidelines. It was difficult to pretend I wasn't fascinated by the way he moved, then. How every flex of muscle seemed completely planned out and intentional, like he carried his studiousness around with him, even in acts of solely physical strength.

What was harder was pretending *I* knew what I was doing. I struggled to keep up with him in that regard, so keeping my cool was quite the task. Afterward was the cool down and meditation. In Light training, cool down was taken in quite the literal sense. By wrapping up the entire session, you reestablish the connection you formed at the beginning of training and receive your reward. A little surge of Light and euphoria passes over you, and for me, a glimmer of hope. I usually felt like I was in a better mood after practice and felt much freer. The weight of Dark wasn't as pressing in those times. For most Light supporters, the process is supposed to literally *chill* you.

While we closed off for the night, Rengas muttered something under his breath, then opened one eye cleverly from his previous meditative state. He leaned over and grabbed my wrist, guiding it to touch his sand-dusted forearm. It was slightly cold to the touch. He had goosebumps.

"I'm so cold, and we aren't even outside. I can feel Her. Light's taken a liking to me." He grinned, staring down at his own arm.

"You must be doing something right then." I tried to smooth down the fine white hair on his arm and to brush off some of the dirt; it only stuck upright again.

"Did She *not* like you before?"
He sniggered, looking up to the sky. "I don't know, did you?" Rengas asked the air, grinning at nothing- then he made a sharp intake of breath as a shiver went up to his spine. His eyes turned to me, wonderstruck. "Did you feel that?"

"Not really- did you feel something?"

"Yeah. Just got another chill." He burst out in a fit of ecstatic laughter that lit up his entire face, and when he calmed down, he added, "Come on, Guno. Let's go get cleaned up."

We reached the little bath that was built into this courtyard. A small stone path through the trees that led to it nestled beautifully into a clearing. It had places to put your spare clothes and a towel so they wouldn't get wet. The bath question was a nice-sized pool, only really big enough for one, with a waterfall that ran over one side that you could go under. There were also a few soaps left on edge to clean with. I had brought my basket with me.

After we had removed our bandaging, we were both happy to see very little scraping. I held the basket close as we entered the clearing.

I stood rigidly by the poolside, awaiting his instruction. Rengas positioned himself beside me, looking into the water.
"You want to go first?" He offered, his towel and change of clothes tucked under his arm.

"Sure." I stared at him awhile, raising my eyebrows pointedly.
"Oh. Right. I'll just sit over here. I'll turn away."
"Right." I nodded, hesitating even after he situated himself in the corner of the clearing. *As if seeing him without paint wasn't enough*, I thought, *now this?* I wasn't sure how much more I could take. I stripped and shook out my sand-filled clothes before folding them up haphazardly and rushing to get in. I had plenty to look at in here. The scenery was beautiful, and most of the plants that surrounded the clearing were sorts I'd never seen before, not in my wildest dreams.

● ● ●

Instead, as I was washing and wringing out my hair, I found my gaze lingering on Rengas situated in the corner. How he trembled slightly, his hand coming up to rub the back of his neck out of nerves. What made him so tense? What compelled him to be so outward and expressive one moment and then shy away the next? I frowned to myself, stepped out and started to dry off. Once I was all dressed, I crossed to Rengas and tagged him in.

"Your turn," I noted. His eyes wandered up to me, lost, and he stood.

"Hey, you alright?"

"I'm okay. Just in thought. I've had a lot to think over lately." He said, giving a tepid smile.

"I have to. Take it easy, alright?" I don't know why I felt the need to reassure him. I guess he was the kindest to me, out of anyone here. I laid my towel on the ground and sat down, taking his place. "Do you want me to leave?"

"No, ah- you can stay. I don't mind." His voice came from behind me. Then there was the sound of rustling. I fought myself not to look. After a while, Rengas piped up again.

"How are you feeling? Light and Dark wise, I mean." He said.

"I dunno. It's kind of muddied right now. Like they're melting together inside me. It's better than nothing, I guess." I shrugged, separating a piece of my hair from the rest to braid. It would keep my attention for a bit.

"Does your faith seem sort of lost? Aimless?" His words met my ears luxuriously, relaxing my nerves. "Because even though I've never had an altercation with Dark, I've felt the same way." He trailed off.

"Why is that?"

The prince took his time before speaking. There was careful consideration to it, just as with his fighting. "At the time, I had no motivation to pursue Light at all. I had almost given up on trying to achieve Beaconism completely. I no longer cared for it." I listened to the sounds of rushing water, maybe being wrung out of his hair.

"I was technically Light but not nearly as much as I am now. I felt like I was lost in this grey area." I nearly turned around then to face him, to read his expression- but I resisted.

"Was this recent?"

"Several years ago. I was a naive teenager." He chuckled. There was more rustling. He must have been nearly done. I gave him a moment before turning around. He was still dressing, pulling on a thin shirt. As he adjusted it and tied it off around his waist, he caught me looking and smiled. His hair was still somewhat wet. It was strange seeing it this flat and out of place. Still grinning to himself, he said:

"Something bad would happen to me, and I would ask, 'Light, why me? I do everything I can for you.' I would expect things to just improve on their own. I would sit there, moping over my morning tea, just wondering what I'd done to deserve all the things that had come to pass," His look became distant as he picked up his towel and threw it over his arm. His eyes wandered back to mine and came back into focus.

"Kind of pathetic, huh? I'm the prince; it's a little selfish to think I don't have it good."

"No, it's not pathetic. You deserve to feel things like anyone else- no one's gonna deny you that." I shook my head, getting up to meet him and placing a hand on his arm. Rengas's gaze fell to the floor as he tensed slightly, his smile fading. It was hard to believe that he'd do something like that in vain, but it did make me wonder.

There was a long pause. I let him think before he spoke again quite suddenly, with a new thought.

"How many unlikely coincidences does it take for you to believe it's a pattern? Like there must be something there as a catalyst, at the very least?"

What a vague question. How would you answer something like that?

"It depends. Do you- do you want to talk about it?" I offered, still holding his arm. He shrugged me off.

"No. Don't worry about it, I'm fine." He shook his head, starting toward the path that led out of the clearing. I watched him go, packing up my things. "Safe-night, Guno. I bid you well."

    I soon had been training for almost ten months. The castle staff knew me and my doings and no longer stood on guard or pointed their spears at me as I passed to go to the library or the garden or to get breakfast. These days Rengas was seen less and less. We didn't cross paths as much. I would often wait up for him only for Ginger to find me and advise me to go to sleep.
    "Our Prince won't be down for a while," She would say, "It's best you got your rest."
    And I did. Whatever Rengas Averell chose to do was none of my business. Yet it felt odd for no one to tell me, and it felt even stranger that *he* didn't tell me before locking himself up someplace. The first time I saw him after those dry weeks, I caught him by the arm before he could disappear into a side room.
    "Ren! Where have you been all this time?" I questioned him almost frantically, making him hold a bundle of something closer to his chest. He avoided my eyes for a moment, then relaxed. He smiled faintly at me with one of those secret looks. That sort of privacy in his stare always rendered me breathless. I tried not to show it.
    "I'm not allowed to tell you, Guno, as much as I would love to."
I considered this, releasing his arm, my hand trailing down it. His skin felt like it had been heated in the sun.
    "Will you at least tell me when you'll be back?"
    I watched the prince swallow uncomfortably, peering into the door where he was headed. He put the bundle down inside the room and closed the door. His face was written over with uncertainty- over what I couldn't tell.
    "Soon, I will be gone for a good while, a few weeks at the least. I will leave the capital to," His eyes flickered about as he chose his words. "To complete my princely duties. There is a certain requirement I must pass."
My brow furrowed. *What requirement?*

"I'll admit, I'm a tad apprehensive over being gone that long, too." He exhaled deeply, and I was about to reply when he stepped forward and took me in his arms. His embrace wasn't tight, but it lingered. I could feel my tension ease in the comfort and Light of him, and when he let go, I wished it had lasted longer. "I will miss you, friend. I think I'll miss you the most." He hesitated, as if about to reach out for me again, but ultimately decided against it. "If I don't see you again before I leave, I bid you farewell. Talk to Ginger, okay? I don't want you to feel alone," He frowned, then reached into a pocket in his coat. "Oh, and will you take care of this? I'm afraid it will fall ill if I bring it with me."

He produced from his pocket the MP3 player he'd gotten for his birthday, an object that rarely left his hands. It was a great responsibility to be given, no doubt.

"Of course. Is there anything I need to do with it, or-"

"Just keep it close. You can use it to listen to Earth music if you want. Here." He pushed a button on the device, making the screen ignite with a soft glow. "That's how you wake it up and put it to sleep."

"Oh- okay, thank you." I didn't care to remind him that the thing wasn't alive, so I nodded. He bowed his head and disappeared behind the door.

That night I took his advice. Ginger would probably know what was going on the most out of anyone. Directly after a session of training alone, I planned to meet her. But first, I cut through the courtyard, stepping through thick shrubbery into the deeper forest to get clean. I had to look presentable in front of the General.

I did different things each time I trained, but most times, it just meant moving about the space as it feels right, trying to reach out into Light's embrace. Sometimes I felt pretty close to Her, but most of the time, I only felt slightly safer.
It was as if all this work was just preventing me from going completely under the veil of Darkness. My work held me aloft over His rancid pit, just out of Dark's reach as His great tendrils lashed out at my feet.

All of this being said, I felt secure enough as I dressed and prepared to meet with Ginger that day. I wasn't having nearly as many violent thoughts. I didn't feel as if I'd split in half. Training had been conditioning my soul to be more elastic so that when Dark feelings came, I wouldn't crumble. I would only flow and reach out like water along a smooth surface before returning to my real faith.

After tying up my hair to bathe, I peered into my reflection in the water. I found my hands moving to my own arms, feeling over the new curves and broader dimension I'd developed over the months I'd been there. I looked into my own eyes, one it's deep earthen brown, the other the stark, pained ring of pure Dark power.

When would it fade? Would I always be marked for my mistakes that weren't even my choice to make from the start? I smoothed my hair back and out of my eyes with a resigned sigh.

Once I had dressed in a clean change of clothes, I reported to my planned destination. The doors to Ginger's office were tall and often left open. I assumed that meant she was accepting visitors, and my thoughts were reaffirmed when I peeked in the doorway and saw her conversing with the captain. His deep sunken, mean eyes glared my way only once. I thought the severe tone of it meant he was commenting on my appearance, causing me to hesitantly touch my still-damp hair that had been pulled up out of my eyes.

I realized it was probably the eyes in question that were the issue. I gave him a courteous nod and continued up to her desk while their conversation slowly died out.

"Plenty of other sectors don't even bat an eye when sending their heirs out to- what I'm saying is, it's fine, Captain. We'll continue this later."

He moved his glare to Ginger, his mechanical Light cannon arm stiff by his side, then briskly left the room. He'd gotten enough vengeful looks in, for now, it seemed.

"Good afternoon, Guno. Just back from training?"

"Yes, how did you-"

"Your hair is wet, and you look exhausted. Good to see our prince wasn't the only thing motivating you to train." I scrunched up my face at her, and she chuckled. She sat back down at her desk, gesturing to a large chair positioned in front of it. "Sit. Is this about him?"

"Well- yes." I obliged, combing through my hair while it was still damp so it would be easier to brush later. "Is Rengas going to become a Beacon? He's been gone so often. Why didn't he tell me? Or you. You could've told me." I knew it was rude to ask in the first place. One's beaconism pilgrimage was a deeply personal experience.

"*This* is exactly why, Lamplight." Ginger waved her hand in a circle around my face. I blinked crossly at her, shifting back in my seat.

"What?"

"If I told you he's walking into the middle of the Farlands, you'd never let him go," She folded her hands on the desk. When I could supply no response, she nodded.

✦ ✦ ✦

"You care about him. It's sad that I have to be the one to tell you. It's alright. He needs someone to care about him besides Rocky and I."

"What are you talking about?" In reality, I had a pretty good idea of what she meant. I understood every word.

"You're from the ground, Guno. You, more than anyone, know the dangers of venturing into the Farlands. We were afraid that if you were allowed to have a goodbye, you'd end up convincing him to stay." She huffed quietly. "You do have quite a sway on him. He'd believe you and stay at the capital instead of following his path: one he's been trying it for quite a while, might I add."

I couldn't bring myself to look at her after that. *Would I stop him?* I'm pretty sure Rengas would stay even if I *looked* at him in the wrong way. At least Ginger was right in that respect.

I did want him to go. This was important to him, as a chance at Beaconism would be for anyone. I wondered exactly how long he'd been trying at this. I thought back to the Beacon elder I never got to meet, a woman that likely tried half her life to get to that point.

I also didn't want him to die. From that point, I was already expecting that thought to haunt me for weeks, maybe months on end; however long this trip took. When imagining what would happen if Rengas didn't make it back, I couldn't even think over the details without feeling sick.

"I guess that's fair." I pressed my eyes closed with a sigh. There was the sound of calm footsteps, and when I opened my eyes, Ginger stood over me and was kindly rubbing my arm.

"Just concentrate on your work. Train, read up on Light as you usually have, write in your journal. He'll be back in no time."

She ended it with a firm pat before leaning back on the desk. She looked off toward the wall, decorated with maps of the sectors and a closer map of Ninth Sector alone. Her eyes grazed over all the empty areas that comprised each, inhabited by no intelligent life forms. Farlands dwelling people who robbed you of everything you had then ripped you apart too. People that used your bones to pick their teeth. Greater moles and living hills and Limbers. Dangerous things no one should be forced to encounter.

Ginger's face echoed everything I felt: utter helplessness. She pushed up her monocle and turned her head solemnly back toward me.

"Care to have tea and dinner later? We can sit on the balcony above the ballroom."

❊ ❊ ❊

"That would be nice."

I met her that night as she requested of me, parting the delicate curtain and peering out into the night, creeping up to the railing of the balcony. Every once in a while a support on this railing would contain a Light lantern, whose soft glow illuminated the writhing shapes of the night. They knew well enough not to attempt to scale the mountain this palace was built on, in its whole scope, with its grand balcony stretching all the way around like the deck of a ship. If this was anywhere else but the capital, I'd be afraid to be out in the open like this, especially at this height.

It was beautiful out here, but the General was nowhere in sight. I'd realized by then how nonspecific "balcony" was as a descriptor, especially since there were *multiple* ballrooms in the capital. It would be impossible to tell which, for she could be in any one of them. I didn't mind the walk, though. I got to see the palace from all angles as I rounded it, sometimes weaving in and out of the archways on the interior side of the balcony. Eventually, I did find her lounging on a little chair at a tea table in a sitting area that jutted out from the rest of the floor. The only things on this table were another Light lamp, a small pot of tea, and two cups.

The whole scene was rather poetic, or at least it would look to be so if my mind wasn't racing so much. Ginger's long military cloak gave her a unique silhouette with the jacket's tall, popped collar. Ginger's face was illuminated from below. She smiled, which appeared somewhat menacing in the low light, and beckoned me over with just a slight tilt of her head.

I met her at the table and sat across from her, giving a small thank you as she poured me a perfect cup of tea using one hand. She didn't spill a single drop.

"What precision." I breathed, leaning forward.

"I was taught with the best of them. Raised with castle etiquette since birth, strangely enough."

"You're not originally from here, are you? The question had been lingering at the back of my mind for quite a while. Ginger had a sort of different physique than most Dashaners, But of course, that could just be her military background. What really stood out was her hair. I'd never seen something so bright from a Dashan native.

"I'm not; you're correct." She replaced the teapot on its little tray. "I immigrated here from Afferas, the same place where Rengas's junk trader friend is from. The one who gave him that." She pointed to the MP3 player in my hand. I placed it on the table.

"Well, that makes sense," I replied and was met with a chuckle. I don't think she was offended; her gaze into the darkened horizon remained reminiscent.

"Does it, now?" There was a pause. Ginger took a wistful sip from her teacup. "I was drafted to Ninth in a courtship program Rengas's parents started seven years ago. He and I were only fifteen- though I'm eight months older. Not that it matters." She smiled bemusedly, giving a short, clever glance my way.

Wait, was Ginger and Rengas betrothed? It couldn't be. If they were betrothed, she wouldn't still be the General, right? If it were true, she'd be with him, decorated with royal markings.
For some reason, merely entertaining the idea made me slightly uneasy as I hid my face behind my teacup to drink. Ginger paused for a moment, then said,

"No- we're not together. Not like that. Not anymore, at least." She made sure that point was clear as she waved a hand dismissively about. "He picked me to be his bride, but I knew that leading our army was my true calling in the end, even if it meant leaving him." Her clever smile fell a little as she swirled the tea in her cup. "He was devastated, but I think he understood that it was best for both of us." This came as a relief. I hadn't even realized my grip on my cup had tightened until I released said grip, setting down my drink.

"Is he still upset about it?" I found myself mumbling, and Ginger stopped me before I could dig myself any deeper with that thought.

"No. He's gotten over me. Light, could you imagine? Holding onto the memory of someone for seven years."

To be honest, it didn't seem outside the realm of possibility for him. Prince Rengas undoubtedly seemed the type to hold onto things like that, but it eased my nerves to hear that it wasn't the case.

• • •

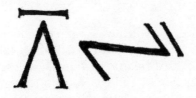

    I wouldn't see Rengas for weeks. I tried not to pay too much attention to how much time passed. I didn't tell Ginger that when Rengas eventually did leave, early in the morning, I heard the distant scraping of the front gates and rushed to watch him go. I quickly threw on a tunic and took the stairs down my spire two or three at a time, veering for the quickest exit leading to the balcony.

    Sure enough, there he was, descending the stairs down the mountain of the capital until he was only a shiny speck in the sand. I watched this small shape move across my vision before eventually disappearing behind a hill. I watched him go with a heavy heart, touching the MP3 player stowed away in the pocket of my trousers. Almost immediately as the prince left, there came a twinge at my chest: a tugging sensation not dissimilar to the ones I often got at night when Alice would try and pull me around. I was lucky that she wasn't strong enough to venture anywhere in the capital besides my head.

    She was pestering me about that book again. Fortunately, now I knew why. I wouldn't skirt around the idea of her anymore. I was in place of Light now. My *heart* was in place of Light, where she'd never reach me.

    Well, hopefully, I thought.

    The beckoning feeling pulled me toward Rengas's bedroom this time. Odd. Why would he put the book in there? Sure, he'd been working on translations, but why take it out of the library?

    Was it because of me?

    That couldn't possibly be true. Rengas would never *double-cross* me like that, I thought. That's not how he thinks of me.

My hands clenched into fists, crackling with electrifying warmth. I rolled my head in a circle as I tried and failed to shake off this presence that kept reminding me that it belonged there, feeding off my consciousness like a parasite.

I am, and I always will be, It seemed to say. At that point, I couldn't tell who had sent the message.

• • •

Now go. You know what you must do.
 It would be fine, right? If I snuck in just for a moment, took a quick look at Alice's book? Just a little peek?
 Maybe if I read too much, I'd go too deep. Maybe there was a point of Dark where sinking to the bottom of His pit was inevitable, and you had to stop kicking and screaming because it would only tire you out to no avail.
 I found myself at the base of the stairs leading up to the prince's quarters. From what I could gather, the room was similar to mine but much larger. As I ascended the top steps of his spire and came to the magnificent upper landing, I was greeted by two guards. It looked as if they knew I'd be here.
 "Good day, Lamplight. Do you have a reason to be here?" One of them droned, lowering their head slightly to regard me. I swallowed and took a step back.
 "Ahhh yes, *ummm*, the prince? He..."
 "He left already." One stated the obvious,
 "And?" The other noted.
 "He told me to, *uhhh* put this back? Yes." I brandished his MP3 player, "And to, to get some books he has picked out for me. He assigned me a few things. Part of Light training." The two guards flanking the door looked at one another for a tense moment that lasted far too long before one spoke.
 "Very well. But we will follow you in."
 I released a breath I'd been holding for the entirety of the time they were silently discussing my plea and kept my head low as the two let me into his quarters. I didn't like at all how I could feel their gaze on my back while I searched the room for my target.
 His room was just as you would imagine: vast and spacious, with luxurious fittings and a circular bed overwhelmed with pillows. I became greeted by the scent of him in mass quantity: rosemary and fine incense. This human element nearly caused me to come back to my senses, but the book was so close. The smell of the tome alone quickly overpowered anything else that could've stirred up some guilty response in me.
 There were candles- way too many than one person could ever need- sitting on pedestals of different sizes about the room. All of the windows had boxes at the bottoms for vines to grow along the windowsills. Rengas always seemed quite fond of plants, just as I was.
 Rengas's desk was the only messy part in this gigantic room. Adjacent to a wall entirely made of bookshelves, his workspace overflowed with what looked to be discarded projects- countless

✦ ✦ ✦

crumpled up notes and scraps decorated with a beautiful, swirling, delicate script. I couldn't imagine how anyone could throw away writing this pretty, even if the words themselves weren't exactly right.

Once I found the book among many loose pieces of parchment and clutter, I took it and grabbed another book for good measure, stacking that on top. I could only pray neither of the guards had seen or heard of the prince's translation project before this. If so, they would recognize the book in my hands immediately. I set down the MP3 player in its place. I would come back later if this position weren't being patrolled and return it. Part of me didn't want to.

Even though I felt the wrath of Dark begin to course through my forearms, I couldn't bring myself to make eye contact with either of the guards as I left, instead giving them both a quick thanks before skittering off down the stairs.

I took the books over to my own room, tossing the storybook I'd grabbed as a decoy in favor of the plush pink ledger underneath. I opened the cover and read through the translations on the front page once more.

Property of Alice Walker. Do not touch.

And then, a date at the bottom which I had not picked up before:

Started on March Eighteenth, 1922.

I stared at this page for dozens of minutes. I stared for so long without blinking that I lost myself for a moment, trying to listen in for anything. A startlingly familiar stillness hung in the air.

Something, *no, someone-* needed my full attention on this book.

Even so, I couldn't get myself to look farther. Dark itched to turn the pages, to dig deep into whatever secrets Alice had in store, reading and reading until the late hours of the night over every last sinister word.

I fought myself to close it. I'd just keep it in my room and have it nearby. Maybe then Alice and anything else that had decided to burrow into my brain would leave me be. I set the thing down on a shelf suspended across a window and kept the storybook with me instead. It was an adaptation of The Limbernal, a common creation myth over how the limber was crafted as a combination of both Dark and Light's will. It set much of the foundation for why limbers were so respected and feared. No one could harness both forces and live to tell the tale.

Just look at me, for instance. I feared if I continued like this and let Alice guide me, I would tear apart.

Maybe that's what Rengas saw in me. A sympathetic monster whose corrupted nature made him vulnerable. I flipped through the pages idly. I'd never read a physical adaptation, only heard it retold in story circles. By the time I was a teen, the story had become so over-embellished it had gained several offshoots from the main plot and had become more of a saga than a fable- yet I can't say I complained.

It went from simply: Man gets exiled to the Farlands, almost dies, calls upon Dark and Light, and is saved as a Limber. Into: Man receives a prophecy from some fae in a crevice underneath his house, goes to Escuro (Unclear how he got there- I might not have been paying full attention that day). Is about to die when a woman saves him? A good-bad girl? I mean, she was a Dark Supporter, but she wasn't all that bad, morally speaking. This part was definitely told by someone younger. A villager my mom's age would never allow for Dark Supporters being shown in a heroic light like that.

Anyways- then he goes to another dimension, a rich one like Itasnia or Vileth- the details get blurry there. I think he meets a band of adventurers, and somehow they disagree? Dark and Light make them each go on a journey to find themselves?

... And somehow, they all end up as giant skulking horse-dog creatures with lights for eyes. Now that I remember correctly, it didn't make much sense at all. At least there was variation, right?

I went to sleep that night reading The Limbernal by candlelight. My mind kept wandering to our prince. He, too, was lost to the expanse of the Farlands now, just as Limber the Exile had been- yet Rengas did this by choice. He looked all those sand creatures dead in the eyes and decided to face them, not even for the first time. *This wasn't his first try.* Who knows how many takes came before this.

Even if he did have practice, it filled me with great unease to imagine him out there as the beings of the night began to stir. I could see some from my tower when I looked up from my book. Where would Rengas sleep? From what I saw, all he took with him when he left was a hefty rucksack and a Light sword.

Light, I was becoming like Cypress, obsessing over every little detail of him. Perhaps now I understood where my friend was coming from. Ren did have this infectious quality to him that was hard to describe.

I just didn't want him to get hurt, I concluded. He seemed to be the only one who cared that I was alive and the reason I was here and not dead in some ditch, or worse- in Ninth Sector Penitentiary where they'd throw me over the fence for Limber feed.

Maybe this would motivate me even more to pursue Light. The thought that if I built up enough worth in Her eyes, maybe she'd keep our prince safe out there.
What was I talking about? He wasn't called "Son of Light" for no reason. She already *was* protecting him. Or at least that's what I had to tell myself so that I could sleep that night.

The next few nights, I didn't fare much better. I could feel Alice or whatever Dark presence in my mind circling at the edge of my consciousness, but never acting. It remained like this for nine or so days, Light training having little effect on lessening the discomfort it posed.

At the end of the week, she chose to strike after I had finished training and had just gotten ready for bed. The burning sensation in my hands had returned, unprovoked. Knowing what it must mean, I slowly stopped right where I was, getting back up from the bed and turning my eyes toward the windowsill where the lace-edged book sat. I tried calling out to whatever was taunting me.

"What do you want with that book? Is it yours?"

Clever boy. Why yes, it is. I would like it returned to me. But not before you take a look inside. A voice entered, slithering, into the forefront of my thoughts.

"Why would you want me to look in *your* journal?" My own voice came in a husky whisper. I pushed a lock of hair away from my eyes, squinting through the dark.

To show you how much you will improve if you continue to follow me. To show you that we aren't all that different. Except for your foolish attachment to Light, that is.

"I *am* Hers! No matter how my bones might shake with Dark, no matter what sinister desires may cross my mind, I am Hers." I asserted with a quiet huff, "I know it. I don't want to know anything else about you. Is that so hard to understand?"

It was true. Occasionally, when I got angry, something deep inside would tell me it would all be better if I just struck out at the thing bothering me, then continued striking until I was satisfied.

The mere fact that those thoughts and impulses existed scared me. It meant that some part of me actually wanted to do those awful things.

I hope you realize you'll make no progress without me. I hold the only key to a Portal device, remember? Light will never take you back after this. The pain in your heart, it is truly that of a natural-born Umbra.

"A what- you know what, I don't care to know what it is because I'm not one. I'm not a natural-born anything when it comes to Darkness." I stood, whirling around. I knew that nothing could get into the capital, yet this voice -Alice's voice- became clearer by the second. My eyes darted wildly about the room, searching for shapes in the tapestry on the wall, in my wardrobe, in the windowpanes, and in the view outside, dully illuminated by the moons. "And how do I know you can make Portal devices? As far as I've learned, Dark and Light cancel one another out. Someone the likes of you, would never be able to handle a tool of Light like that! A tool filled with Light's very essence!" I didn't even notice as I started to raise my voice. I hoped no one would hear. I don't know what I'd do if anyone were to come in. I was scared of myself. What would I do if I lost control?

She was laughing, now. A triumphant laugh that filled my senses and blurred my vision, causing my chest to tighten.

Very clever. So clever indeed. Do you remember the other thing I offered to you as well? She told me.

"Yes, I do- agh, *I wish a Limber would have its way with you! I wish a swarm of pygmy beasts would tear your skin off! I wish a greater mole would take you and-*" I stopped myself, and there was a pause. She'd gone completely silent... and I'd voiced my urges aloud. *Should I tell someone?* I thought. *What will Ginger think- what will Ren think? Oh Light, what have I done.*

Alice's influence returned only as a squeezing in my lungs that caused my heart to race and for me to choke up. I fumbled to the floor, ready to slowly fizzle out into my demise. Yet I only struggled, breathing irregularly until I somehow drifted to sleep right there, curled up on the rug, one hand clutching at my chest.
Waking the next morning came as a surprise. The dull ache in my ribs remained but seemed to be only a phantom of the damage caused the night prior.
I didn't tell anyone about what happened. I couldn't trust anyone, including myself.
The next night Alice didn't try to contact me again. I still kept my body tense, waiting for the moment she would come back for me.
I ended up pulling the covers most of the way over my head, like making a little den for myself would keep me safe. All it did was put me to sleep faster.

My dreams came to me at an unbelievable clarity. I found myself in the library, with Rengas sitting across from me, only wearing a thin dressing robe. I looked down. Alice's book was in my hands. Rengas leaned in and took it from me, easily making my grip

* * *

loosen when he touched his soft hands to mine. He stowed the book behind him, and it vanished. I became furious. He kept doing this. Taking away what was rightfully mine.

Wait- rightfully mine? The book wasn't mine-

He was taking it away from me. When I looked down, my hands had been coated in Dark; Dark of my own creation that extended my fingers into points.

"Guno," The prince purred, scooting forward so much he was practically on top of me, "Don't hold back." He took one of my Darkened hands while slipping the robe off his shoulder to expose his chest, then took my hand and started to bring it close to his heart.

"Don't be afraid. Come on. Show me what Dark feels like." He whispered against my ear. Everything was heating up. He was pressing my hand against his chest, letting my dagger-like fingers drag across his flushed skin, making deep marks in black. He held me close while Dark continued to wound him.

Then I woke up in a garden, an oasis in the middle of the Farlands. I cut through low-hanging trees and stepped over bushes. The desert past the trees looked too calm and too devoid of life. The only noise was a soft whine from the center of this oasis, from a little pool with crystal clear water becoming polluted with black. The prince was here again, lying on his back at the bank of this pool, taking labored breaths. A Dark, gaping wound sat in the middle of his chest. He clutched at the sand around him but otherwise appeared quite resigned. I didn't hesitate to rush to his side, falling to my knees beside him. I seized the front of his tunic, stained with a mess of ichor and blood.

"Rengas! Oh, Ren, who did this to you?" I cried, trying to lift him into my arms. His gentle face had become more peaceful. He'd simply accepted his fate, surrounded in wild foliage even more vibrant than those at the Capital. He was too heavy. I couldn't possibly pull him up. I couldn't recall when or how, but I'd done this.
He'd come apart and didn't even mind.

I felt myself beginning to sob, and I held him close, knowing more than anything that what came next was inevitable.

I startled, struggling with my covers before throwing them off and away from my face. My breathing was still shaky and irregular, and from touching my face, I gleaned that I really *had* cried, not just in my dreams.

I couldn't tell if Alice was influencing my dreams, yet it would make sense if that were the case from the way my mind bounced back and forth between deep sorrow and fiery rage.

I turned my sights toward the window. It was still dark, yet not as deep as the dead of night. The sky had begun to gain a purple tint. It must have been dawn or nearly there. I swung my legs over the side of the bed, wiping sweat from my brow, then the tears from my eyes.

I would have thought the noises from outside my door had influenced my dreams too. It wasn't uncommon to hear the sounds of footsteps and muttering late into the night. Sometimes, even, I picked up the distant tune of one of Rengas's songs. I often found myself pressing my ear to the door, desperate to try and make out the words. I never could.

This being said, it would make sense if I'd heard the indistinct tones of the prince's voice and subconsciously worked them into a nightmare; but then I was reminded once again of his absence.

It would take a while to get used to, and unfortunately, I had a while to spare.

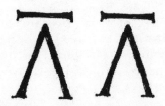

As day after day, week after week of training came and passed I was ready to give up. None of this was helping. In fact, I was beginning to feel worse about all of this. Dark and Light acted as two separate forces in my body, each independent from one another. I felt like a different person in the presence of Dark than I did when Light was around, such as during training or meetings with Ginger.
Light was so fragile. I couldn't keep up with Her. Every time I let myself lash out, I felt Her break into tiny pieces and slip through my fingers, and every time I was overcome with the cataclysmic guilt that followed.

Was any of this worth it if I was going nowhere? Would I ever pose a threat to Alice? Would I ever be free?

These thoughts lingered as I packed my things for Tenth Sector. The Light and Portal Ball had approached much sooner than I had anticipated.

I awoke early that morning when Rocky came in to rouse me personally. He had brought breakfast to eat in my room before instructing me to prepare for departure.

"Just take this and pack whatever you might want for the trip to Tenth. It will probably take us eight or so hours to get there." Rocky told me, handing over a hefty carrying bag roomy enough for a week's worth of things even though the portal ball only lasted a night. "Ginger has food and things, so don't worry about that." He stood next to the bed where I sat and laid out something flat covered in cloth along with a small box that he set next to it. "Here's your ball ensemble. All the pieces should be here. Your eyepatch and jewelry are in the box. Gosh, I hope the coat fits. Hazelgrove spent days on it."

"I'm sure it's great. I'll wait to open it when we get there." I took the clothes and folded them over so they'd fit in my bag. "I'm glad she helped me with color swatching and all. I'm not the best with things like that." I remarked, tucking the box into my bag as well.

"Hey, Rocky?"

I looked over my shoulder to the elf, who blinked in surprise, bringing his fists to his chest.

"Yes, Mister Lamplight?"

"How are they going to keep me safe out there? From Alice and Dark, I mean. As soon as I step outside the bounds of the Capital, she'll be able to take me." I scrunched up my nose. "I feel like her powers have strengthened since the time we first met. Who knows what she can do."

Rocky swallowed with a wearisome look on his face, turning to look out the window. A scaly, shaking hand went and adjusted the little hat on his head.

"I'm certain Ginger will be able to protect you. She has her Light blade an' all that." He looked back to me, walking back around to see what I was doing: staring at my staff, figuring out how and if I would take it with me. "Plus, we'll take a few guards with us, Rioh too." He gave me a sharp-toothed half-smile that he could only manage to hold for a few seconds.

I hadn't thought about the fact I'd have to be locked in a sand drifter for *eight entire hours* with the Ninth Sector's captain. What fun.

"How big are the Sand Drifters we will be taking?"

"Pretty big. These are the nice long-distance ones, not the little ones we take to the villages. They're faster too, I think."

"Oh, good." I smiled vaguely, "One more question."

"Go ahead, Mister Lamplight."

"Do you know when Rengas, er- our prince will be back?" Rocky gave me a blank look before his dusky red cheeks flushed a deeper red. He made an odd humming noise.

"Umm, I, uh- I'm not too sure. He should be back soon, but I don't know how it will work out with the Portal Ball and all that," He cringed, scratching the back of his neck tensely, "I wished he would be here in- *It would be most convenient* if he were back for the ball. It's one of the most important events for people like him to attend." I would imagine so, I thought. "He's been fighting to get more power in our sector. Only people like Kalesse Limbernal can make that happen, and it's a long trip all the way from Fourteenth Sector to here."

"Kalesse Limbernal?"

"Yes. Kalesse is not only the empress of her own sector but serves in a council of overseers to make sure other rulers do their job correctly." He took a deep exhale. "The council isn't exactly liking how Rengas had been conducting himself these past few years, and so they revoked some of his princely responsibilities." His eyebrows furrowed, his flushed face screwing up. "Which I don't think is fair at all! Rengas is doing a *fine* job, and they can't just-" He fell silent, breathing deeply again. I made a few understanding purrs and clucks under my breath. Rocky's face went a bit slack in a questioning sort of way.

"Sorry- I agree." I translated, "That's what I'd meant."

"Ah, my apologies."

"No, you're fine. Don't worry. I completely understand the confusion." I chuckled to myself to help him relax, and it seemed to work at least some. His shoulders loosened up as I buttoned my bag closed.

"Alright- well, report to the entrance hall in two hours." Rocky bowed deeply and left the room. While considering if taking my staff was necessary at all, my sights fell on the windowsill again.

Oh.

I completely forgot to put Alice's book back. If Rengas came back to see his stuff had been rooted through and it was found in my room, it would mean bad news.

Imagining the disappointment on his face made my blood run cold. I took the books in my arms and started to make my way over to his wing of the capital.

"I thought I could trust you." He would say, his eyes beginning to brim with tears, *"How could you do this? Maybe you weren't meant to return to Light after all. Maybe I should give up."*

I would try and comfort him, but he'd only push me away like he did that one day at the bath. I'd be done. Maybe I'd get thrown in the penitentiary after that, but the worst part would be that that look would be the very last one Ren gave me. The last before I was taken away without a chance to redeem myself.

I came back to my senses at the door to his quarters, and *thank Light,* the guards were busy getting ready for the ball and weren't stationed there that day. I quickly returned the books to the place they were when I borrowed them. I replaced the books as close to where I remember them being as I could. I didn't remember very much from the night I took Alice's book. Hopefully, my memory would be better than Ren's in that regard. Then I took the MP3 player. It would be dangerous to leave it pretty much alone in the capital. I packed it in with my other things when I got back to my room.

Ginger had cautioned me before I began getting ready to wear layers and a long-sleeved tunic, probably a hood too. The sand drifters didn't have very much shade and were built for safety rather than comfort. When the time came I heeded the General's warning, dressing fully and pulling on some light boots before tying my hair back and making my way to the entrance hall.

Just as Rocky said, Ginger, Rioh, and several guards all were congregated at the front entrance, and Rocky himself stood with a cart carrying the bags.

Ginger clapped me heartily on the shoulder once I'd put my things in the cart.

"Ready to get going, Lamplight? Ever been in a sand drifter before?"

"Yeah, I think so." I smiled brightly, as tense as I still was from that close call earlier. "No, I've never been in one."

"Really? Well, I think you'll find you like it quite a bit. It can be very exhilarating- but I suppose after a day's travel, it does lose some of its novelty." Ginger wore a multi-layered cloak over her usual General's coat. She looked up toward the high ceiling and took a deep breath or reflection before she regarded me once more. "What do you say we get going, then. We don't want to waste daylight, as you must understand."

"Of course."

I held my breath as we all left through the front doors, descending the steps past the first outdoor platform. It still felt cool here and must have still counted as capital bounds. Ginger warned me as we came to a certain point down the mountain, holding an arm out in front of my chest. She gave a signal over her shoulder to the rest of our entourage.

I saw Rocky and Rioh pull on their hoods, and Ginger did the same before brandishing a longsword from a holster at her hip. It looked *right* in her hands. Do you know how some things just *fit* with a person? That's how Ginger is with swords. Or how Rocky is with his hat. Or how Ren is with flowers, especially pink or purple ones.

I followed their lead and pulled the hood over my eyes too.

"Stay behind me. If that witch tries anything, that will be a mistake on her end." Ginger growled, pushing up her monocle with her shoulder before stepping over the barrier.

Our party remained tense as we crossed the line. I could feel it. Some guards came to walk on either side of me while Ginger kept watch of the front, sword at the ready. The sun had not come up yet, so it didn't feel terribly hot on our way down. That also meant creatures would be more fearless in any attempts to take us before we reached the safety of the sand drifter. It waited for us at the bottom of the stairs.

"If you don't mind me asking General, why don't we just use a portal or something to get there? Don't you think it would be a lot quicker?"

"It's too unpredictable to try traveling that far within the same dimension, and with this many people to boot. We'd rather not take our chances." She glanced over her shoulder at me but really seemed more interested in watching whatever was *behind* me. I turned around too, reading the coarse expression on Ginger's face- yet was only greeted with the sight of Rocky and another maid struggling to get the baggage cart down this ridiculous flight of stairs. It had been difficult thus far just keeping my own balance on the weathered uneven steps, so I didn't doubt that it was difficult.

We eventually made it to the bottom of the mountain, all the while Rocky tripping over himself and Ginger jabbing and swinging her sword into air like a madwoman. The sand drifter still awaited our arrival in the most gentlemanly manner a boat could.

Sand drifters most resembled boats, from what I knew about water vehicles. It had a round bottom for navigating through sand like it was the thinnest of liquids. For some creatures living beneath it, the sand really was liquid. It bowed and filled up space wherever needed, languid and elusive. But this drifter wasn't made to go under the sand, thank Light- only cut across the surface.

Ginger undid a latch on the side of the sturdy cage that made up most of the vehicle's top, and a section swung up from the rest like a doorway. She ushered me inside first, guiding me through the middle compartment of this drifter that served as a little sitting room up to the front, where there were two pairs of seats.

She strapped me down in the front passenger's seat, patting my chest before disappearing behind me to help everyone else get in. There were more seats that you could strap into toward the back. All the rest of the seating in the middle didn't have the same safety equipment, but there was a place to put the baggage cart and a spacious table to sit at. Over that section was a solid ceiling to provide some shade, but other than that, everything was just a cage of thick iron bars.

Ginger used this cage of a ceiling to hold onto as she came to situate herself in the driver's seat. The dashboard consisted of several levers and a panel on the right of a dozen or so light-up buttons. She pushed one, and lights flicked on from the front of the drifter with a heavy *thunk,* illuminating some of the path ahead of us even more in the dawn's light. I craned my neck to see who sat in the other two front seats behind us- in the one behind Ginger sat Rocky, scrawling hurriedly in a little leather-bound notebook- and behind me sat Rioh, whose Light blaster arm shifted menacingly as soon as we made eye contact. I made sure not to look again after that, holding my arms to my chest and looking straight ahead. Ginger buckled in, then raised an eyebrow at me a moment.

"Everyone all set?" I nodded, and there were a few grumbles of confirmation from behind us, along with a small "Yes, General!" from Rocky. She nodded and thrust forward a larger lever on her left side. The entire vehicle clunked and shook with life, raising what must have been a foot or two before Ginger took hold of another lever and made the great machine creak into motion. Ginger allowed us to unbuckle for short amounts of time if we wanted to get something to eat or sit in the center portion of the drifter when we gained enough speed.

Once the sun was high in the sky and we had been traveling for several hours at the very least, my mind had wandered deep into my imagination. It was the only thing that could distract me from the heavy feeling of defeat in my chest and the sweltering heat of the Dashan sun.

I imagined something hopeful for a change: what would happen if Ren *did* make it back? What if he made it back *as a Beacon?* Where would Light choose to mark him? Would he let me see his markings? Touch them, even?

I bet they'd be cool to the touch, like Light. It would surely be a big deal if Ren finally reached beaconism. I reckon all the villages would hear about it; it would be talked about for weeks, and Ren being a Beacon would only make him more of a spectacle for those like Cypress Cadler.

Oh Light, I missed Ren. I hated admitting it, but I really did. After he left, there was really no one to talk to. There were Ginger and Rocky and all, but they were much too diplomatic about conversation. Rengas could hold a conversation like the most relaxing thing in all the sectors was talking to me. Words just bloomed and spilled from his lips. It seemed so *easy* for him.

Rocky pulled me out of my trance with a gentle shake that he delivered to my shoulder.

"Mister Lamplight, Are you hungry? I can make some simple preparations. I can teach you how to play peg and chips, too- if you'd like, I mean." He stammered over the grinding of the ship's engine. I blinked up at him, squinting through the sun's glare, and nodded. In the center of the sand drifter, at least it was quieter. That was good because it was soon revealed that peg and chips were a game that required a lot of concentration and talking. Rocky explained the rules while slicing up a roll of cheese and some fruits for me.

"The game is all about multitasking. You have a minute and thirty seconds to stack all of the chips on each person's turn, so their faces match by number. Each chip has two random numbers on each side. There should be sixteen of them." He pointed to the stack of discs on the table in front of the little bench I sat at.

"After you stack each chip, you also have to push a peg into one of their respective slots. One hand does one task, the other hand does the other." I looked at the other game pieces- wooden pegs with the tops painted red and a pegboard with holes for each- the fit would be tight by their size. *Fun.* The heat didn't help my willingness to do any of this. I almost preferred to stare off. My gaze wandered past Rocky, over the lamps that hung from the drifter's ceiling.

Rocky paused his cutting and nudged me on the shoulder.

"Hey, Mister Lamplight- are you listening?"

"Huh? Oh, uh- repeat that last part?"

Rocky frowned as he finished expertly cutting a dwarf apple into thin slivers. He sighed deeply as he returned his attention to me.

"If you don't want to play, Mister Lamplight, you should just tell me."

"No, no. Keep going. I'm sorry."

"Okay. While you are doing both of these tasks, I will be asking you questions to try and distract you. If you don't know the answers, say 'pass,' and I'll think of another." I squinted, pushing back a loose curl and attempting to fit it back into my ponytail. As I did so, I asked,

"So, is there a *winner?*" I sat back, trying to get comfortable even with the cramped nature of the bench I was on.

"Yes- If you don't complete all three tasks on your turn, I get a point. If you win, you get the point. The first person to five points wins." He cleaned off and stowed away the cutting knife in the box with all the kitchen supplies in it. He then settled down next to me, pushing over the wooden slab that held the snacks. "Have at these, if you want."

I took his offer, reaching for a few and stuffing them in my mouth. Did that make a *fourth* task I was meant to do? I wasn't feeling all that optimistic about this. It just seemed stressful, if anything.

I don't know. Maybe it was better than nothing. Rocky set out the pieces, making sure the chips were mixed up while compiling the pegs beside the pegboard. They kept rolling away with the jostle of the sand drifter, and he huffed impatiently every time he had to put them back in place. He reached to grab a slice of marbled cheese, then regarded me.

"Alright, would you like to be the question asker or the multitasker first?"

"Uhm, question asker. I want to see how it's done before trying the tasks."

"Alright. Remember, your job as the question asker is to ask as many questions as you can to try and make your opponent slip up! They can be personal or factual, as long as you know the answer to said factual question." He slid the tray that held all the game pieces over to himself. There also sat a small sand timer on the corner of the tray. He handed that to me. "Countdown from three, then turn that over." He instructed, and I did so, after a bit of hesitation. I took down my hood. Underneath the cover, it wasn't as needed.

"Okay. Three, two, one-" I began. Oh. Questions. Right. Rocky was already expertly sorting through chips until he found a match, sticking in a peg- then another matching chip. "How many siblings do you have?"

"Eight." He replied without looking up. Rocky had taken down his hood as well. All I could see of his face past his dark fluffy hair was his protruding nose.

"Nice, uh- *wow, that's a lot*, uh- do any of them work with royalty, too?"

"My older sibling Torrid. They're a General in Eighth." I raised my eyebrows. Rocky was already six- no, seven pegs in.

"Um, hm. what's the best sector?"

"Th-that's subjective, Mister Lamplight."

"Your favorite, then."

"Seventh."

"Why?"

"Born there." Rocky pushed the last peg into its slot- after a beat, the timer ran out. One point for him.

"Good job," I said; he thanked me, sliding the tray over and taking a few more snacks into his hand. After the chips were mixed up, Rocky counted down and flipped the timer.

"What is the Limbernal's first name- the dashaner man from the myth?" A topical question, indeed; I fumbled to get the first peg into its place.

"Yes, I know who he- uh, Gryndo."

"Correct. List three things you like to do in your spare time. Skills of yours."

"Uh, Let's see," Any hobbies I once kept had since been replaced with work since I was brought to the capital. "I kept a garden back home."

I glanced at the timer. Already halfway through, I'd only managed to stack six of the chips. "I like to adapt stories, and, uh- I do a lot of baking. Or I *did.*"

Now that I was reminded of it, I began to miss my garden. It was small, tucked into a little space behind our house that was protected from the sun. My mother and I managed to cultivate a few gentler and softer plants than the tough-skinned fruit plants, shrubs, and cacti that would typically grow any place else. It was probably dead and barren by now. That thought alone could have been enough to make me cry.

In the end, Rocky won the game by a longshot. He knew how to draw his questions out so that I had to both listen and do the two tasks. Even if I wasn't thinking of an answer, I had the job of paying close attention to what he was saying.

After Rocky and I finished snacking, Ginger called over her shoulder to return to our seats for safety's sake. I made a point not to look at Rioh as I passed him this time. I pulled on my hood, buckled in, and turned back toward the wall of the drifter to watch towns pass by through its caged exterior. It wasn't long before I started to see the vibrant colors of sun fall spill across the sky, pooling vibrantly at the horizon like a portal fluid. It wasn't long until the mountains we passed through became increasingly close in proximity, and Ginger made another announcement to the rest of our crew.

"We will be entering Tenth soon! Get ready to get out quickly. We need to change in our guest chambers and be out in," She inspected a point on the dashboard-

"About an hour and a half! Is that enough for all in attendance?" She waited a moment before concluding, "Good. Now hold on- we are going to be slowing down soon."

I had a feeling that most of those details had been included specifically for me- Rocky and Rioh probably knew full well how to brace themselves in a sand drifter and how to prepare themselves for a party like this. I, on the other hand, not so much.

A massive shape steadily approached the drifter: a swell in the sand that would have registered as another hill if not for the oddly shaped holes punched in its top. When we came upon it, the area was so massive that it completely consumed my field of vision. Our vehicle advanced toward an opening in the side of the mountainous shape, just as the last of the sun disappeared behind it.

As the hill swallowed us, we were immediately greeted by another sight: a glittering city, with its settlements curving around the inside walls of this cavern and coating the floor. The capital extended straight from the middle, positioned atop a ginormous stalagmite.

An entire sector contained just within this pocket beneath the sand. The sand drifter creaked and lurched forward as it slowed to accommodate tight twists and turns between buildings and down paths. I let my hood down once more. It felt so much cooler and more comfortable down here beneath the cavern ceiling. I leaned as far as I could toward the cage, holding onto the bars to try and see the strings of multicolored lights and floating lanterns suspended from the tops of stores and cottages. My eyes kept wandering to the capital building, however. Its towers extended straight into the top of the cavern's ceiling, and it had large circular platforms jutting out from the sides like mushrooms from a tree trunk. What could they be for? I supposed I would find out soon enough.

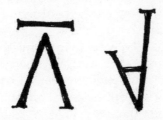

Ginger pulled into a tunnel at the base of the stalagmite that supported the capital. It served as a port where other sand drifters and smaller transport vehicles dropped off passengers. It was brightly illuminated along its walls, and Ginger parked us along the wall of the port. When she pulled the large lever back into its original position, the drifter once more made a cry and sank back into the ground. She had the maid and our guards get out first, then Rocky, so they could unload our things. After that I was allowed to unbuckle.

As I stood, my legs weakened. After eight hours of barely using them at all, they felt brand new- and very, very wobbly. I held onto the doorframe of the drifter as I stepped out, Ginger spotting me as she stood on the loading platform. She caught me as I struggled to move over the small gap between the edge of the drifter and the platform, nearly missing the ledge. She held my arms and waited for me to regain my balance.

"You got it, Lamplight?"

"Yeah, uh- sorry. Yeah." I shook out my legs and stretched. Now that I was on solid ground, it felt so good to walk again. "Where are we changing? Is everything within the capital building?"

"Well, yes, technically. There are smaller settlements within this stone structure for guests. Kind of like a very exclusive, members-only hotel." She gestured above us as a guard pulled open a heavy door in the wall of this port, revealing an inner chamber with flimsy-looking mesh doors that opened up for us as if they awaited our entrance. All the chamber seemed to contain was a lever that stuck straight up from the floor.

The guards entered first, then the maid and Rocky, then Rioh, who took hold of the lever and waited for Ginger and I to join them. The space was just big enough for us to fit. The whole thing rattled when I stepped in, as if this room was just slotted in or was hanging there by a tether. I gripped onto Ginger's arm as a source of comfort against this worrying thought.

My suspicions were reaffirmed when Rioh cranked back the lever, and the whole room started with a mechanical groan, both sets of doors closing. We were moving upward- I could tell because of both the feeling in my gut and the cracks and imperfections in the stone encasing us that whizzed in and out of view from behind the mesh doors. The doors opened once more to reveal a brightly lit, cozy foyer. I fully clung to Ginger's arm to keep from stumbling. Ginger's professional stance did not falter, her hands still folded in front of her as she looked up at me and chuckled warmly.

"Are you going to be okay, Lamplight? We can take a minute to regain our balance if you need." She guided me into the entrance room, allowing me to hang onto her.

"Yes, that would be- Thank you." I shook my head and waited for it to clear, then took a look around. Other groups of Dashaners and Ground elves occupied the space with us, one maid carrying a cart filled with cooking utensils for a ground elf royal- or at least I *assumed* she was royal, from the two deep navy spots decorating her cheeks. The maid and the royal bickered over how to get the thing up the stairs to their room, the royal tensely skittering around the maid to make sure she didn't drop her things. They were clearly understaffed. Ginger saw them in the distance and patted my hand to signal for me to let go.

"You guys go to our room without me. I'll be up shortly." She jogged over to the two, easily picking up the back of the bulky cart and helping the maid lift it the stairs without jostling the contents around. I watched her before Rocky tapped me on the shoulder.

"Come on. Our room's this way."

We took a smaller flight of stairs up to a little landing with three doors, and Rocky fished out a key from his pocket. He unlocked the first one and pushed it open. Rioh gave me a passing glance of distaste as he entered before me, making himself comfortable on one of the ornate sofas around a sitting area. To the left of it was a set of changing rooms with a full-length mirror in the center, and on the right more mirrors with a long counter for cosmetics.
Rocky and the maid stopped the cart in the center of the room. Rocky handed me my bag, which I pulled over my shoulder.

"The ball starts shortly. As soon as we're all done here, get ready to leave." He said, and I thanked him, quickly stowing myself and my things away in a changing stall.

I knelt on the ground, unbuttoning my bag and laying out the bundle of clothing that I'd received from the tailor. I very carefully unwrapped Rengas's MP3 player, setting it aside as I opened up the bundle of clothes. Inside was the coat Rocky had been so worried about: a beautiful, intricately made piece with golden embroidered plants all along the chest and shoulders, with more intricate patterns as trim. The brass clasps crossed over the chest elegantly. I anticipated I'd look just as important and knightly as Ginger in something like this, in its dignified midnight blue, with its long coattails. Also included in this package was a transparent, silky royal purple piece of fabric to go around my waist. The other items were less flashy- some flexible lace-up boots and an undershirt, along with some loose trousers. As I started to unpack my little box of accessories, I heard the door to our room open and some quiet conversation too distant to pick up. It was okay- I didn't want to eavesdrop anyway.

    I started to dress. Upon pulling on the undershirt, I realized how tight it was- when my eyes flicked over to the coat. The loose sleeves revealed the lighter color of the shirt underneath. Wow, Hazelgrove really thought of everything, didn't she? I clasped the fastenings over my chest, then wrapped and tied off the piece of cloth. I thought about doing a bow but ultimately decided against it. I popped on the boots, tucked the seam of my pants into them, and took the box with me out into the main room.

    I was met with the sight of Ginger talking with Rioh, already in a completely different outfit. Her coat was tighter than her usual one, and her collar shorter. This time she was given a half- cape split into two that reminded me of a bug's wings. Ginger turned to me when I approached the scene, breaking into a kind smile.

    "You look stunning. The ensemble suits you well." She observed, folding her hands. "Now, let's get these situated." She reached for the box, and I handed it to her.

    "How do you want your hair to go?" She asked as the maid skittered up to us. Her soft, round eyes stared up at me with uncertainty before moving in Ginger's direction.

    "I can do it, miss." She practically whispered.

    "Alright, but I'm coming with you. I've never seen Lamplight this put-together." And she did follow along behind us on our way to the counter with all the mirrors. They sat me down on a plush stool, turning me to face my reflection. The maid brought over a big basket filled with various instruments, one being a brush that she gently dragged through my hair. I'd brushed my hair that morning, but it still felt nice.

    She pulled some hair from the sides of my head, then twisted the pieces and tied them behind my head with a length of string, making sure to configure the eyepatch so it sat nicely over my hair. The eyepatch was made of the same blue-with-gold-embroidering as my jacket.

After a few more adjustments, the maid reached over my head and clasped a heavy gold plate necklace around my neck, fixing it to sit nicely atop my chest. Viewing myself now, it was clear that there was planning put into every component of this outfit. I made a *very* convincing Light supporter.

I mean- I *was* a Light supporter, but not as far as the rest of the people at this party would be concerned.

Just a few expensive fabrics and a piece of gold had suddenly turned me into someone important. I could well be some military General or posh noble, and no one would be able to tell otherwise. It would feel nice to be treated like someone worthwhile, even if it was just a disguise.

The maid wasn't done. Ginger eagerly handed her a little jar of something and a brush. She dipped the brush in, lightly brushing matching gold specks onto the corner of my normal eye and a bit onto my cheeks. I blinked in mild surprise.

"Do you like it?" She said softly. I nodded.

"It's a lot more than I'm used to, but I'm not opposed. Thank you." In the reflection, Ginger whipped her head toward the door. She set a large hand on my shoulder. I clicked a wordless response, trying to crane my neck to see.

"*Kevik -*" Ginger cursed under her breath, waving a hand for me to get up, " It's time to go. We've waited here too long. We need to get to the guest entrance before the general public."

I got to my feet, and Ginger kept a hand on the small of my back as she guided me all the way into the foyer. She released me, and our group sped up to a brisk walk up the stairs and through various passageways.

On the way up, Ginger explained that if Rengas were here, they would take the royals' entrance and have an announced arrival when they came through the door. Since he wasn't here with them, the prince wasn't technically on the list for announcements, so neither were we. Because of this, we had to take the normal way in- through a beautiful, gargantuan archway that opened up like a giant mouth, lit up with all sorts of warm lights. The floor had been sprinkled with vibrant confetti made of petals and leaves and paper strips, creating a trail that beckoned the gathering crowd inside.

Similar to the crowd at Rengas's birthday, I could see folks of all dimensions as I followed Ginger. I became overwhelmed with the

● ● ●

scent of spices and warm pastries that filled the air. The narrowing entrance opened up into a great hall with archway exits on all sides leading out into the glittering night. I tipped my head up, viewing the maze of vibrant cloths adorning the tall ceiling. My wandering became interrupted with Ginger seizing my shoulder and a shadow cast over me by a large figure. I flinched with a small bark.

"Meet General Harthene." She gestured to the startlingly massive figure, who bowed. He must've been several feet taller than Ginger and I, with canine-like facial features that made his brow angular and many areas of his face and arms thick with fur. My eyes looked him up and down. A frilled tail gently swayed between the separation in his coat. I brought up the courage to meet his eyes and extended my hand.

"Guno Lamplight." I managed, with all the professional gusto I could pull together.

"He's a student of mine. Back at Ninth we've started a military internship program. He flourishes more every day." She lied eloquently, clapping me heartily on the back. That must have been my cue.

"Yes. Ginger's an excellent teacher." I smiled to make it seem more genuine. Harthene smiled back with a mouthful of pointed teeth.

"I wouldn't expect anything less. Say, Ginger- where's your boy? I was relieved of Corvid just a few minutes ago. Hope they'll fare okay with just the guards." He briefly craned his neck to look over one of his massive shoulders, his posture remaining almost comically perfect.

"He's out for Beaconship, actually." Ginger said, pride gleaming in her tone. "It's a great shame he couldn't be here to keep Corvid company."

"It's okay. They have plenty of friends." Harthene smiled once again. "Well, Ginger, Lamplight- what do you say we take a look around?"

General Harthene started toward one of the open archways, and as he did, he slowed down to point behind us.

"See that corridor, Guno? That's where the actual dance will take place. Only higher nobles and capital officials are allowed." I slowed down from the jog I'd been maintaining to keep up with him. "It has gotten to the point where the dance has cultivated its own culture. Different dances- and even particular moves- can convey quite a lot. It shows the person you're dancing with what your intent is with silent communication."

● ● ●

I was staring at the entrance even as we stepped through the archway and into the cool night air. I was hit with a much stronger wave of the scent- and looking to the right to see a giant cooking fire on this enormous party balcony, I could see why. Carts filled with all sorts of sweet and savory hors d'oeuvres flanked the fire pit, which illuminated the faces of a group of young partygoers. One small Dashaner boy was clearly marked with royal paint. Princes and princesses must have been everywhere. I felt like every breath I took was inferior.

To my left were more kids and young adults making paper crafts, little gliders that they tossed around, and some which they pitched down over the side of the balcony. The crafts slowly spiraled down into the cities below. For Light's sake, there was even a young teen with Beacon marks all down her throat! How one could achieve it at such a young age, I couldn't even fathom.

Perhaps the most enticing were the sounds of song and dance filling the atmosphere, the source of which I could not yet see. Ginger must have sensed my interest.

"You can go. Just come back to the cooking fire by the start of the theatrics show." She blinked at me decisively, Harthene still standing politely behind. "Or I can come to get you. Have fun, and don't take that eyepatch off. We're in big trouble if you do." I nodded and found myself breaking into a grin as I took off toward the sound of music. I could see figures around the bend of this circular platform.

I turned and grabbed a piece of fruit from the cart before moving to where the paper toys were being made.

I was going to meet a beacon.

I have to admit; the thought alone did keep me on edge. Would the youth here view me as an enemy? They couldn't *sense* Darkness, right? After a small debate with myself, I approached the group of teens. The beacon turned as if on cue, looking me up and down with large, lanternous eyes. Her kinky hair fell just past her ears, and she wore loose fabrics wrapped over a short top. For a beacon, her clothing remained relatively simple in nature. I quickly addressed her Beaconsip by holding both my shaking hands to the middle of my chest, pressing one over the other, and giving my chest two soft pats. I never thought I'd get to put the many times practiced gesture to use.

"Safe evening, newcomer. I don't think I've met you before." She began, squinting slightly, "What is your name?" The markings peeking out from the collar of her shirt pulsed, showy and spectacular in every way. The details were so finely put together they seemed to shift and flow the longer I looked.

"I'm Guno Lamplight, a General's apprentice from Ninth." I bowed deeply. The half-lie only came naturally because of Ginger's assistance prior. "I'm a villager. Or at least I was. I wanted to meet a Beacon. How does one do it?"

She squinted at me again, her lip curling slightly. Some other kids, appearing only slightly younger than me as well, paused in their playful bickering. She didn't pay them any attention. "Well, Guno, now you *have* met one." Her expression softened. "Thorn Acker." She was still doing a routine check around my general area. Was someone behind me? I turned to see-

"Sorry. I just don't know what to make of you. I guess the suspicion isn't very virtuous and Beaconly, is it?" She joked, gesturing to a sitting area beside us. "So, you want to talk. Let's."

She must have seen clean through my facade.
But it wasn't a facade. I was a light supporter, I reassured myself. I sat down on a cushion, and she took the one beside mine.

"So, what do you want to know?" Thorn was adjusting the emerald-tinted draperies to sit neatly around her legs. "How I got my marks? Is that it?"

I shook off the slightly accusatory tone, straightening my posture. "Well, yes. But you don't have to; I'm happy just to talk as well. Uh, what do you think about-"

"No, no. It's fine." The beacon stopped me before I got ahead of myself, clumsily waving a hand that landed on my shoulder. I fell silent.

"A lot of nobles and uppity citizens of Light will make it seem like any old village folk can get their beacon marks just by being good or *believing* hard enough- but through my time in this dimension, I've found it's a little more complicated than that." She continued to hold my arm as she wistfully gazed up to the cavern ceiling, maybe even through it. I followed her gaze up to the cracks and holes in the stone sky.

"Your upbringing also plays a factor. I grew up with two gracious mothers who were fantastic role models, one of them a beacon herself." She let go of me to shrug, then lean forward, her hands on her knees. She glanced over her shoulder at me passively. "All of my family is still intact, closely knit. I have siblings who my moms took under their wing after a Dark attack in our village. I've experienced *very little* feeling of Dark. You know what I mean?" When I nodded, she added on, "Dark is a feeling, in more ways than one. I have a close friend who fell prey to Dark. *I can almost feel His burning secondhand.*" She didn't watch me anymore, yet I could feel she awaited my response.

"That's a very realist approach to Her influence. I've never heard it phrased like that before." I tried to change the subject. She was trying to show me she knew.

I can see it, Thorn would say. *Your eye. Who do you think you're fooling?*

My fingers itched as they waited for Dark to pour in- yet in this place, with these people, nothing happened. I was confident it never would. It would take a whole lot of effort for Him to get in now.

"What's the use in glorifying Light? As much as I love Her, the world isn't all black-and-white as our capital officials may make it seem. But *you* know that already." She gestured in a flourish around my face while still looking in the other direction.

"What do you mean?" I asked pointlessly. I already knew, as Thorn said. And she knew I knew, which became apparent as she gave me a knowing smile that curled up at the edges.

※ ※ ※

"I have to go. Enjoy the ball, Guno. And keep what we talked about in mind."

She stood smoothly and went to join her friends, all jeering and pointing over the edge of the balcony at something below. I brushed off my piquing curiosity in favor of the music, which continued. I made my way past the food, not really watching where I was going as I did.

I bumped into the ground elven heiress from earlier in the lobby downstairs, who had set up her equipment here. Feeling my cheeks burn, I apologized before speeding up to a jog.

The platforms extending from the core building of the capital were made up of large semicircular sections that served as outdoor "rooms." They were all quite expansive, but the one I encountered next made the others' size pale in comparison. There must've been a crowd of at least a hundred people all clapping and beating the ground with their feet along with the infectious tune that drew me in.

I very quickly got caught up in the thrall of the crowd, watching beautiful people dip in and out of the center of the dancing circle with ease.

I remained off to the side until I was forcibly yanked into the center by a pretty ground elf noble with a stripe of bright yellow down her nose and chin, whose long ears were well decorated with gold and jewels.

"Newcomer! Do you dance?" She shouted over the noise, moving in jingly circles around me just to keep the groove going.

"Yes, a little bit! I'm a villager; I haven't been trained!" I yelled back, starting up an awkward jive that didn't quite suit the music. She giggled brightly, shaking out her long hair and pulling me into one move after another, making me dip under her arm and teaching me a few simple moves I was not familiar with.

Clearly, these were used in starkly different circles than mine. Wealthy, Light-rich circles of class and vibrance. By following her, I eventually got into a groove that fit. It was like a switch being flipped. In a moment, everything occurred in a timely whir of color and sound. It didn't feel awful and clunky anymore, and with all the cheers and clapping, it almost felt as if I were being admired by the people around us. It felt as if I did something right.

"Lamplight-!" A voice cut through my trance.

I twirled to a stop, the girl still holding my arm and laughing erratically with her high of adrenaline. My cheeks hurt from smiling. I turned to squint into the crowd with my one free eye, my smile

• • •

loosening as I caught a glimpse of flame-red hair. It was Ginger, pushing through the crowd toward me. "Let me borrow him a second, Pranta. You can have the boy back later." Ginger broke into the middle, grabbing my wrist. Pranta, it seemed the elf's name was, released me with a mock frown.

"Alright, suit yourself, General. You should join me when you get back, though! You're too stiff." She teased, already jiving back into the circle to allow more people a turn. Ginger pulled me out of the ring, where Rocky waited for us.

"Oh, Guno! You'll love the theatrics this year," He said. They sat me down in front of an elaborate stage, where pillows and cushions were set on a vast woven rug for people to sit on while watching the show.

Actors dressed in beautiful costumes and handmade masks came onstage. Their clothes rattled and jingled as they told the tale: the creation of this very sector.

After swallowing a nation of people in its belly, a great beast was struck down, then set ablaze. Its skin turned to hard leathery rock, and by Light's blessing, all of the villagers inside survived. Now its stone belly provided refuge, rather than the overwhelming terror it once meant for those inside. Even if Tenth was only a sector away from us, the mythos here was different enough to be completely unfamiliar to me.

Once the show had ended, and the actors took their bows, Ginger turned to me. My body was already itching to get back on the dance floor.

"I thought you ought to see a professional capital production. I understand you want to go. Go on ahead; you are dismissed." The corners of her lips pulled into a small smile. I didn't move as the playgoers around us gradually cleared out of the carpeted area. I stepped forward but was hesitant to take her with me like when she grabbed my arm earlier, so I simply waved my hand in a beckoning motion.

"Come with me. You heard, uh..." I didn't think I caught the princess's name.

"Pranta. Miss Nunez does this sort of thing with everyone, Guno. She's incessant."

"Come on, General. It'll be fun." I insisted, attempting a charming look. She heaved a sigh, pushing up her monocle, then took a step past me.

"I'll watch you."

It was better than nothing. All in all, I just wanted to see Ginger get out there into this scene she was so familiar with, yet acted like she wasn't. She was an Afferian noble, raised with Dashan royal customs. She knew how to conduct herself, how to lead, how to handle a sword, which means she knew how to *dance* just as well. Even though she was no longer an heiress, I was sure there had to be a shred of that royal training still in her.

Seeing me, Pranta immediately perked up from the opposite end of the ring, waited for a dancer to exit the middle, and came to drag me back in. I saw Ginger break into a pained smirk as she crossed her arms, staying put.

Then, to my surprise, Pranta left me to pull Ginger in against her will. Ginger could have easily protested, for she was much larger than Pranta- but she didn't. The general lazily allowed herself to be guided to my side, her hand being placed in mine. I shuddered with uncertain apprehension.

"You two have fun! I'll dance with you later, newcomer." Pranta caught my gaze from behind Ginger, shooting a clever wink my way. I could feel my cheeks burning.

As soon as Ginger entered the ring, the band had picked up a much less jaunty and much choppier, ballroom-like tune. Ginger's dark cheeks reddened too, and she rolled her eyes.

"You can never argue with her," Ginger growled with soft annoyance, her hand coming to rest on my hip. She started to make slow steps. My hand lingered in the air as I followed her lead. "Place it here on my shoulder- well, for now." She chuckled.

Our simple little waltz soon evolved into an entire series of foreign moves, all of which she led me through. As with Pranta, it became a bit easier the more we went. I had been correct in my assumptions. Ginger was skilled, in her own right. Sure, a much different type of skill than Pranta had been, but I enjoyed this too. Ginger took a deep bow after a final move in which I unfurled and released from her arms. I awkwardly moved to do the same.

It wasn't much later when Ginger looked up to the sky with alertness. We'd gone back to the fire to eat something with Rocky before the more exclusive dances began.

"I think it's time." The General leaned forward, tossing her empty roasting stick into the fire.

"Rengas isn't here. How will we officiate anything?" Rocky piped up through a mouthful of gourd; a hand raised over his mouth.

Ginger's face was tight with embarrassment. She wrung her hands over the flames. "As the General, I'm listed as his emissary." She said vaguely. Rocky's eyes went round as he nearly choked on his food.

"You're saying you'll have to-"

"Yes, Rocky. Don't worry about it. I can conduct myself." She pushed up her monocle.

I swallowed my bite of greater mole sausage. I had no clue the reason for Rocky's concern. Did this mean she had to talk and dance for Ren? She seemed completely capable of such. I put my stick in the fire as well, and we started off to the royal's ballroom.

The room was almost completely devoid of furnishings; the only thing filling the space was probably hundreds of people trickling into the room in groups.
However, the room had a loft at the far end that held a full-size band, practically an orchestra. They played a calm tune as the assembly continued to gather.

Each royal member or royal family had its own entourage of guards and couriers. However, sometimes I saw a royal didn't have a family accompanying them-only a team of five or six people guiding them in. For instance, there was Harthene's Corvid, the Dashaner kid I soon met as Harthene guided them inside beside us.

Their choppy, thick black hair obscured their eyes. I caught glimpses of the royal paint on their forehead every time they brushed their bangs away. This was the only way I knew they were not a member of His ranks. This move also exposed both of their perfectly yellowish-orange eyes just long enough to reassure me. Even then, I glanced their way every so often, hoping to catch this reassurance once more. As my people watching continued, it prompted Ginger to give a firm tap to the side of my head, then wave her hand in front of my eyes.

"Stay alert, Mister Lamplight. Stay alert and stay with Rocky. I'm not sure how long I'll be here for." She grimaced into the crowd.

"Oh, that's right! Your Rengas isn't here." Harthene smiled. "Don't worry about the dance. I've seen what you can do. You'll be fine. You do remember your speaking points though, yes? The ones Ren was supposed to conduct."

Ginger's eyelashes fluttered as she received the compliment. She cleared her throat before responding. "Yes. Pass first through fourth. Just a quick greeting, then move on. Fifth, we need to speak about some of their policies." She began to mimic some moves with her arms vaguely; just a preview of the real thing, I presumed. "I have a sneaking suspicion that Twenty-First has a Dark problem, and I need to tell Kalesse- I mean Fourteenth- about Rengas's progress." Her arms fell back to her sides. "I'll explain why you're here." She said to me.

"Should I worry?" My hand raised to make sure my eyepatch was still on.

"Not at all, Lamplight. I've got this all under..." Ginger started with another glance toward the center of this room, where people were now gathering in a line. There were markings in the tile floor indicating where the representative from each sector was to stand. "I can handle it for you."

I wondered if she said that in part to reassure herself. After Ginger, Corvid made their way into the center, hiking up their deep green robes as they came to stand beside her. In the distance, I could see Pranta lining up, too, already bouncing on the balls of her feet in anticipation.

A bell rang in the corner of the room. It had come from a slender Dashaner man in a tidy suit, who set the bell down as soon as he had allowed it to chime. With his cue, the band above us picked up pace and volume. I watched as the line of royals and other representatives shifted, with Ginger in particular taking a calculated step forward. Turning to face my left, they began a seemingly complex series of steps, each person weaving in and out of this line without any miscalculation. I must have been leaning a good bit out of the place where Rocky and Harthene were standing because Rocky's scaly hand came to hold my wrist and pull me back into the perimeter.

"We will get to join soon enough, Mister Lamplight. It's just a little longer." The elf stumbled on his words. He was staring off. He did that quite often, so I wasn't too concerned, and continued to watch the people who spun off of the line and met up in pairs or threes. One moment you could focus in on someone, then the next, they'd disappear into the stream of dancers and join another sect. They all somehow functioned individually and also as a unit.

How did Ginger do it?

The grand double doors opposite us that we'd all come in through had been opened. When partygoers began to separate around it, I noticed someone cutting through. Someone in a sweeping cape and heels, with things tucked into their short white hair- a beacon, striped with Light.

XT

I'd taken off for the other side of the room before Rocky could stop me, keeping to the edge as not to disturb anyone. As I cut through the dancers, it was clear who'd come in late to the dance.

His soft eyes went over the crowd, searching. Once we locked eyes, the prince started to rush toward me. I was too floored to move; I only took a few dazed steps forward to meet him, taking in the new patterns of shining white that flowed across his chest under the sheer material of his top. As he extended his arms, I also saw the patterns that twisted in knots at his fingertips and across his wingspan.

"Ren-" I practically cried, my face screwing up as I met his embrace. When he took me in his arms, a refreshing chill went over my body as my feet completely left the ground. He set me down, muttering my name and incoherent nothings, keeping me close by my arms.

Rengas's expression told me that I was the beacon who crashed the ball, not him. As if this were just as surreal to him as it was for me. A pretty tear rolled down his cheek. My hand nearly lifted to wipe it away. His eyes were creased with longing for something unsaid.

My gaze found its way back to his chest. Though his ensemble was flashy, this was certainly the most glaring thing about it. I struggled to muster any words.

"You-you're a- Ren, bless Light!" I put my hand there instead. I could feel the chill of his hands through my sleeves, so this sensation was especially cool- in a sweet, honeyed sort of way. It wasn't a stinging cold, really the opposite. Just a radiant one. It matched Ren nicely, I found. It *fit*.

Ginger and swords. Rocky and his hat. Ren and Light marks. The prince nodded, moving one of his hands from my arm to rest over mine, holding it fast in its place.

"Yes, bless Light. She has finally heard me." He sobbed once through a bright grin, more tears peppering his thick eyelashes. They glistened under the lantern light.

"Dance with me, Guno. You have to." Rengas told me. Of course, I'd oblige.

"I will-" I was cut off by other dignitaries wondering things about him just as I did. I stepped aside and allowed them to take his attention. His hand hesitated, even then, to slip away from my arm.

"So you actually did it," I could make out, or "Which try was that?" or "Rengas! Well done!"

Occasionally Ren would protest or try and respond, but often it got cut off by another disapproving quip or a bit of eager praise. They brought him to the edge of the group of spectators, close to the dance floor.

As Ginger passed us and caught a glimpse of Ren, I saw her eyes widen. She stumbled and missed a move: a stomp that the rest of the representatives did in perfect unison. Then the General was swallowed by the crowd once more.

She couldn't speak to us until the bell rang again, signifying the end of that round. She immediately made her way over along with everyone else. She held her hand out to keep back a tall half-ground elf beacon woman. She pursed her lips but waited patiently behind Ginger's arm.

"*Rengas!* How did you get back so- Bright Saint Parkeyre." The General's gaze was focused on his chest, one hand over her mouth.

"I used my ring. Ginger, don't worry, I can tag in for you! Is this the second round next? I need to- oh, hello, your highness." His voice quieted once his eyes locked with the taller beacon woman. He chuckled in a deflated sort of manner. "Miss Limbernal."

Her stern expression quickly softened. Ginger stepped aside, and the half-elven queen lowered herself slightly to pull Rengas into a tight hug. The markings on her neck and the ones on Ren's inner forearms pulsed with energy. I saw him shiver before pulling back. He was chewing on his bottom lip, holding back more tears.

Since Kalesse Limbernal went to speak with him, most of the party guests kept their distance.

"Rengas, I am so proud of you. This is the beginning of your ruler's journey." She told him. "Now that Light has recognized you as one of Her own, it's only a matter of time before everyone else here recognizes you too." Now with his beacon marks, Ren and Kalesse could have looked like family. Kalesse was hurriedly wiping away his tears before they could ruin his paint. She took a handkerchief and pushed it into the palm of his hand. He went to dab it to the corners of his eyes.

"Kalesse, can I talk to you later? After the speaking dances. I have other things to tell you."

"Of course you may." She kindly petted at the locks of hair adorning the sides of his face, then set her hands on his shoulders, her head turning toward the bell and the band loft.

"I can go another round if you need rest, Rengas. I would completely understand that." Ginger added from behind Kalesse's towering form.

"No, no, I've got this. I've been looking forward to this ball since last year." He sniffled, pointlessly brushing off his pants and adjusting the scarf around his waist.

"A little bit of sleep deprivation isn't going to stop me!" He dismissively waved his hand in the air, then handed the handkerchief back over to Kalesse. I nearly began to follow him as he made his way to the center of the room, but Ginger stopped me before I could. I watched Pranta get back in her place- then spot Ren, and skitter over to him instead, holding his arm and putting her hand on his stomach as she owned him. A fleeting itchy feeling went over me. A feeling that told me I had to do something to stop her.

But what? I asked it, and it faded away as soon as it came.

The half-elven queen had not yet left for her post. Instead, she asked me,

"Are you Rengas's friend? I saw you in the General's company earlier." I looked for the woman in question, but Ginger had already left to join Harthene. The fact Kalesse considered him my friend felt like an honor in itself.

"Yes. I train under him and Ginger." I told her, holding out my hand. She shook it in both of hers. She was a beacon, too, just like Thorn Acker. Could she also feel the Darkness in my heart?

"Ah, the prince's 'project.' Yes, I've heard quite a lot about you, but I'd love to hear more." To my shock, the queen *smiled*. A motherly, prideful smile that chipped away at my building unease. Then, she turned, still viewing me from over her shoulder. "I'll see you later, yes?" With that, Kalesse joined the others. The bell rang.

Ginger's dancing had been skillful, but Ren's was eloquent. Every turn of his wrist and curve of his body told leagues. Though I wasn't familiar with the language, I could tell he was conveying a story. I wandered back to Harthene, Ginger, and Rocky in a daze, trying to catch glimpses of the prince as much as possible.

● ● ●

"The prince may have his irresponsible moments, but no one can deny he is an *exquisite* performer." Harthene's deep growl of a voice rang out. Rocky lowered his head, rubbing the back of his neck. He didn't seem all that eager to discuss it.

"Yeah, all of this is impressive. I've never seen anything like it." Rengas had disappeared from view again, so I turned my gaze to Harthene. "How long does it take to dance like this?"

"It depends. Most capital leaders learn this dance from the time they can walk." He raised his bushy eyebrows at me.

"Holy Glow," I remarked. For Rengas, that could have meant over two decades of dancing.

There were a few more rounds of what Harthene called "formals" after this. For most of each turn, two representatives were paired up. From there, they took turns making the more complicated and showy moves while the other watched. Sometimes, the active speaker would engage lightly with the other: for instance, Rengas took Kalesse's hand and lifted it daintily in the air before moving under her arm and around her. The instant Rengas was done, he found us and rushed over to me, taking both my hands in his.

He looked like a god with his white hair backlit by the bright lanterns above us. I wanted to hold him close and let his Light sink into my skin. I yearned for the heat plaguing my heart to be extinguished. I fully believed then, at that moment, that Rengas had the power to do so. He was the key. The missing piece to this whole charade that would *finally* cause everything to make sense. But he'd never allowed me to get that close, surely. If he would allow me, Ginger wouldn't. Rocky wouldn't. Rioh wouldn't.

"Dance with me." The prince ordered.

"With *you*." I voiced with a timid cluck, peering to my left at Ginger. I didn't think he meant so soon.

She'd gone tense; a fist raised to her lips. The fist loosened, turning into a dismissing wave.

"Yes! You said you would, so come on! The next song is starting; there's no time for delay." He released one of my hands but used the other to lead me to the center of the room. I could feel every chilling line Light had traced in his skin. Perhaps that's why a nervous shiver went up to my spine as we reached the middle. If this hadn't been a place of so much joy and Light, Dark would certainly have taken hold of me by now. My muscles were tense. I could feel hundreds of eyes on me, tracking our every move.

Who is this? Some noble would say, *Just another one of His Majesty's playthings?*

* * *

I had a gripping feeling that I wasn't supposed to be here. I wasn't allowed. The sense of inferiority hadn't been nearly as bad earlier when I was free to blend into the crowd, but now that security blanket was gone.

Rengas didn't let me stray too far into my mind. However- he squeezed my hand, making me look into his eyes. The lights were too bright. I had to squint just to see properly.

"Hey. Just watch me, alright? Ignore them. They don't matter." He soothed, holding out his other hand. His ring hand.

Most of the marks originated from where the ring sat on his finger, a cluster of tightly wound lines that competed to share the ring's company. From there, the marks loosened from one another. I took his hand as it was offered, but my fingers hesitated over it first before I pushed myself to commit. "These are the informal dances. Policies and inter-sector matters have already been handled. Now it's just," He grinned wickedly, barely with any of that shakiness he possessed less than an hour before. "Fun. Meaningless fun." He was still startled as the bell rang. He released my hands but kept close. "Take a bow." The prince instructed. Rengas held my gaze all the way down as I mirrored his polite move.

Maybe he was right. All I needed to do was focus on him, and everything else would melt away. Reality would slip through my fingers, airier and thinner than Light herself on those nights where I'm all alone, and there's no one there to hold my nerves fast.

He straightened again, folding an arm behind his back while the other raised flat in the air. I copied, pressing my hand against his. He stepped forward, and so did I, and we rotated in a circle. The music sped up in pace. Rengas laughed brightly and twirled away from my hand, beginning what I assumed was his turn.

The prince's tone was much different with me than it had been with Kalesse and the other officials. He gave me taunting gazes over his shoulder and maintained eye contact when turning abruptly to face me with one smooth roll of his body. It became difficult to keep my own little stationary groove going. For my own dignity's sake, I tried to match his playful attitude. The only thing that slightly concerned me was how similar his glances were to the secretive ones we shared back at the capital and how those looks would be under intense scrutiny. Yet, I was implored to keep my eyes on him and keep my focus steady. I would try not to think about what the others saw.

Ren approached me, a sharp grin spreading across his face and coloring his cheeks with each languid step. Well, two could play at this game; I turned away from him, continuing my smooth little jive before

* * *

striking a dramatic pose with my arm outstretched. I couldn't help but hear the crowd quiet in surprise. Somehow, it did quite well for my confidence. I heard a few more footsteps behind me, then the sound of fabric pooling on the floor. Looking to my left, I saw Ren's cape, which had been discarded on the ground. Rocky scurried to pick it up as soon as it made contact with the floor.

It must have been my turn. I continued to face the other way. I recited things I already knew, just little steps from my village. Now and again, I'd glance at the crowd. Some individuals seemed to have some intrigue for what I was doing, but most were indifferent. In my loss of focus, I fell offbeat for a few moments. I bared my teeth, working on getting back on track with sharp juts out with my elbows. With a powerful stamp of my foot, I'd turned to face the prince again. He'd shifted all of his weight onto one leg and viewed me through heavily hooded eyes. As soon as I came to face him, the prince came even closer, slinking toward me while lowering himself as if he were melting. The prince pooled at my feet.

It was getting hot under this coat- maybe be the prince had the right idea by taking off his cape.

I felt my heart jump as his leg shot up, and suddenly his heeled shoe was inches away from my nose. I stumbled back in a motion that I attempted to turn into some sort of groove that I continued as Rengas laughed wickedly, rolling around my legs and making fluid moves while on his knees.

"I heard these dances have meaning, Rengas," I told him cautiously, stealing looks to the nobles around us. Many of them had gone pale. Rocky clutched the cape to his chest and looked as if he were going to faint at any moment.

He brushed against me quite a few times, and I was almost certain it was on purpose; this was confirmed when he became still in a crouch in front of me and began to rise to his feet. I swallowed coarsely and struggled not to recoil as he ran his hands along the sides of my legs all the way up.

I couldn't stop dancing. This was a two-sided thing. I leaned into it, poising my hands above my head and rolling my body a little. It was clunky and probably didn't look great, but by the pleasantly surprised look on Rengas's face, it was enough.

"Yes, they do. Who told you?" The prince blinked at me once he was at eye-level. He didn't stop moving, and neither did I. We circled one another so I could respond,

"Ginger," I answered, taking his hand as it was offered to me and twirling under his arm. "So what about these? What do they mean?" I asked calmly, taking two purposeful steps back as he separated from me.

The prince began to delve into strange dances once more, moves where he felt his own body and incorporated subtle motions of his hips that nearly made Rocky drop the cape.

Rengas's hand, glittering with all sorts of rings and bracelets and Light, trailed down his thigh. "Telling you that would ruin the mystery!" He giggled, raising his voice so I could hear over the music, his face bright as the lights above us. Rengas spun around, throwing his hands in the air to frame his face in a final move that made it seem as if he were helpless to his own movements. As if they were some primal urge that just happened to overcome him in that instant.

I wasn't going to lie; the act was pretty convincing.

The music died down. I let my body relax from its ending position. Who knows what I'd chosen to do then -some amateur bend backward as if I were being dipped- except I was dancing alone.

Upon letting my gaze settle into the crowd for a second time, I could see that many onlookers didn't know what to make of the prince's performance. Many of their faces were slack. Ginger pinched the bridge of her nose with a neatly gloved hand. I watched as a group of nobles began to congregate, muttering to themselves. I gritted my teeth, clicking under my breath at them. Sure, whatever Rengas was choosing to do might not have been the wisest choice, but this was a party! Wasn't he allowed at least a little bit of self-expression? I thought his dances were beautiful, even if they didn't align with the protocol.

But then again, he never did tell me what the moves meant.

"Come on, Lamplight, care for another go?" The prince had come to meet me again, the gold pieces attached to his belt glinting as they swung with each step. The words themselves brought back bitter memories from Escuro. Memories of failures and debts you could never pay off, of long nights spent grieving over the life you could never get back. Not in ten millennia.

"I'm not so certain." I began, but he was already rolling his shoulders, putting his arms around my neck, and shimmying against me while laughter spilled from his mouth.

I really did miss him, didn't I?

"Come on; a little more dancing couldn't hurt a taka mouse! I'll let you lead this time." He said, hands running down my arms so he could grab hold of mine. The bell rang.

I decided to give in; it hadn't been that bad. Well, aside from the nasty looks I caught every time I came to face the crowd, that is.

* * *

With the fluttery feelings and surges of adrenaline that coursed through my body with every fast-paced move and well-timed gaze from Rengas, I found I didn't mind them so much.
Our second dance came to a close in a giggly frenzy, his hands still gripping mine. His grin faded as Kalesse approached him. She leaned close to his ear, muttering something, and then sent him off with a pat. Trying not to let whatever the queen said shake him, he started. Rengas didn't let go of my hand. I didn't mind that either.

"What did she say?" I questioned as the prince started to lead me away from the dance floor.

"She wants us to wait outside and enjoy ourselves while she and the other inter-sector officials discuss something."

"Why? What is it?"

"She didn't say, specifically, yet I have a hunch." His eyes flickered to me as I stepped out into the night.

Here, in dimmer lighting, his Light lines really stood out; stark white bolts through the firelit darkness. Rengas was clearly tense; his arms were held stiff at his sides. I took a few more steps out, beckoning for him to follow.

"Just don't worry about it," I tried to reassure him.

I was reminded of something in my pocket; I could feel it against my leg. "Oh! I forgot," The MP3 player had been in there this whole time. I'd almost completely forgotten it; good thing that my pockets were deep enough that it didn't fall out while we danced. I carefully took it out and presented the device to him.

"You remembered!" He took it in his hands just as gently, stowing it away as soon as it was given to him in a pouch attached to his belt. "I can't believe- how did you know I would make it back in time?" His silvery eyes flitted back up to meet mine.

"Well, the thing is," Dark-filled regret festered at the pit of my stomach. I hadn't known he would be there at all. I just thought of bringing the device because I was hopeful- and because I didn't trust the castle staff enough to leave it alone. Yet I entertained him through a tense expression: "I kind of got a sign from Light. I could feel Her. She gave me hope that you'd be back soon."

His eyelashes fluttered as he quite literally lit up. His genuine excitement only made me feel worse.

"Really? Oh, my induction into Her ranks must have reached quite the audience." He chuckled deeply. A fleeting grimace passed my face, along with a slight sting in my cheeks. The fact he believed me was much more terrible than the lie itself. A passing lie with no

※ ※ ※

impact would be much different, no harm done, but *this*- this felt horrible.

"Yeah, really." I was digging myself a hole here. "Hey, how long do you think they'll be talking? I wanted to see you dance some more." I'd tell him the truth eventually. Now just wasn't the right time. The comment seemed to have struck him the right way once again because his cheeks were going a deeper pink beneath his red stripe.

"Oh, you silly mouse- you know you can see me dance anytime. It doesn't have to be at a party." A breath left me as my head swiveled to check my surroundings. Once the initial wave of panic passed, I met his eyes again. I never could keep away for too long.

"So, who did you tell them you were? Only Kalesse knows you're being nursed back into Light's image."

"Ginger told everyone I was working for her. A General's apprentice." I shuffled my feet. Kalesse already knew the truth about that one. It wouldn't take much for the rest of the party guests to find out I was tainted by Dark, especially those who were beacons.

"Hm. It does seem plausible, given the way they've dressed you." The prince cracked a smile at my jacket, straightening out the lapels with steady, Light-laden hands.

"Hey, *I like it.*" I raised an eyebrow, pushing his hands away from my chest.

"And I never said *I* didn't like it. The look suits you, as stuffy as it may be."

"You're one to talk- what you're wearing barely counts as a top! I hope Hazelgrove gave the capital a discount because they didn't use much fabric at all." I cackled with a birdlike chime to accompany it.

"*Ooh, ouch.*" He looked all too pleased, even as he crossed his arms. "Well, I am one for material conservation, but I'm afraid that isn't why I chose this design."

"Oh, of course, *you* chose it. Ginger would never allow this much-" I paused, noticing I'd taken a step closer to him as we were bickering.

"*This much what?*" His indulgent grin spread, "Go on, say it." Rengas blinked down at me, waiting for a response. Waiting for me to give him some sort of praise on his appearance. I didn't entertain him this time. I only turned my flustered scowl to the fire at my right. Luckily I didn't have to stall for much longer. Kalesse returned, giving a suspicious look to Rengas, who immediately dropped the grin. I clumsily gave her the Beacon's greeting, which I'd forgotten earlier when I was caught up in Rengas's return.

"Lamplight, do come with us a moment." She extended her arm to me. My hands moved away from my chest to take her offer when Rengas piped up again.

"Just him?" He said it quietly, merely testing the waters.

"Unfortunately, we are still deciding on what to do. We need Lamplight's opinion here. Hopefully, it will only take a few moments." Rengas gave me a pleading look as Kalesse led me back inside, my arm hooked around hers.

I tried not to grip Kalesse's arm too tight as we approached what I could only assume were the inter-sector officials, deep in discussion. With them also were Ginger and Rioh. That made me the tensest: Rioh and his Light cannon, which he seemed ready to fire at any moment.

I took a bow as she opened up the circle for us to join in. I paid respects to those of them who were beacons, this time pressing my palms to my chest in much more of a rush. Rioh's steely, cold eyes fell upon me. I tried not to show how much it unsettled me, moving my arm out of Kalesse's.

"So, Lamplight. I've disclosed to the others your purpose at Ninth's capital. Your *real* purpose." Her hand was now on my shoulder. Light's cool steadiness radiating from Kalesse was a good reason I was still upright, I was sure. I blinked to attention. "Tell us how you came to the capital. From the beginning, please."

I cleared my throat, afraid to step away from her hand. That small noise was the only thing that broke the silence since the band stopped playing after the formal dances. I found my eyes lingering on Ginger's face, which provided a sense of safe familiarity as I recounted the whole thing.

"Well, my teacher of Dark- I would say kidnapper at the time, pardon me if my language is too harsh-" I worried my hands, "She took me to a, uh- a Dark place. A dimension of twisted, *evil* intent like none I'd ever seen. She wanted me to fight." The royals and beacons around me were completely silent. Listening for any crack in the film, any detail that seemed off.

"The prince found me soon after. I was beaten. When he, uh, took me back to the capital, he fixed me up. Then Ginger, the prince, and I started training together. Conditioning me with Light."

"Yes, the General has told us that much." A king said. I felt my pace quicken with embarrassment.

"Y-yes, well-"

"Rengas started this whole charade *without permission*. What sort of prince does that?" Rioh growled, playing with his cannon. It clicked intimidatingly.

"Light has recognized him. She clearly knows what She's doing- She knows that this time he means to make a difference! Besides, he's *the prince,* Rioh. He isn't obligated to answer to us." Ginger contested.

"*Of course he's obligated!* Rengas isn't a full Prince. He's a *limited* one. We do his job, Ginger! Why do you think that is? He needs to learn to listen to orders before he can give them." Rioh bared his fangs at the General; this was an argument that I was sure they'd had countless times when the prince wasn't watching. I couldn't bear to imagine what would happen if he overheard.

"Rioh, no need to raise your voice." Kalesse lifted a hand. Rioh put *his* hands over his heart, this time.

"My apologies, Miss Limbernal." Even as he bowed his head, there was a nasty bite in his tone. "But you all must understand- *and I mean no offense, Lamplight-*" He gritted his teeth. I steeled myself for the worst. "Allowing people such as *you* into places of Light is dangerous. You must understand, as a Dark one yourself."

I didn't. Not quite. I didn't tell him that, though. I kept quiet.

"That is what Rengas doesn't seem to get. He's too soft. He can't comprehend when someone can hurt him, and he won't until it's too late." Rioh preached like this was a grim omen, his watchful eyes landing on me once again. I clenched my fists.

"I'd never!" I found myself getting heated too. "I'd never hurt him! How can you assume- I didn't choose this! Tell me, why in the Afterdull would I ever choose this life? You speak to me as if I wanted to have my freedom taken!" My ears burnt red hot. Kalesse put a hand on my shoulder, squeezing.

"Lamplight. Steady yourself. Focus on the topic at hand." Kalesse said- yet looking at the officials around me, it only made my face burn more with all their terrified faces. Thank Light we were in the capital, or else I didn't know what I would've done.

I didn't want to think about it.

"And this is exactly what I mean." Rioh mused. I looked at Ginger for help, but she watched the floor and didn't catch my eye. At least I knew she was just as strung out about this as I was. I didn't know how much longer I could bottle up my anger.

"They're temperamental. The fact that Rengas is so lenient on the boy; he lets him wander wherever he pleases." Rioh continued, "He has easy access to *anything* in the capital. Are we going to let Rengas continue this blatant act of nepotism?" He shrugged as if everything he said wasn't up for debate, a mere fact out of his control. The mention of "access" was what really got me. It was as if Rioh had been watching the whole time and had been watching when I took Alice's diary from Ren's room. If he really didn't see me take his things, he was making a dangerously insightful guess.

Quite a few inter-sector officials seemed to agree with Rioh's point, some pensively nodding their heads.

Maybe Kalesse saw that this talk wasn't making me seem any more docile because she patted me twice dismissively.

"Go back to the prince. I think we've got it from here, Lamplight. Thank you." The queen bid me off. I left quickly, ignoring Rioh's fading voice as I went.

"Well, what'd they say? does it look good for me?" Rengas begged for an answer, biting his lip as he pulled me to the side. He hadn't moved from the spot I'd left him in.

"Uh," *Kevik, where to even begin?* "I don't know."

"You don't know? Were you even listening in there?" He poked my forehead. I swatted his hand away.

"Yes. I was. There were just a lot of points being made. They seem to be discussing your power. Your position in the capital."

"Well, duh! They're seeing whether or not to give me full princely rights and duties! *I haven't been promoted since I was fifteen!"* His eyes were wide, almost manic, as he looked me up and down and seized me by the shoulders, shaking me. Needless to say, I couldn't shrug him off that time. Ren's grip was strong. I shook the stars out of my eyes.

"Yeah, okay. Still. There were a lot of arguments. If you haven't noticed, I'm not really *in* on inter-sector policies." Sure, I was letting on a little dumber than I actually was.

I didn't want to wrongly assume the outcome of their meeting, or worse, be the one to break his heart. His grip softened, his hands slipping from my shoulders.

"Fair enough..." He dropped his gaze to the floor in that same repressive manner Ginger had moments before. There was a period of silence where I decided what to do from there.

* * *

"Hey, you wanted to dance, right? Let's do that." This time, I was the one who took the prince's hand. We moved back to one of the dancing circles. His expression seemed to ease the whole way there.

"Yeah, I suppose you're right." His smile was readily returning as we came to the edge of the ring.

My eyes went round as he used my shoulder to steady himself to pull off his shoes. I wobbled quite a bit under his weight but still tried to keep him steady by holding his arm. I watched him remove his shoes without any protest. He was about to pull me in when I rushed to pull off my boots as well. I looked up just in time to see how pleased he was before he quickly averted his smile to something else. As soon as my shoes were off, I was being pulled into the crowd. Their hollers and clapping grew in magnitude, seeing Ren enter the circle.

The prince took a bow with a prideful flourish, then held out his hand. That intimidating, competitive spark was back. I took his hand.

I was almost glad Pranta Nunez wasn't here this time around. I found I liked having the prince's company to myself. I thought about the thing he'd said earlier, a passive comment that almost seemed like he was making an offer.

You can see me dance anytime. It doesn't have to be at a party.

I let him have the spotlight first, as he, along with the partygoers around us, clearly anticipated. He continued the loose, fluid movements from the ballroom, with sharp moves that melted and slowed when the music did. Rengas twirled around, teasing the audience by grazing his hands against some of theirs, but didn't pull anyone else in. Instead, he took his last few moves, tossing his hair and feeling up his body once more. He seemed to think it would do something- disarm me, maybe?

I wasn't so persuaded. I waltzed right up to him, looking him straight in the eyes as I continued to clap along with the music, mimicking the ring of people around us. I tried to add a lot more competitive, sharp moves this time. We continued like this, back and forth, until another pair was led in. We stumbled, giggling, out of the crowd like a pair of drunks, clutching onto one another as we waited for our heads to stop spinning.

"Come with me. Let's explore." Rengas told me, his skin speckled with lantern light. I couldn't keep my hands off of his palms and forearms, feeling every little indent and curve She had carved into them. So naturally, I couldn't refuse when he started away from the circle, not bothering to get our shoes.

"Where are we going?" I held his hand in both of mine. We ended up circling the center building, crossing each of the circular platforms until we came across a staircase, leading up the tower's side. Rengas held onto the banister as he shot a look back at me. We took off, ascending the spiraling set of stairs, the cave's inner wall twinkling and rotating above. Up here, we were greeted by yet another outdoor space, all under an intricate golden canopy where vines grew between curls of metal and little lights. The perfume from the flowers above hung thick in the air with luxurious pungence that drowned out even the scent of the food carts below. His eyes lingered on me as we came to a stop at this uppermost platform.

"What-" I muttered so that he'd take his eyes off me. They were too much, always had been.

"Nothing, uh..." Wordlessly, Ren released my hand, jerking his head toward the edge to urge me to follow. This time, his gait was much slower. "How do you feel?" He asked as I approached the platform's railing. I knew he meant within Light and Darkness; I didn't need clarification this time.

I ran my hand over the rail's smooth finish, worn down by generations of nobles and party guests. "Do you want me to be honest?" I slowly lifted my head to address him. His hands twitched.

"Of course I do." The prince said. I took a deep breath.

"I feel like I'm more Light, but the Dark side of my heart has been," I furrowed my eyebrows at him, blinking with uncertainty at how to word it. "It's become more awakened. It's more alert. Harder to ignore."

Rengas was a picture of such clean-cut obedience. It must have been so simple for him. Just do as he was told, and everything would go alright. "I feel like it got worse when you left for Beaconism. Even when I train, no matter how hard, I feel no results. I feel like- like-" I pulled at my hair, then thought against it- I didn't want to ruin the staff's work. "Like I'm just broken. For good."

"Are you kidding? You're not broken! Why would you ever think-" He turned to me so sharply I nearly jumped back. He gently retook my hands, running his thumbs over my knuckles. I let myself give in to the touch, my eyes falling closed for a moment. I took a step closer to him.

"I wish I could just forget anything ever happened. Just for a moment. Something always finds a way to remind me of what I've done." My worries spilled from my mouth before I could hold them back. They would have run on in circles forever if Ren hadn't gently held the back of my head, letting me lean into his chest. I lightly held his waist to keep him close, yet I didn't genuinely believe he'd leave anytime soon. I just wanted to feel safe knowing I had so much Light around me, even if it wouldn't keep me out of harm's way in the long run.

"Do you think there's any hope for me?" I asked vaguely, half posing the question just to myself.

"Do I really need to-"

"Right. Of course, you think there is." I chuckled, leaning back after a long moment. The prince's expression showed that of dreamy helplessness as I kept him there. I noticed how his posture relaxed, muscles loosening. It didn't get me nearly as worked up as it made him, but I could still feel the pulse in my chest. I kept worrying about where to put my hands. "You're *too* hopeful sometimes, you know."

"It will be my downfall." His hand cupped my cheek, sliding up into my hair. I cherished the feeling; it dulled the swelling of my eye, even. I leaned closer yet to him, my hand gripping the front of his ornate top. I'd waited so long for his return that it hurt. I spent hours recounting and re-learning his teachings just to recall the tone of his voice. The moment I'd longed for had arrived, but so had the end to Rengas's mission. My purpose at the capital had been fulfilled: helping Ren connect with Light.

How did I not think of it before? All this time I'd spent wanting time to pass quicker when really I should've been enjoying my time safe within a barrier of Light. I should've made my last encounters with the prince count. I was fortunate, at least, that I was getting to see him one last time. I touched my forehead against him, frowning as I tried to keep my composure.

"I'm very happy for you, Rengas," I spoke quietly. The prince watched me, the petting of my hair slowing. "Though I'm really going to miss you. I'll think of you often when I'm gone." I was finding it difficult to keep the stinging in my throat at bay. I couldn't bear being face-to-face with him, instead of returning close to bury my face into his shoulder, holding him close as I restrained sobs.

"Gone?" His voice wavered too, though in confusion. The prince held me tighter as well.

"You're a beacon now. You- you did it. I have to go home." He'd done so well, too. He'd outdone himself. Even if I didn't know why this was important, I knew it meant a lot to him. It took him ages to get here- and he'd even saved me in the process.

"Oh, Light. We did say that, didn't we?" He tried to comfort me through quiet shushes and more rubs at my back. "Surely we can figure something out, sweet mouse! We don't have to rush into sending you anywhere until we're- until we're certain you'll be safe, right?"

I shook my head into his shirt.

"I don't know! I was never in control of any of this!" Any ferocity in my tone was undone by my sniffling and the fact that my voice broke whenever I spoke up.

"I don't want you to go." Rengas took my shoulders, pulling back to see me. I caught my breath. "I really, truly don't."

There came a squeak from behind us. I reeled back so fast I would've fallen over the edge if it weren't for the railing that caught me. I was fully ready to fight before I saw it was only Rocky accompanying the platform with us. I took a last glance at Ren- *poor Ren*- the prince was so deeply shaken, not even his furious dancing made the jewels at his neck and wrists tremble that much. He was an even deeper scarlet than when I was close to him.

"Rocky- good evening!" He tried desperately to straighten his posture and make it appear as if nothing had happened.

"Looks like you and Lamplight are havin' fun." The elf's tone was almost accusatory- he growled out speech from the corner of his mouth, his arms stiff at his sides. He caught a glimpse of my tear-freckled cheeks before I could dry them.

"Lamplight, are you okay?" The elf seemed to be caught off guard by the sight, unprepared to console me. I nodded and muttered some assurances. Rocky paused before clearing his throat.

"Well, in any case, they need you, Rengas. Maybe you shouldn't wander off." Rocky, too, was flushed. His rage was uncomfortable to watch. He was so bad at hiding it that I began to feel bad for him. "They've made their decision. *I advise you to come down as soon as-* you forget that. Follow me, your highness."

We did, keeping an arm's length distance from one another for good measure. The last thing I wanted was yet another member of the castle staff on my case.

This time I was the one told to wait outside. Rocky and I stood side by side, saying nothing. Nothing I said still when Rengas emerged from the ballroom with the most defeated expression I'd been yet to see from him. Any of that "hope" we'd spoken of only minutes ago had been drained from his eyes, his cheeks devoid of their natural flush.

He walked right past me without as much as a sideways glance. It was Ginger who finally broke the silence.

"It's time to go home, Lamplight."

"Is he okay?"

"There will be time to ask on the ride back."

There would be time, plenty of it. I prepared myself for the feeling of Dark to return as soon as we left Tenth's capital while I strapped into my seat. I could feel Rocky's stare digging into me. That alone would be enough to stir Dark from his slumber if I wasn't careful. Ren had insisted on sitting in the middle of the drifter where he could have a little more space.

As soon as we were off and out of Tenth, I found myself prickling again, and the weight of my Dark eye became heavier inside my head. He was trying to catch up to compensate for missed time. How silly of me to think I'd ever be allowed a break.

I hastily unbuckled and rushed back to Rengas's side, where he was curled up on a bench, his hands holding his arms. I tried to pull them away, tucking my fingertips into the palms of his hands, which weren't nearly as cool as they were before.

"*Ren,*" I uttered to him, the sound drowned out by the whir and rattle of the drifter's machinery. "Dark has come for me again. Can I rest my hands here?"

The prince's head had been lowered away from me. Once he finally lifted it, I could see tears shining off his red-stained cheeks. His face was scrunched up as I attempted still to bring him out of his hidden away state. Begrudgingly, he offered his arm for me to hold. I scooted closer to him on the bench. The prince said something too indistinct for me to pick up. I hummed for him to clarify.

"I don't really want to talk." He grumbled. I could feel the muscles of his arm tensing underneath my quieting hands. Even though it was much darker now, his glowing was very faint.

"That's fine. I'm here for you, though, if you ever feel like it." I tried to show that I was holding his arm for his comfort as well as mine, gently brushing my fingertips against his skin. He shuddered and frowned at me a little before turning away again.

It was going to be a long night.

It pained me to see him like this, but I didn't want to overstep any boundaries. I couldn't risk the prince shrugging me off for good. I avoided the looks Rocky gave me over the back of his chair now and again with persistence. I didn't know his intent with those looks, and I didn't intend to find out. I needed to keep my focus on Ren and Dark. Those were the only things that mattered.

I was relieved beyond words when several hours into the drifter ride, Ren shifted on the bench to face me, his quiet sobs only worsening. He was here. That was good.

● ● ●

"May I?" I lifted a hand to his face. He nodded softly, permitting me to wipe away his tears. I only did so above and below his paint, too afraid to touch the sacred material itself. I kept my other arm close to his; my fingertips still pressed into the palm of his ring hand. His lip trembled with heavy grief. He still constantly avoided my eyes; at least I could make sure he didn't stray too far into his mind.

"Sleep." I whispered, leaning back on the back pad of the bench, "I'll stay awake and keep a lookout. You need rest after your travels."

He mouthed something. I was too afraid to ask him to clarify, and I dropped the thought after the prince closed his eyes, a hand closing over the one I had held his arm. He must have meant it as some sort of acceptance.
I kept myself awake to watch for a few more hours, but mostly to feel. Feel how I responded once Ren's hand slipped from mine in his sleep, and take in how Dark could pull me without the safeguards keeping Him back.

The wave of burning was so strong I had to return to his touch almost immediately. What if my shaking hands would wake him up? Or my heavy breathing? *Kevik, why couldn't I just keep still for him?*

Ren had stressed enough already. I just needed to keep still and silent just until we got back, just until sunrise.

I only realized I had fallen asleep because Ginger had to rouse me come morning. I remember feeling the heat first, a raging smolder all across my flesh burning tenfold from a regular day in the Dashan sun. It was then, when my fear and anger mounted, when I knew something was truly wrong. Rengas wasn't beside me.

"Stay back-" I snapped as I came to, pressing myself flush against the wall of the drifter- Ginger took a step back at the same time as I did, her hand reaching for the blade at her hip. My hands gripped the cage behind me. Ginger's eyes went wide.

"Guno, come on inside, alright? You're not in your right mind." She held out her hand. I let out another low grumble.

"Where is he?"

"Huh? Guno, who-"

"*Rengas!* Where is he?" I watched Ginger's face grow increasingly slack. She kept looking at me with that same stupid, dumbfounded expression like she didn't know how to handle me. Like I was just another lowlife that needed to be *contained*. I heard a creak from the bars I was holding onto.

My head whipped around to see I'd created a good bend in the bars just with my Dark- covered hands. The stuff nearly reached my elbow...

Likely the only reason I was able to come down from it was because of my own fear as I looked away from Ginger. I was reduced to a small, panicking mess once more as the General pulled me to my feet and led me back inside, taking extra care to ensure Dark didn't reclaim me on the way up. A few steps in, Ginger muttered something dismissive about traditional values and raised her hand to her monocle. Once she twisted it, a yawning portal opened up, cooling my face and making Ginger's coat billow in the breeze. Ginger pushed me through before I could resist- not that I would. Not on purpose, at least. These days it was getting harder to say that for certain.

"To answer your question, Rengas is in his room. I know you've missed him, but he needs time to process the news of his position." To my surprise, Ginger held her hand out to a guard, and

• • •

they gave her their Light staff. She put the thing into my hands. Even though the portal had scrubbed it away, the coolness of the staff's polished white wood felt nice and safe in my grasp.

"What news?" I asked, knowing the answer before the words left my lips. Ginger looked at me over her shoulder, then started walking. I followed.

"They've decided to keep his job as-is: in its limited state. The inter-sector officials weren't confident enough yet to grant him the full range of responsibilities that a typical prince would."

I felt myself grip the light staff a little harder. "Why wouldn't they give him some slack? He's a beacon, for Light's sake." I breathed incredulously, holding my head.

Ginger blinked hard. "If I'm being completely honest, Lamplight, I don't know." After a while, the General cracked a smile but didn't look back at me as she continued to lead me to where I presumed was the direction of my quarters. "But the dances he was doing might have had something to do with it." At the mention of his dancing, I felt my coarse expression relax. I brought the Light staff closer to my chest.

"Huh? What about them?" I asked, and was going to leave it at that- but a glance from Ginger prompted me to add, "Well- he told me they had meaning, and I was suspicious for sure, but he refused to tell."

Ginger shook her head. She stopped at the bottom of the stairwell up to my room, leaning against the archway and crossing her arms. Her distant smile didn't falter. "The only reason I think it would have been off-putting for the Inter-Sector officials is it could have been deemed as inappropriate for him to do that, or perhaps immature," She met my eyes, raising her eyebrows pointedly. "The dances he did were intimate courtship dances for royals, Guno. They usually aren't performed outside, you know. *The bedroom.*"

A hot flush rushed up to my neck and face faster than I'd ever felt- I tensed again, gripping the Light device even harder. *"He- why would he-"*

"Oh, come on, you know why." She shook her hesd bemusedly. As she passed me, she took back the Light staff, grabbing my shoulder to give me a little friendly push. "Still, try and give the prince space. He needs it." She advised. After that piece of information, I wasn't sure if I could. I needed to ask- just to make sure, of course.

I was left stunned in the doorway, just me and my loose thoughts.

● ● ●

So he'd done that on purpose? This probably wasn't just a regular occurrence. Could it be that the prince had done those dances for *me*? I'd had inklings for sure; the way Rengas moved his body the night before had certainly lended to a more promiscuous tone. I guess I just thought he was making it all up for fun.

After a minute of standing there at the base of the stairs, I finally came to my senses, blinking back to attention. I wiped my eyes blearily to try and rid my mind of any stray thoughts about the prince. I made my way upstairs.

As soon as the Light device left my hands, I knew I'd be in danger soon after. Halfway up the stairs, I broke into a sprint, steadying my breath as I felt the prickling in my face reach my hands. I knew by now someone was trying to get in. Being upset would only make things worse. I had to keep in mind everything I'd been taught. I needed to act with the best intention in mind and only make choices that would, in the end, hurt as few people as possible. But that isn't to say I can just let people like Alice and Prue push me around. I leaned against my bedroom door, pushing my hands up into my hair.

"If you want to talk, let's talk." I said, biting my cheek with an uneasy growl, "I had a night with some beacons. Is this why you're so upset?" My head swiveled side to side in search of a source of the feeling. As soon as I spoke, I found my lungs tightening, a surge of burning going up my body.

"Oh, so," My breaths came short, "So that's it. I see." I managed between wheezes. I really shouldn't be pushing my luck, I thought, but I wanted to see how far this could go. The last time I had a run-in with the witches, they hadn't done this much. They could only cause so much as a mood swing or creep into my head, like when Alice influenced my dreams. This was much more physical. Even when I'd become short of breath earlier, it wasn't nearly this painful. The witches had grown stronger, for sure. I could feel it like a change in the wind.

"Are you going to puppeteer me around now? I can take-" I can take it, I would've said. But their grip tightened further, making me sink to my knees, eyes watering. I pulled at my chest in a futile attempt to relieve the pressure, but of course, there was nothing there to tear away.

Maybe I *couldn't* take it. Eventually, I sat there on the ground long enough prostrating myself to Darkness for her to let me go. I heaved my own body into bed that night, feeling as if I'd doubled in weight.

• • •

The feeling didn't leave for what must have been nearly a week. It was only Alice and me, day-in and day-out. I'd wake up with a clear head, but by the time the afternoon hit, I was being barraged with piercing thoughts that weren't mine. At least, not at first they weren't. There's a certain point in my "Fits," as Ginger likes to call them, when regular Guno recedes, and something else takes hold. I tried to dismiss the thoughts Dark gave me before as simply a curse- those urges weren't *my* urges. Those violent thoughts weren't *my* thoughts. But now I could see more than ever: Alice was right. Dark, in some respect or another, made up a part of me. When my hands overflowed, the things I did were things a person would consider but never act on; little repressed, intrusive thoughts.

Oh, it would be silly to do that. You'd think, with a clear mind. And Dark asks, *Why would it be silly? Have you ever tried it?*

Wouldn't it feel so good to have release?

Having realized this, I dreaded having to tell Ginger. I didn't think I ever would until I was face to face with the General. She had been handing me, for the first time, a Light sword. Not a fake- the kind *she* used. The kind that fit her so well. Here she was, trusting me completely, yet I hadn't done *anything* to earn it. I was keeping back the truth.

"Uh, General?"

"Yes, Lamplight." She didn't look up from polishing her own sword; mine felt heavy in my hands while Ginger examined it as if the blade weighed nothing at all. I shuffled on my feet.

"I don't think I'm getting any brighter." I lowered my gaze to the ground. I could feel her watching me now.

"And what makes you think that?"

"The witch has spoken to me a lot more. My outbursts are getting harder to control." I let her process that as I deliberated how to present my vicious tendencies to her, how to gently and neatly package them so they didn't hurt. "And I think about wanting to hurt people a lot more often. It's bringing out something in me, Ginger. something that's-" I pressed my eyes shut, letting the sword's lethal tip sink into the sand and allowing my hands to relax a little as they held the hilt. "*Very* hard to ignore." I allowed myself to assess her face fully. Ginger was deep in thought; her watchful eyes turned upon the stars through the arena's massive skylight. She sighed in a way that made my heart wither in its silent disappointment, and she spoke.

"How long have these impulses been here?" She asked, just when I thought it couldn't get worse.

I had to egg myself on to get it out.

● ● ●

"A long time! A *real* long time." I blurted, and took a step aside to lay the blade of Light safely on the ground. "Three months into training, at least? I don't know; I don't." I clutched my hair, beginning to pace—anything not to meet the General's eyes. "I can't tell what Alice put in my head from my actual thoughts, it's- it's-" I could feel something warm and sticky seeping onto my scalp where my hands had held it.

"*Guno.*" Ginger dropped her own sword and rushed over to me. Before I knew it, she was holding my shoulders and guiding me to the sidelines. "Take it easy, boy. Easy." My hands had tightened around chunks of my hair.

How dare she-she doesn't know what's best for me. I let the wave of rage come and go. Then, Ginger had a lantern held out in front of me and surgically removed my hands from my mess of sticky hair to hold it. The cool exterior smoothed over the stinging in my limbs quickly. I let my head hang as my pace slowed and my vision broadened. As soon as my head picked up, it had caught Ginger's attention, and once again, she paced back to me.

"Come, we're going to talk to Rengas and the captain." She began pulling me to my feet. I didn't try to fight it. She pulled me out into the hallway, giving orders to guards which didn't make sense in my dazed state.

"Go get the prince, please. Have him meet us in the high tea room- oh, and have someone prepare refreshments. Lamplight is tense."

"But Rengas is in..." A voice came from inside their helmet, which quickly fizzled out.

"He can finish his music lesson later. Give Mr. Dhegai some tea and fruits in the west sitting room. Let him know he can finish his session with Averell afterward." Ginger kept her hand steady on my back. Several times I caught her checking if I still held the lantern.

"Yes, General." The guard she had been speaking to and a couple of their compatriots departed, leaving Ginger and I alone to find our way to where Ginger was going to have us all "meet."

The high tea room, I soon would discover, was a cozy place. The place had a similar structure to the library in that the walls were round. It had an almost three hundred and sixty-degree view of the ground level outside, apart from the open archway leading back into the rest of the capital. The dressings were simple: plants suspended from the impossibly high ceiling made a sort of leafy faux-roof and a large and equally round tea table was in the center of the room. Ginger had me take a seat. My legs trembled as I got settled in one of the short tea chairs. The general took the seat beside mine. I fidgeted with the lamp, afraid it would turn off if I held it too tightly.

"Do you miss the village, Guno?" Ginger asked. I took a deep breath; the question had caught me off guard. The General hadn't been watching me. Instead, she scrutinized the patterns in the wood of the table, trailing a finger along its lines. The answer came more quickly than I had expected it to.

"Yes," I said, "Yes, actually... I do miss it."

"What do you miss?" She turned to me with patient regard, leaning on her hand.

"I miss a lot, I guess. I miss my friends, mostly Cypress. I miss my garden..." There wasn't a week that went by without me thinking of it at least once. " I miss talking to the elders when I had free time." I snorted a little in recollection. "I don't miss being tense all the time. It's nice having your meals prepared for you, though I suppose I'm tense anyways, with," I gestured to myself with an impatient waggle of my hand. Ginger smiled slightly.

"Yes, I understand." She sat up and folded her hands together atop the table. "It seems you've been away for quite some time now. I'm sure your friend Cypress misses you too. Although I'd be interested what he thinks about *how* you've disappeared- to hear that you committed a murder, only to discover later you're the prince's apprentice!" She shook her head in disbelief, "I mean, I don't write the papers, but I'm fairly certain that's how it got down to them." She jabbed her thumb toward the window, where the sun was just beginning to set. "I bet you'd never thought you'd become a legend, huh?"

"I didn't even think about that." I admitted, "I can't even imagine what Cypress is going to think." That is, assuming I'd ever see him again. In my urgency to get out of my village, I didn't think of the connections that I'd leave behind when I did.

A legend. That is worth more than a story. A man who is a legend has not only one story but ten. Twenty. He is a wealthy man. Ginger was right to think I never thought I'd become that fortunate. Imagining having that many stories to my name eased a deep ache in my bones that had kept up ever since I left home. It was something to be grateful for, yet the circumstances under which I was being immortalized were still bittersweet.

I looked up just in time to see the prince enter, his look distant. He wore long robes that trailed behind him in two intricately embroidered pieces. Rengas silently and obediently sat far from the both of us.

● ● ●

"Sorry to interrupt your lessons, Rengas. We won't keep you for long." Ginger greeted him as a maid brought around some tea and plates. I thanked her as I was given my tea, a deep orange-colored one this time. It was too hot to drink right away. I busied myself with blowing on it as I watched Ren.

"That's fine." He said distantly, blinking slow. Rioh entered after him, with his usual dark visage, throwing out his chair to sit down.

"Safe evening, General." The captain took his tea with a heavy hand. "Will you allow me to speak today, or am I sitting in just for the record of being here? Because I'll see myself out if it's the latter." Ginger squeezed her eyes shut, grinding her thumb into her temple.

"No, Rioh, this includes you. I would like you to be gentler to Lamplight, however." Ginger told him. I started to sip on my tea to avoid making eye contact with the captain, keeping my head down.

"I'm not sure if this is the time to be *gentle*."

"I see where you're coming from, but I assure you, it *really* is. If we use force, this is going to turn out a lot worse than if we use a steady hand." Ginger rubbed my back. I could feel my shoulders relax with both the gesture and the warm feeling of honeyed tea going down my throat. "But it seems that this alone hasn't been enough. I'm not sure what other route to take."

"What is that supposed to mean? Is he getting more evil?" He raised the arm with his canon gauntlet on it, though we knew he'd never fire. Still, the taunting gesture really got my blood pumping. Ginger raised a hand to get him to settle down.

"Well..."

"I guess so." I started, and Ginger gave me a panicked glance, "That's definitely one way to think about it. But I- I don't want to be! Have I ever tried to hurt you, Rioh?" I set down my tea, finally raising my head to address him. The captain's face had gone slack. He cleared his throat, shaking his head a few times.

"No. But I can't be certain you won't." He grumbled. I nodded.

"Yes. To assure I don't, we train! Though that hasn't done much but make me a better fighter." My hands found my own arms, feeling the muscle there. Ren still had not spoken since he came in and didn't seem to be in any hurry to either.

"I have a few things we could try, but every one of them is going to be experimental. We can't be sure what will work, as none of us are *super familiar* with Darkness as a whole." Ginger sat back, hands folded in her lap. "For one, we can adjust where you sleep if you're feeling more unstable at night. We could have someone monitor you." I thought I saw the prince look up for a second. "We can also put more lanterns powered by Her brightness in your room instead of regular candles."

"I can sleep in the dungeon if you guys are really paranoid about it, too." I hated to suggest the idea, but I knew it was what everyone was thinking. I watched Rocky shuffle in and hid behind Rengas just as I said it before taking the seat beside him, keeping a hand on the prince's arm. His gaze bored into me at the mention of the dungeon. *As if I didn't already look like a huge portal traitor to everyone in the capital,* I thought with irritation. I didn't want to explain myself. Someone else could do it for me later.

"There's no need for that, but yes, it is an option available to us." Ginger insisted. Rengas still watched the liquid in his cup with glazed-over eyes. Rocky's gestures of comfort didn't seem to do anything to bring him back to reality. "I suppose, Guno, just tell us whenever you have a particularly bad episode. Preferably as soon as you can."

"But what if I become hostile toward you? Won't traveling across the entire capital to get someone's help make it worse?" I wrung my hands, trying to avoid provoking Rengas by staring too much. The General paused in thought.

"How about a bell?" Rocky suggested, now properly massaging Rengas's shoulders. The prince didn't seem too enthused but didn't tell him to stop. "Like one that Rengas or Rioh would use to request service. It's no different, right?" I nodded. That could work, couldn't it?

"Yeah," I told him, "There's no harm in trying."

It was later that day when I couldn't hold it in anymore. I couldn't stand Rengas Averell of all people looking so placid. It got on my nerves how upset he was. I knocked on the door to his chambers with too much haste. The guards weren't there. I wouldn't be surprised if Rengas dismissed them himself.

There wasn't an answer for a long time, so I tried again.

"Rengas, let me in!" I let my head rest on the heavy wood of his door. "Please?"

It opened, catching me completely off guard. I stumbled a little, and Ren didn't try and catch me.

"Guno, do you need something?" The prince's eyes were slightly puffy, and he was dressed in a sheer robe over some simple nightclothes. His cheeks were flushed more than usual- the glint of them was unmistakable. That, and the fact he didn't bother to put on his royal paint.

"*Ren.*" I lifted my hand to his face. He tensed and pulled away-

"Come in." He said in almost a whisper. I did as I was told. The prince crossed the room and sat down on his bed. Then, to my surprise, he scooted over.

Was I supposed to sit beside him? I made sure to keep my head low as I approached. I wasn't good enough to sit beside the prince, on *his* bed, whether he did courtship dances with me or not. Rengas's hands were folded in his lap. He was stone-cold for a while, letting me live in this awkward silence I didn't dare interrupt. I watched him fidget with the numerous rings on his surprisingly dull fingers. His Light marks were there, for sure, but much fainter than that night at the portal ball.

Rengas trembled now and again. I itched to touch him; anything to soothe the ache that neither of us had spoken on and that neither of us seemed to want to.

"Were your parents strict?" Rengas was the first to say anything. He still twisted his rings around his fingers, but his actions were becoming increasingly stiff. I cleared my throat and scooted back in my seat.

"No, uh, I don't think so." I found myself answering obediently, "I had a good bit of autonomy, at least as far as I thought?" I stopped myself from asking why he brought it up.

"That's good." He nodded a little. Then, his hand extended to me. I looked up at him in my puzzlement, and he only glanced in my direction before adding, "Hold my hand."

I once again followed his orders, gently taking the prince's hand in both of mine. I felt along the gentle recesses of his Light marks. Rengas allowed me to do so but turned his head away. I would come closer if he would allow it, but who knows what step was a step too far.

"I've been thinking a lot lately about where I went wrong."

"Ren, you've done nothing-"

"No. You don't understand, Guno. You don't get it." He bit his bottom lip and pressed his eyes shut. He sniffled, quietly. "I'm not all that you think I am." My hands tightened their grip around his. I could say the same about myself, I thought.

Ren shook his head, "That time I told you about? Where my faith seemed so lost? I'm beginning to realize it was my fault. Everything I waste time worrying about- everything that kept me from joining Her- that's *my* doing."

• • •

I squinted down at his hand as I ran my fingertips over his knuckles. I took a few deep breaths to try steadying myself.

"How so?" I encouraged him to continue, trying not to interject this time.

"I'll just start at the beginning, I suppose." Rengas came closer, his eyebrows pushing together with clear embarrassment. "The story about your father is similar to how I lost my family."

I'd always wondered what had happened at the back of my mind but had never brought up the courage to address it. It seemed rude to.

"They went out on vacation when I was fifteen, when Ginger and I- did she tell you?" He paused to ask me, and I gave a quick nod of my head. "While, yes. We were arranged to marry. Anyways, they were planning to visit a few resort dimensions, a week in each, and then return." His voice trailed off. "You can probably tell where that went. They somehow didn't make it back. Kalesse was over to take care of me while they were away, I remember, and I was given a choice to go look for them." He met my eyes, at last, frowning deeply. "I didn't. I didn't look for them. I didn't even try."

"I guess we have that in common, then."

"No, Guno! It's not like it was a futile effort, either! I had the resources! I had the firepower! I was just too much of a *keving coward* to do anything about it." He cursed himself, gritting his teeth as if he could become so angry that his tears would subside. "My mother was with child. I could've had a sibling." Rengas took my other hand without looking and rested his head on my shoulder. I don't know why I didn't choose to hold him closer. I could see the spots where his tears wet my tunic. The air was thick with the scent of his perfume. When he spoke again, his voice was even more broken.

"If I hadn't been so cowardly, things would be much different than they are now. I'd have a family, or at the very least, I'd have answers." Rengas nudged his face into my neck, a gesture that made me shudder with the sensitivity of the spot. He didn't seem to notice. "Even though I don't have answers, something's always told me they didn't make it. That they've joined Her." He released one of my hands to gesture up to the sky. I could've sworn his markings ignited with a new brilliance, then. "But I did hold out hope for a very long time."

No wonder it took him longer than other royals to reach Beaconism.

I thought back to what Thorn Acker told me at the Portal Ball. How did Rengas go through all of this, and none of the inter-sector officials considered that his journey might take longer? It was plain and simple now: it *wasn't* anything he did. He was predisposed by all that guilt, all that grief, to be set back a few years.

"What made you change your mind?" I asked, trying to crane my neck to see his face.

"My mother started to visit me in my dreams." He straightened to look me in the eyes again, tucking his legs up on the bed. I did the same. "Sometimes it was my father too, but most often it was her. She said, 'Do not look for me. Do not look for your father. You will regret it if you do.' But that doesn't change the fact that I regret not looking for them." Though his tone was confident, his expression was uncertain. There was something about this that made him feel lost in his lack of control. "Nothing will ever be fixed, and I'll never have the closure I'm searching for. That made me so angry for so long. It distracted me even further from Light's path."

I could imagine it already: a young Rengas, trying to be coarse against the world despite his inherently soft nature. Using crass, cutting words by the day before praying sun fall and sun fall again to hear his mother's voice in his sleep.

I glanced at the scarred fingertips that I cradled now.

"I don't blame my father for staying silent if my parents really are in the afterglow and not somewhere else. It isn't unlike him to watch from afar." He smiled a little, and I gave in as I lifted my hand to his flushed cheek to once again wipe away his tears.

"I don't blame you, if that means anything. I don't see you any different." I smiled back. He leaned into my hand. His warmth was the gentlest kind I'd ever felt. It was like thawing out after the coldest night.

"I'm thankful for it, Guno. Truly." He even treated my name with care and quiet consideration as he pronounced it. How he could go from doing controversial dances in front of hundreds to *this* was something I would never understand. For once, I was content with not understanding.

"My father was a fearsome and rough-mannered man. Rioh reminds me a lot of him, actually." I let my hand fall away from his face. He retook it. "Malecai Averell, Son of Light. He held the title before me. Objectively speaking, he did a much better job than I have." His reminiscent smile faded a little.

"That can't be true. Ren, you just compared him to *Rioh*." I told him, shaking my head. He burst out laughing again, his face regaining some of its life. Against my will, I exhaled with relief.

"I can understand that. Still, if I ever came across him again," He rubbed the back of my hands in slow circles with the pad of his thumb. "I don't think any of that would matter. I would regard that scornful demeanor of his with so much love. I do *miss* him, no matter what his beliefs were at the time." He paused.

"Did you think of either of your parents' absence as much as I did?" Rengas's head tipped to the side, a strand of white hair falling into his eyes. I shook my head and released his hands to tie back my hair. Rengas slowly brought his hands back to his lap. "I know it's a little different on the ground level."

"Yeah, not nearly as much. I told you about all there is when we were training. I was sort of told not to think about it, I guess, and so I didn't." Ren's gaze was fixed on me like I was a spectacle. "It's easier just to cast those worries aside. Think about other things, like Brightness, or how your garden is doing, or what ingredients you need for your meat pie." I tried to keep my tone light and in jest, but Ren didn't smile.

"This worked? You were satisfied with 'not thinking about it?'" The intensity of the prince's gaze caused me to look away.

"I don't know," I admitted quietly, "It's less satisfaction and more co*mplaisance?"* I paused, "Did I say something wrong?" Rengas shook his head. "No, of course not. It just, *pardon me if I'm rude-"* He briefly prefaced.

"I'll be fine."

"It seems such a shame to erase what someone meant to you, even for self-preservation. Wouldn't it be selfish, then, not to think of them? Your family is so much of who you are." It was steadily growing dark, and the natural light from his windows was becoming too little for the prince's liking. Rengas stood, going down the steps to the bed to the candle stand next to the window. He took the bit of flint and steel by the candle's base and struck it beside the wick, gently guiding the candle to a flame. He coaxed it into being, steadying the flame with his hands before using that candle to light others around the room. He handled each with incredible patience. My answer came late as I became transfixed in watching him move.

"I suppose so."

"I'm sorry, Guno. That *was* more of an accusation than a question, wasn't it?" He laughed warmly as he lit the last candle, his face pulling back into a grin. He set the first back onto its stand. "Say, I'll make it up to you. Why don't I take you down to the royal garden?"

I sprung out of my seat at once. Ginger had never permitted me there.

"*Really?*" I searched his face again. He giggled, covering his mouth with a hand.

"Yes. Just allow me to get dressed. I'm not decent." He pulled his robe tighter around him, as if that would make the material any less sheer, and stepped behind the dressing partition that separated the room. That, too, wasn't completely solid; I could make out the silhouette of him behind the screen, which left just enough to the imagination not to be profane. It wasn't long at all until I had to look away.

"You're still in your day things. Will you be cold, Guno?" He asked, barely hidden away.

"Ah, no. I'm fine."

"Hmmm," He hummed vaguely. I looked back just to see what he was plotting. He had finished by then, dressed in a heavy imperial coat over his tunic. It did get freezing at night, especially during the Scarce Months. Still, I thought this was a bit overboard. Slung over Ren's shoulder was another coat.

"Stand for me?" He held out the coat. I shook my head and did so slowly, walking over to him. I could feel my neck burn as he helped me into it. "If not a gentleman, I'm a lady. I won't have you catching a cold. It would be out of character." His eyes narrowed mischievously. Seeing him now, I would've never guessed that he'd been crying only ten minutes earlier. I held up my hair so it wouldn't become tucked under the collar. I shook my head at him again, though I couldn't hold back a smile of my own.

"I don't need to be taken care of, you know. I'm nearly twenty-five coming up, I suspect. Did you know that?"

"Just because you're older than me doesn't mean you don't need help! Poor old man." He put on an air of pretend concern, clasping his hands together before reaching for my face. I batted his hand away playfully.

"Hey, only two years!" Just like that, my teasing argument had been flipped on me. After stepping away from Rengas's nitpicking touches, I rolled my eyes, scratching the scruff at the side of my face. "Let's go to the garden. Or has the idea become boring to you already?"

The prince's face scrunched up a little. He turned up his nose. "No. It hasn't. Come along; I'll show you the way."

The royal garden was everything I'd dreamt of and more. Really, the place was less of a garden and more of a *jungle*. If it weren't domesticated and walled in, it probably would've been one of the only wooded areas in Dashan.

And the prince had been right- it was quite cold. For once, his insistence on fussing over me was completely justified, I thought, as the back doors were opened for us and we were brushed with a wave of air. The prince held a lamp in one hand, which he held aloft, although lanterns of Her origin had already been lighted in the enormous trees around us.

"You mentioned you had a garden. You're rather fond of plants, yes?" Rengas asked as he turned over his shoulder. He walked a few steps ahead of me, descending the steps into the thicket of the garden as I followed behind.

"How'd you guess?" I remarked, raising an eyebrow quizzically. Rengas paused for a moment, seemingly unprepared for what I'd said. I saw him lower the lantern a little.

"Funny, Guno." Ren said, "I'm sorry we had to keep you out of here for so long. I guess Ginger was afraid you'd get lost. The garden takes up miles of land, you know. Have you seen it from the east balcony?" His voice was distant now. I'd fallen back to gaze at a flower with a bioluminescent core that lit up its curled petals. It was tempting to stick my fingers into it if I was honest, but I didn't want to tamper with anything in here.

"Guno?" He called. I saw his figure pause from my periphery.

"Uh, yes. Yes, I've seen." I pulled my eyes away from the flower and jogged to catch up with him. I found my eyes lingering on his hand, still stiff at his side. *"Are you? Do you?* Like plants." I shook my head a few times, squeezing my eyes shut- "I mean, *doesn't everybody,* but you know what I mean. Are you good with them?" I laughed along with the prince as he gave a well-meaning chuckle, throwing back his head.

• • •

"Doesn't everybody." He echoed, "Yes. I do love them, although I'm reluctant to, you know. Touch them, and care for them, and things like that. I doubt I have the same magic touch that you do." He shrugged, "I couldn't keep anything alive on my own, not even a plant."

"Oh, I doubt that."

"Plus, who knows what all these outsourced Elscarade species can do. I haven't studied their flora enough to trust it." He waved a finger at the canopy above.

"I think that's the best part." I grinned, "Learning what they *do*. It's like magic, sometimes." He looked at me as if I'd said something else funny, which is when he turned off the lamp and tied its cord around his belt. There was plenty of light without it.

"I was a gardener back at home. I worked for the Farmer's Guild, and in turn, I got a good cut of the crops. That way, my mother and I would never go hungry." I turned my smile up to the prince, and feeling a leap in my chest, decided to grab his hand. It was different, somehow, in these circumstances. It was harder to do and less of a casual, spur-of-the-moment action.

Rengas met my eyes, and he seemed to be holding something back in his coarse expression.

I guess I was, too.

I pushed my fingers into his, letting our hands intertwine and feeling the cool against my hand. The prince's long eyelashes fluttered, and he turned his face away.

"Seems like a decent deal." I thought he would have forgotten our conversation completely by then. It surprised me that he remembered enough to pick up where we left off. "Farming is such a profitable industry nowadays. Must've done well for you." I nodded, agreeing with the last part at least. My mind had begun to wander again.

"Sorry for bringing this back up, but," I tugged on his hand a little to get us to stop our walk. We had come beneath a thick trellis that formed an archway of twisting vines all around it. There seemed to be a little sitting area in here, but I didn't have us sit. A twisting feeling in my gut told me we wouldn't be here for long.

"If you remember my discomfort with that diary you're translating, I think I know why that is." I pulled a loose curl behind my ear, "No. I *know* why it is. Not think. I'm almost completely certain." I didn't release the prince's hand. In fact, I held it a little tighter. It brought his attention back to earth. "I know you don't want to talk about that sort of stuff, but I think it's important. Especially given what we talked about today."

Rengas's eyebrows pushed together a little before his expression relaxed again. My other hand twitched, and I quickly grabbed his other hand- anything to get in a little extra talking time. I was sure Alice could power through even Ren's cooling abilities if she tried hard enough. I wondered what level she was at now.

"The "Alice" that your book belongs to *is* the dark witch. I lied to you. She seems to want her book back. Whatever you do, *don't-*" I steadied my breaths as I felt my chest constrict. I squeezed my eyes shut, my other hand tightening into a fist.

"Guno." Ren's eyes became rounder as he scrambled to release my hands. For a fleeting moment, I panicked while I opened my eyes again. I thought he was going to flee from the fear in his face and how quickly he'd recoiled. Instead, he was taking off his portal ring and slipping it onto my finger. He squeezed my hands.

"Keep going. Don't what?" He asked. I exhaled shakily in sheer relief, letting my head hang.

"Don't let me touch it anymore. Lock it up someplace. Who knows, it might have some sort of... power? Significance?" The prince wheezed a little; his voice was worn and fatigued.

"I've only gotten a quarter of the way through, yet it seems to be simply a typical diary, Guno. An adolescent expressing her woes in a misunderstanding household. I really doubt it's some evil crypt." I tugged away a little in protest, but didn't have the heart to pull my hands free.

"Even so. Please do this for your own safety, okay?"

"Of course."

I left the garden quickly, giving Rengas back his portal ring. He'd wanted to stay in the garden some more. I did too, but I had a feeling something was coming. It was in the minutes before one of Alice's visits when my body didn't feel mine completely. It moved in unnatural ways. My walk was a little too rushed and inconsistent. Even my speech patterns wavered as if my voice was artificially creating each word, though I believed I was talking normally otherwise.

I was quick to slam the door to my room once I was alone. Already, a golden bell had been placed on a pedestal beside the door. Without thinking, I closed my eyes and turned away from it. I couldn't ask for help. Not yet. I wouldn't drag them into this. I needed to ask her something first.

* * *

"Alice?" The sound of my voice fell dead, so stale and muted in the air I was uncertain if I'd said it at all. I could feel her ahead of me, standing right next to my desk. As I walked, the air became thick. My footsteps and my pace slowed as if I were trudging through quicksand. She came closer, put a single-pointed nail to my chest... and pushed.

My breath left me as I was sent backward, and I fell- through the floor, and deeper- my vision blackened, yet I could feel *everything*. Gravity was so heavy; I was becoming compressed underneath the floorboards. I was in the walls. She'd buried me six feet deep beneath the sand. And still, there she stood, unphased, untouchable. Just a few feet away.

"Who?" She asked. I didn't respond. I didn't have a throat to speak from anymore, nor lungs to produce air for that throat to use. I should have felt scared, yet somehow, I wasn't. Maybe she'd taken away my heart to feel the terror I should have felt, I thought. "Who, Guno."

Maybe it was *her* that smothered me, now. Her dark cloak had enveloped me and left nothing to speak for. *Is this how she felt, too?* After all, she was in here with me.

Your diary is more than what Rengas said, isn't it? I managed to phrase, though it definitely didn't come out in words. I couldn't guarantee it had come out in the right order, either, like some sleepwalk-spoken phrase.

"More than... isn't it? Rengas, diary...your..." It could've been, or perhaps, *"Rengas is more said... than isn't it, said..."* What an embarrassing thought. Communication was futile and foolish; subjects and prefixes ran together. She answered with something filled with malice, so much that it made my heart burn a little more furiously than it had been. That, I was sure, was the only thing that made me certain I still had a body at all. A body I was so far away from.

Yet I could tell clear as day what she was trying to tell me. The diary had always contained more than what Rengas saw. Much more. And Alice thought I was stupid for thinking any different.

Learn... think, do you... from insistence? Why you can... are-
No, that wasn't right.

Maybe I *was* as stupid as she thought I was. Maybe even more so. Maybe I had always been a fool. I tried to pull together the dissonant parts of my being that seemed to be tethered together only by thin pieces of thread, each drifting out to be their own. My mind, heart, body, voice was each trying to be free. The Light and Dark even tried to cut ties with the useless mortal form that binds them to the ground.

"*Do you think I can learn from it?*" I struggled to sort the phrase properly. "*Why are you so insistent?*"

She's insistent because she knows better than you what's right.

She's insistent because we're so close.

She's insistent because you're not so righteous as you think you are.

She's insistent because she's just like you.

Each rolled in like a gentle wave, each pushing me farther out than I was before. I would die out here. That was the only thing of which I was certain. I would become another legend, someone who meddled too much in the two forces' affairs and paid dearly for it. Just as I began to feel the pieces of my soul dissolve into nothing, they all snapped back at once, and I had a body again—a buzzing, rattling, inconsistent form.

Still, there Alice was, just out of reach. She'd taken down her hood, pushed her bangs to the side...

Six eyes. She had six eyes.

"Do you feel it yet, Guno?" Her voice echoed through whatever sick chamber she'd put us in. I was on my hands and knees, elbow-deep in something sticky. It weighed down my hair and glued my eyelashes together. I started to speak only to emit a low groan as my body fuzzed out. My left shoulder and hip began to slide out of place, then my jaw. I wish I could stay together just for a moment. My left eye was melting out of my skull, but my hands were too sticky to collect it all and scoop it back inside.

Did talking usually require this much effort? It felt like I was trying to learn how all over again.

"I... feel... bad..." I creaked, my head teetering on the brink of rolling off my shoulders. Alice took a step closer. The breeze from her cloak was enough to make my body fall apart like a juvenile block tower. It didn't hurt as bad anymore, though it was hard to look her in the eyes from such a low vantage point. The side of my face was sticky. I didn't like it. I began to weep as my face sunk further into the ground, further into oblivion...

"*Imagine how I feel.*"

● ● ●

Rengas was the piece that caused it all to make sense. I'd felt it at the ball when both our forms were lively and warm, and I felt it now. Though feint, even the recollection was enough. I could be lightyears from real and still remember the face of Rengas Averell. I could be separated from my body by several dimensions and still be able to recall how his Light marks felt against my fingertips.

I was dissolving into nothing. Soon even those loose parts of me would break apart until they were too small to see, too small even to be given a thought to.

Rengas, though, was whole. I pictured him holding me, sheltering me, and through that being put together from scratch. To be held, you too have to have substance.

He surely wouldn't mind, in all his beneficence, having to teach me how to be real again.

Rengas? I called to him, using whatever modes I had left.

Rengas, please, I remember you. I told him, because I did.

Alice had left me to come apart on my own. For all I knew, she had come apart too. I got no answers to my calls. I was only accompanied by memories of what reality with the prince had been. In my ramping panic, I called louder and willed all of my pieces to vibrate together, even if so far apart, even if they'd never existed at all.

Rengas! Rengas, I'm trying so hard; please tell me if I'm real.
Come get me, Ren.
I want to go home.

    My manic wailing dwindled as I woke up with a start in the healer's room. Someone held me up, and eventually, each of the people around the bed came into focus: Rocky by the bedside. Rengas at the far wall, staring off, and-
    "Someone get Fyrnie. The boy is up." Ginger's voice ordered. It seemed she'd been the one holding me fast. I curled into her as my screams turned back into sobs, and she held me there. Her coat felt like a coat, my hands felt like hands, and the only reason my face was sticky was because I had been really, really sweaty.
    People were rubbing my back, and I was real. Yet- something remained off. Maybe it was the possibility that now, I knew she was getting stronger and that she could take me at any time-
    Ginger held me by my sides, pushing me to get me to sit up. I'd been stripped of my coat and shirt, and the blanket had been taken off the bed I sat at. Rengas came to my side when he noticed I was awake and held out a glass of water for me. I drank just to feel the cool liquid wet my dry, sore, but very real throat. Then I finished the glass. Ren stared on, then took the glass back.
    "I'm so sorry Guno, I shouldn't have left you alone, knowing you were feeling dim."
    "Aaahhh," I warmed up my voice. Though hoarse, it worked, and I could feel my neck vibrate again, changing frequency with different notes. I pressed a hand to it just to feel. "It is, okay. I didn't want to worry you."
    "Are you kidding-"
    "You'd never worry-" Rengas and Ginger tried saying at once. Ginger waved her hand to let the prince speak first.
    "It's more important that you're safe! If you're safe, we're all safe, right?" Rengas nodded, getting me to agree and nod along with him.

"I... I suppose..." I tried to get up. Rengas slid off the bed and easily pulled me to my feet. My shaking hands went to hold him closer.

Oh Light, he was so tangible. So warm. I'd been right to think of him. I couldn't even see through all my tears as I settled into his embrace. He cupped the back of my head, gentle in his support.

"I was so worried for you." I heard him whisper into my hair, "Thank Light, you're safe."

After a long moment, I backed out of his arms to see a bespectacled healer walking into the room. He looked from me to Rengas to me again, smiling awkwardly. Maybe with a good bit of worry, too, seeing as I still had wet tears on my face and was wobbling like a baby limber learning to stand.

"Easy with him, Averell!" Fyrnie gasped as Rengas let go. My knees felt a little weak, but I stood fine. "What happened here? He looks exhausted. Let the boy sit down, your highness." The lanky Dashaner straightened his apron and produced cloth for me to wipe my tears and sweat off on. He nudged Rengas aside with an elbow. "Do you feel faint?" He asked with urgency, lifting a hand to my forehead. "Too hot? Too cold?"

"No, no, no, I'm okay." I felt quite awake, actually, once I'd recovered from the initial shock. I let the healer prod at me and feel my heartbeat. "You said you found him face down in his room?" Fyrnie pushed up his glasses, holding up my chin with one hand.

"Yes, and he had a very slow heartbeat, and," His rambling paused for a second. "Fyrnie, I was really worried! How long do you think you can be out before it starts to-"

The healer cut him off with a raise of his hand. "He seems fine now. It could've been he just got too dizzy from the Dark coming on so quickly, or perhaps it was a simple cold." Fyrnie gave a charming smile and a pat on my shoulder. He had messy hair and a lot of freckles, and a badge on his tunic denoted his role as a medic. "Let him rest. He needs it." He told Rengas while looking at Ginger.

"Anything that hurts?"

"My head," I whined, rolling my shoulders back.

"I'll make you some pain relief tea, then. It will only be a few minutes." With that, Fyrnie was off, and as soon as he left, Rengas sat beside me again. Rocky sat on the bed adjacent to mine. The elf's ears were trembling like a bug's antennae as he fixated on a point over my shoulder.

"I'm glad Ginger arranged that meeting yesterday, Guno, but why didn't you ring your bell?" Rocky leaned forward in his seat.

• • •

Rengas grabbed my hand; I couldn't be sure if he did it for his sake or mine. It took every fiber in my body not to make up some excuse. There really was no reason to lie; everyone in the room cared about me, and Rocky asked because he was concerned. If I told the truth, what was the worst that could happen?

"I- I didn't think I needed your help." I crossed my free arm over my chest, "I thought I could handle it on my own."

"Well, that's kind of stupid." Rocky said bluntly, before locking eyes with Rengas and going a deeper red, "I mean, we gave it to you for a reason." He fell silent and excused himself from the room. I heard a small wheeze from Ginger and turned to see her hiding a smile of amusement behind her hand.

"I'm sorry about that," she muttered, "But he does have a point." Rengas had the sort of shifty look on his face that clearly showed he was trying to avoid conflict by being non-obtrusive, so I left him be but let go of his hand. I did feel a sting in my fingers, but it was faint enough to keep down. I wasn't going to blow this out of proportion- there were plenty of tales of needy children who made a limber out of a fyrbex just because they were scared of the sparks near their family's hay bales. I wasn't going to be one of them, yet it had already been proved I couldn't handle this.

"Most days, I've been fine keeping Dark at bay by myself, so I'm sorry if thinking that yesterday was a bad choice or something. But what if yesterday wasn't a big event? What if I'd called you all to stand around and watch me when there was nothing wrong?" I shrugged, standing and pacing away from the beds, clenching my fists.

Fyrnie had finished the tea and hesitantly held it out for me. I thanked him under my breath before downing half the cup in one go. Relief tea had a sour taste that made your mouth feel cold, and it took effort to go through so much in one sip. My tongue was left with a stinging feeling after. Ginger and Rengas watched me with more curiosity than anything else. I was glad, at least, that they were listening.

"I think I'd rather have that happen than have you pass out again." Ginger sought agreement from Rengas with a jab at his arm, who replied only with a small "Yeah." My ruthless grip on the teacup lightened a little.

"Well," I seethed, clicking through my teeth animalistically, "I'm sorry."

"It's okay. Guno, can I talk to you for a minute?" Rengas stood up from the bed. I held my tea closer to my chest.

"Alright." The prince was still in the clothes he was wearing last night, even though it seemed to be well into the day now. It wouldn't have stood out to me if I hadn't seen the prince change up to four times each day.

He pulled me out of the healer's room and into the hallway just outside, keeping me close. I backed against the wall, finishing off the last of my tea. Already, my head felt less tight.

"I know Ginger and the others may disagree with this, but I do believe you should spend the night with me tonight. My beacon marks seem to be the only thing able to placate your Darkness, right? They sort of level out?" He whispered, checking for any onlookers. He stopped and looked at me suddenly with soft perplexity. I hadn't even noticed that I'd stuck my hand up his sleeve to feel the marks there. I pulled back my hand with a small apology. The prince chuckled, his face lighting up a little. I was more than happy to see his tension ease.

"It's okay. Are *you* okay with staying with me tonight?" He tipped his head to the side.

"Uh- yeah. It looks like it's our best option." I wouldn't want to make another bad choice by trying to tough it out on my own. "Can *you* ask her, though?" I asked with hesitance. Another bright laugh as the prince held his chest. The hand moved to hold my shoulder. When I met his eyes, he winked.

"No problem. You stay here." I nodded with a shaky exhale as Fyrnie came out to take my cup.

"Feeling any better, Guno? It seems you can walk alright."

"Yes, sir. Thank you."

"It's no problem at all." Fyrnie left me alone in the hallway. I sat there shuffling my feet until the prince was back. I perked up with an attentive cluck.

"What'd she say?"

"As long as we're careful, you're allowed. But it's just for tonight until we figure out something else to do." He relayed. Rengas's face was flushed as if Ginger had said something else besides what he was telling me. "Well, Guno, I'll see you later. I have a lesser languages class in twenty minutes. Mustn't be late!"

I waited for him to leave, but for a moment, he didn't. He stood there staring at me with an increasingly reddened face. Just as my mind began to race, Rengas raised a hand to cup my cheek gently- and he kissed it.

And then, just as quickly, he was gone. I don't know why, but my headache dissolved completely after that, and in its wake was a plethora of other disconcerting feelings. *I should put a shirt on,* I

● ● ●

thought, and took my time walking back to my room. There was no way in the Afterdull I was going back in that room with Ginger and the healer.

I pulled on a comfortable top, going to the mirror to draw the laces tight. I could still feel where the kiss had been so carelessly placed. I touched that cheek on the same side as my monster eye. I doubt he'd done that on purpose. Should I go in there early? Would he want to see me? There were so many things to consider. Before the prince pulled me aside, I made a mental list of things I should do before the end of the day, but now I had forgotten them all. I pushed my hair flat to my head, staring uselessly into the mirror until I heard quiet scratching from my desk. I whirled around to see my quill drop onto the tabletop.

It had been suspended in midair. I feared the worst and quickly crossed my arms to feel that they were still attached before running up to examine the damage. Nothing had been broken, nothing knocked over, but my notebook had been flipped open, and written neatly on a clean page, was:

Rengas Averell will die, and you will be his killer. Do this. We all know you can.

After it, a symbol: a "W" like shape with a strike through it that mimics a bow's shape.

As soon as my eyes fell upon the page, the splitting pain in my head returned tenfold. My eyes squeezed shut as I fell against the table. In his room with a tutor, I could see Rengas copying down sigils from a translation table. His skin was bright and youthful, bursting with life. It was enough to make me drool. I'd never seen him this way. He'd never looked so tempting. I bit down hard on my thumb, then shook my head as I was about to head for the door. I shouldn't make snap decisions. I'd see him later. Just a few more hours, then I'd have him all to myself.

He would tear so easily with Dark around, I thought. Sure, I was in less control now that Alice was progressing, but that also meant I was stronger. As Alice was my mentor, my progress would surely reflect hers. I could bend the prince to my will. Kevik, he'd probably let me cause his undoing. But I didn't want him dead, did I? After I was finished with him, what would be left?

Part of me said it didn't matter what was left. The sheer ecstasy in those moments would be more than enough for a lifetime. I held onto the table to steady myself through the vivid fantasy, my eyes wandering- before I caught sight of the bell. It sat there, unutilized, stagnant. Rocky's words from earlier repeated in my head. Was I losing myself? Yes, maybe.

I paced slowly to the bell pedestal, standing over the small brass object. It mocked me in its triviality. So tiny. So low of me to use it. But then there was the reminder from earlier.

Stupid boy. I was stupid not to ask for help.

More than anything, I didn't want Rengas to die. What would they see if they came in and saw the note? They would know it wasn't my handwriting, right? I was thinking about this for too long.

I seized the bell's handle in a fist and shook it as hard as I could muster. A guard came in first, pulling me up and helping me to my bed. Then came Rocky, then Ginger, then a few more guards. The headache had long since faded, replaced with dizziness that wasn't half bad. I was stuck in a daze filled with wantings and images and...
My hands were burning. Then I was holding Ginger's light staff again.

"Guno! Guno." Her voice emerged into clarity as she squinted at me, pushing up her monocle. *"What happened here? What's that letter about?"* As she jabbed a thumb behind her, I could see Rocky standing over the desk where the note had been written. The elf picked it up, brow furrowed. It took me a minute to sit up, and for a while, Ginger had to keep me up by holding the back of my neck. I used her dense arm as a crutch as I blinked to attention.

"Ahh, sorry, I-"

"Don't be sorry. Just tell us, did you faint again?" She asked. I shook my head.

"No. No, I didn't. I've been awake the whole time. I think one of the witches has, uh," I wiped my face, "I think it's a command or something, because I can't stop thinking about it. Maybe it's not even the note itself."

"Are you joking, Guno? This is no time for pranks."

"No, no. Just look at my handwriting on the other pages. I didn't write it. It's not mine." I hadn't intended on anyone reading my notebook, and I certainly didn't *like* the idea, but beggars can't be choosers. I helplessly watched Rocky flip through the pages.

"Yeah, no, these aren't similar at all. The writing on this note is -pardon me, Lamplight-much *cleaner* than the rest of this stuff." Rocky told the General, glancing at the pen on the desk that had been the culprit. "Most of Lamplight's stuff is recipes. And poems, or something? Is that what these are?" Rocky frowned at the page.

"Anyway, it doesn't look like there are any other death threats." I breathed a sigh of relief, falling back into Ginger's support. Out of my periphery, I saw her squeeze her eyes shut and nod.

"Great. Thank you, Rocky." She pushed me upright again with one arm. "Are you sure you can sleep with Rengas tonight?"

"What?" Rocky squeaked, already fuming. He snapped the book shut. "Is this some sort of- what have you all been- *Ginger*- I thought better from you!" The newsboy stammered, ripping off his hat and crushing it in his hand.

"Rocky! No! Literally *sleeping*. We're doing it for the boy's safety. It's been proven that Ren's beacon markings have a cooling effect on Lamplight." Ginger cringed. I remained silent on the topic as Rocky slowly put his hat back on, dropped the book onto the desk, and left. I sighed apologetically.

"For Light's sake," I wheezed to Ginger, "Let's not tell Rengas yet, alright?"

"Why wouldn't we tell him?"

"Well, I've talked to him, and he's already having such a hard time. Just for tonight, can we keep this between us?" I pleaded, pressing my hands together. "If anything starts to go south, I'll tell you immediately, promise."

Ginger's brow furrowed as she considered it, scooting back from me to allow some space. "Okay. *If you really do promise.*"

"Yes. I swear."

I wanted to keep my promise this time, for real. I had meant it. I wondered what had caused the letter to be written. Now that I thought about it, the letter was more likely to be written by Prudence, the material realm witch, than by Alice. Alice had said she had dealings in mind, so physical manipulation such as moving a pen wouldn't be something she could do. Did beacons have specializations, too?

Then there I was, back where I started, thinking about Rengas.

That night I arrived at the doorstep of the prince's quarters with my heart hammering against my chest. Would he try to kiss me on the cheek again? *It's not like I wished for it to happen, but I certainly wouldn't mind if it did*, I thought.

I knocked on the door once his guards had stepped aside, and Rengas let me in. This time there was a little tray of berries, crackers, and juice on the table in the middle of the room, and the prince had already lit all of the candles. He'd clearly put some thought into my arrival.

It startled me, to say the least. What startled me even more was that Rengas had already taken his paint off and was gazing down at me with a special sort of warm fondness. It was another one of his indescribable looks, now *actually* in private, like how they always made me feel.

I think I was finally beginning to understand what those looks meant, I thought, as he offered me a glass of pilocari juice. I took it and sat on a cushion beside the table that was a lot plushier than I'd anticipated; I had to stick out my arm to catch myself before I spilled any. I received another one of the prince's silky chortles as he simply settled on the floor, sorting out his loose robes around his legs. He picked up a few berries to eat out of his hand.

"So, how have you been? Has the headache sorted itself out?" He asked once he finished the handful, untying and slipping off his headscarf, part of his evening ensemble that night. He folded the thing up in his lap. When I thought I'd never get more up close and personal with the prince, he managed to beat my expectations. I found myself watching his face, specifically, studying his exposed cheeks. My hands fumbled with one another as I tried to find an answer to his question despite it all.

"Uh, yeah! I feel fine now, thank you."

"Of course." There was a pause before Ren spoke again, "Guno, do you want to know something fun about being a beacon?"

He tilted his head to the side, grabbing another berry. I wanted to know everything about being a beacon, I thought. I wanted to learn of every new feeling he'd grown, every new power. Even if I'd never been able to feel it myself, sharing in his experiences would be enough.

"Yeah, what is it?" I sat forward on my elbows, placing my cup on the table.

"I can get *star-drunk!* In fact, I got a little caught up stargazing for a while earlier, and I have to admit I started to feel a little tipsy! Incredible, right? Kalesse hadn't been lying when she said it works."

"Really? Is it strong?"

"I'm no lightweight; I can take my stars. I reckon a minute or two wouldn't do anything." He shook his head as if it were silly to think anything else. He stood up, putting his hands in his pockets as he gazed out one of the tall windows. He allowed me to sit and snack some more before he had a maid collect the refreshments. He paid her little regard. I don't think he'd meant any disrespect; he was a pampered kid with a new guest, and his mind was clearly someplace else. I couldn't blame him; mine was too, yet I couldn't imagine in the same way. Since he got up, I noticed there hadn't been another bed or lounge set up for me to spend the night on.

Unless I was expected to sleep on the floor, there was only one other bed arrangement option.

It's not like it'd be cramped, either. Rengas's bed probably had room for twelve, and I wouldn't be surprised if he utilized that space at times from the things I heard about him in passing. I'd heard *a lot* of things about Rengas over the course of my life. I wondered how many of those rumors were true. As if he'd heard my silent discussion, Rengas sat on the edge of his bed and called,

"Do you think it's about time for bed? Also, are you feeling alright?" He asked politely. I hadn't noticed how I'd been glaring at nothing for the last minute, feeling a wave of what felt like a hot static course up my body. Why did I have to remember these things about Rengas now? Couldn't I just have been content in my blind trust of him? He was real, and I was too, and we were both here together.

It was so hard to give in. Complete trust was a leap of faith that I wasn't sure I was ready to make.

I stood and fluffed up my hair as if I were scrubbing the unsavory thoughts clean- I felt the hair stick to my fingers. Slowly, I extracted my hand from the tangled mess of curls I'd made, my mouth hanging open as I looked to Rengas for guidance. His eyebrows raised as he rushed to my side.

"It is getting worse, isn't it?" He said. I felt my hands tense as he took my wrist. I let out a low rumble. I could've sworn Alice's command had set something in motion, just beneath the surface. Even now, I could feel it, slowly edging at my waking thoughts. Maybe I shouldn't have let him in as much as I have. Who knows what sorts of things he'd done with no consequences in this place, where a single room was large enough to conceal anything easily. He was the prince. Whatever he did was under complete cover from the law because he *was* the law. If he had been real, maybe it wasn't in the way he ought to be. Maybe I should've done something about it while I had the chance.

"Sorry, sorry! I didn't mean it like that. You're doing just fine. Here, we'll settle in. Take my hand." He released me, not wanting to be forceful, and I saw his hands pulse with godly energy as he presented them to me palms up. I don't know what it was, but something about the dichotomy of Ren's unscrupulous past against his morally righteous title unsettled me. Now I suppose that title would be:

His Highness Rengas Averell, Prince of Ninth Sector, Son of Light, and envoy to her Holy power-

Or something like that, though I was sure it was even longer.

"No, I- I can't. This was a bad idea-" I began, closing my dirtied hands and turning to the door. Rengas jumped in front of me; his expression had shifted. Something in the way he carried himself was suddenly less sure and confident, replaced with an air of panicked urgency as he presented his hands once more.

Then again, maybe I'd been wrong, I doubted myself, *maybe he hadn't been real after all*. Not this version of him, at least. The real prince would never be this forgiving. He'd never allow me to get so close. To see his face bare. To dance with me alone and share with me the little trivialities of his day.

"Please, Guno, let me help-"

"I can't-"

"Guno! For Light's sake, listen to me!" I froze in place, beginning to shake a little as my eyes widened up at him. "She gave me this power for a reason. To help *you*. She didn't grant it to me anytime else. Now let me use this how She intended." Rengas narrowed his eyes as he presented his hands one last time, his feet planted.

This wouldn't end well for any of us, I was sure. Yet he looked so genuine. There was only one way to know, I supposed. My eyes started to well up with tears as I met his eyes. My hands shook, hesitating over his.

"You're real, right? Do you actually care for me? This isn't some delusion?" The words I produced were hoarse and weak. Rengas's fierce gaze upon me softened. He opened his mouth, and for a second, couldn't manage anything.

"Of course I'm real. Why wouldn't I be?" He blinked a few times, coming closer. "I'm trying to help you *because* I care. That's as real and genuine as it gets, I think."

I took a deep breath.

Decisively, I placed my hands in his.

There was a blinding flash through the room that made both of us cringe and reel back from one another. I could've sworn Alice returned to take my body away, but the light faded, and all that remained of it was little starlike specks showered over my arms and all over the prince, too. They freckled his rosy cheeks and coated his robes. Rengas remained still for a moment before slowly heaving a few rounds of confused laughter. Just as with the portal, I noticed, I'd been completely cleaned of any Dark substance that remained on my hair or fingers.

"That has to be good, right? I- I've never felt brighter!" He wheezed between laughs and shivers. He took a step closer to me just to retake my hands, and we both watched the flecks on our skin die out one by one. "I'm still getting a handle of the power I've been granted under beaconship, but I'm confident it's there. And if you remain open and willing to receive it, as you are now," He grinned, squeezing my fingers, "I think you'll be okay."

I allowed myself to relax. This was the first time in a while I felt truly, completely safe, and I was willing to let it stay that way for as long as possible.

"I think I'm ready for bed now," I told him, only receiving another blooming smile.

"Alright, Guno. Let's tuck in." I had to stay close as he rounded the room, blowing out all the candles. I got a good view of his face there, his fair-featured profile outlined by the yellow light of each flame. When Rengas was done, he stepped backward into bed, pulling me with him and watching me the entire time with heavy, beckoning eyes. I felt my pace quicken. There was no use trying to hide my face, even as it began to heat. I settled beside him, not letting go for a second. I both didn't want to and was afraid of what might happen if I did.

* * *

Rengas burrowed a little into his pillow, his ring hand resting palm up on the sheets between us as I comfortably held it. There was still something I hadn't managed to tell him, something that I was always either too cowardly or distrusting to admit to. I had to tell him tonight. I'd hate myself forever if I didn't. If he really cared and had been genuine all along, he would understand.

But first, I wanted just a few more minutes of undisturbed silence to watch the prince completely at rest, with his hair splayed about him and falling into his face in loose strands, the beacon marks on his chest and arms just now quieting. The ones on his chest formed a tapestry of pictures. I could make out a few shapes of figures or flowers or small animals dancing across his skin. I wanted to feel them again, now that they were exposed.

"Rengas, may I touch your marks?" I whispered. The prince had long since closed his eyes, but he opened one curiously to see what I meant.

"You already are," He said back in an equally hushed tone, seeming satisfied, "You mean, these?" The prince guided one of my hands to his chest. Yes, indeed, that *was* what I had meant.

I felt along the path of one that particularly reminded me of a small rodent, long ears and all. "Yes," I noted simply. Rengas closed his eye again.

"It feels nice; I don't mind." Ren sighed. It did seem that the more I touched the indents in his skin, the more they glowed in that one spot. Light's strangely positive reaction to me caused me to calm a bit, enough to speak up.

"Ren, I have something to tell you. It's something that I did." I bit the inside of my cheek with a small cluck. Rengas's eyes fluttered open.

"Mmm? What is it?" Rengas scooted forward to have my hand closer to his chest, watching me patiently with dilated eyes. Again the hesitation came as I knew telling him would disturb his rest and connection with Her- but I had to, even if it meant getting kicked out of his room.

"I did something bad when you were out on your beaconism journey," I tried to get it out quickly, squeezing his hand, "Alice, the witch, she got me to take the diary from your room. Even so, it's not an excuse. I shouldn't have kept it; I should've told someone." I shook my head, "Light, I'm so stupid. I'm really sorry. Both to you and Her. I'm just not strong enough."

"Strength doesn't have to do with it, Guno." Rengas peeped, his voice hesitant, "I'm a little sad that you haven't told me until *now*, but I'm glad you've told me at all, I suppose." He exhaled deeply. "I forgive you. Hopefully, you know now that some things you simply can't handle on your own. It took me a long time to understand that, too." He nodded. Somehow, his markings retained their glow or perhaps shone a little brighter.

"Thank you." I told him, "And you're right." I was forced to break contact with the prince's chest to pull my hair away from my eyes. Rengas's smile returned full force.

"I know I am." He quipped easily. Rengas slid his hand over the one of mine that still lingered about his sternum. "Is there anything else you needed to tell me?" He drawled slowly, regarding me with silky, quiet patience. The look alone urged me to confess leagues of other things about myself, though before he asked, nothing had come to mind. I pursed my lips, holding my breath.

"No," I said rather candidly. Rengas only giggled, nodding.

"Alright then. Is that safe-night for us?" I considered it.

"Yes. Safe-night, Ren." I told him, turning my head a little toward my pillow.

"Safe-night, Guno," He yawned, and I had to hold back a yawn of my own, *"Wake me up if you need anything, okay?"* His voice trailed off, heavy with drowsiness. I nodded in agreement. As I drifted off, my hand slipped from his chest. Half asleep, I managed to bring both hands back to hold his.

And miraculously, for the first time in Light-knows-how long, I got a good night's rest.

I thought I was still dreaming when the first thing I saw when I awoke was Rengas over me, and the first thing I felt was his hand set gently on my stomach. Once I stretched and let my eyes readjust, the prince's eyes lit up, and he tightened a fist in the fabric of my tunic.

"You're awake." He tittered. I did quick work in sitting up, scooting away from him so he wouldn't look at me like that anymore, at least in not such a compromising position. The prince had brought his morning tea into the room, and it had been placed on the same low center table as the refreshments from the night before.

"Yeah, I think so," I replied. Rengas crawled across and got out of bed from the other side and quickly began to sort out tea. Then, I remembered the witch's orders; and the fact that I'd have to tell him that, too. I was thankful I'd saved it for later. The admission coupled with my confession about the book would have completely ruined the night prior, I was sure. "Thank you for keeping me safe last night," I muttered, "I slept very well." Ren held out the tea, and I received it with yet other thanks.

"I'm glad!" He chimed, "Oh, I'm very glad. I slept well, too." He sat on the stair below me with a teacup of his own. I was perched at the end of the bed. "At least we know that I can assist you, but I don't see how we could make it a permanent fix. The witch, as you've been calling her, can still control you, right?" He blew on the liquid to cool it off before taking a little sip. "I'm afraid that will be a constant until we find a way to stop her or block contact. We've already done all we can on your end. You're fit as ever." The other remarked, leaning back against the bed.

Was the answer really that simple? To break contact? I was Alice's puppet. How could a puppet break its own strings? Even if I did, she could always tie them back on.

As long as she was alive, I'd be in her service.

Oh, Light.

I was going to have to kill Alice. I was going to have to kill them both.

The thought wracked my brain like a fever. I leaned forward, holding my head in a hand. There was no other way. Without a parasite to guide my thoughts, I'd be free. Without a mentor, I'd no longer be a student of Dark. Although there was no guarantee the side effects would go away, it wasn't like Darkness himself was going to give me orders in the night.

I got to my feet in a flash. "I need to talk to Ginger." I blurted decidedly, "I'll see you later, Ren!" And with that, I ran from the room before he could try anything else funny and took my tea with me.

I'd spilled a good amount of tea on myself by the time I skidded to a stop at Ginger's door. She scrutinized me from her desk as if her monocle didn't help her any, pausing in the middle of signing a document. She set her pen down and pushed a stamp and a pad of ink aside, then sat back patiently. I took that as an invitation, hastily coming to situate myself in front of her.

"General, I've come to a few realizations." I panted, setting my quarter-full cup on the desk as far away from her documents as I could. "Well, *one,* I suppose- but still."

Ginger blinked slowly, crossing her legs as if she needed to be thoroughly prepared for what came next. "Let me guess; you're voting Rioh off the capital- NO! You're finally admitting your feelings for-"

"*Ginger! Bright Saint Parkeyre,* no." I exclaimed with desperation, holding both hands out. She moved her head a little to see past them, a small smirk forming on her lips once the shock had worn off.

"Yes, yes. You know I was only joking. Lay it on me." The General stretched, locking her hands behind her head. I gripped the arms of my chair.

This is what I'd been planning all these months for. Training, holding meetings, studying to "bring me closer to Her." So why was I so afraid? I'd been given more than enough time to complete my task. It felt more real now than I ever could have imagined. I guessed back then that I didn't really believe everything I was being told in the early weeks of training.

"Confronting" Alice and Prue was always the end goal. Maybe I had imagined Light Herself was going to swoop in and do the job for me once I'd done enough play sword fighting with Rengas and Ginger. In reality, it was never that way. I just wish someone had told me *that* sooner.

No matter what I do, I'll always be touched by Dark's hand, and there's no forgiving that.

"I think I'm ready." I released the chair to wring my hands. Ginger met my eyes, then lowered her arms slowly, sitting up into a more attentive posture.

"You mean, *ready* ready?" She implored kindly.

"Yes. I'm prepared enough to get out of here. I'd like to do it as soon as possible, though. I don't know how I'm going to hold up if I wait any longer and let those witches push me around." I took in a breath. Held it. "Which is why I think I need to kill them. If it's violence they want, it's violence they're going to get." Ginger's chin lifted a little as I spoke. "I don't think there's a way to negotiate with them. Who knows how long they've been in His ranks. They wouldn't turn so quickly."

"I trust your judgment, Lamplight, if you really think this is the way to go."

"There's no other way. I mean, I'm going to die if we don't. I might die regardless." Ginger furrowed her brow at the table for a bit before her attention drifted away from me to something else. I swiveled around to see the subject: Rocky, who held my gaze for a little too long, then nervously shuffled to Ginger's side without a sound.

"What are you all discussing, General?" He interjected, a small frown tightening his thin lips. He ran his hands over his arms as if he were freezing in here, though it was actually pleasantly warm.

"Lamplight's ready to leave. He's going to defend himself and slay the witch, he says." Ginger repeated to him. Rocky's wide eyes dodged in my direction before returning to Ginger. He lowered his voice considerably when he spoke again. I was unsure if he meant to keep it from me.

"Are we helping him?"

"I suppose that's Lamplight's choice. Yet this seems like a personal endeavor." Ginger spoke carefully. Rocky fell silent and began to fumble with his own arms even more.

"H-how are you? Feeling any different since yesterday?" Rocky pushed his words out. The tenseness was contagious, and I found myself paying little attention to the General just to try and deduce why he was so disturbed all of a sudden. More disturbed than his usual, at the very least. I had a hunch it was me who made him feel that way, but why now? Why not when Rengas first picked me up? Why not during any of my other Dark fits? It had been nearly a year since I came here. Why now?

"I've had a few, uh, feelings? Temptations? She definitely gave me command with that note, is all. I can't shake it. But other than that,

I'm alright, how about you?" I tilted my head to the side a little. Rocky swallowed, his eyes somehow becoming bigger than before. He shuffled his feet.

"Can't shake- yes. Oh, I'm doing just dandy!" Rocky breathed weakly, "I'll see you both later! Goodbye, and good luck if I don't- if I don't catch you before you depart!" He scurried out of the room before the General or I could get another word in.

Of course, why hadn't I seen it before! Rocky was concerned for *the prince,* not for himself. He was scared of what I'd do to him.

Keeping this in mind, I waited until Rocky was well out of earshot before speaking again. I cleared my throat,

"This all being said, Rengas has a right to know what I'm planning on doing. Even if he doesn't go with me, he has a right to say goodbye." It sounded pretty grim saying it aloud, but it was what we were both thinking.

"Hey, Lamplight?"

"Yes?"

"Stand up for me." She commanded. I stood with trepidation, my eyes narrowing as the General stood and paced around the table. She held out her arms. I raised an eyebrow.

"Light, Guno, have you never been hugged before? I'm trying to show my gratitude." She thrust her hands out again. I wouldn't make another mistake by denying affection like I did the night prior in Ren's quarters. I steadily moved into her embrace, holding it for longer than I'd anticipated. Like Ren, Ginger embodied this steady strength that quieted my aches. Her steadiness also made my own power pale in comparison. She patted my back, and I pulled away. "You've come a long way, Lamplight, whether you think so or not." Ginger set her hands on my shoulders, giving them a tight squeeze. I yelped a little under pressure. She gave a small chuckle and let go.

"Thanks." I wheezed, my hands covering the afflicted areas. I rolled my shoulders back and straightened. "Uh, can I admit something to you?" I asked. These past few days had been a string of endless admittances, it seemed- but I didn't want a word to go unsaid.

Especially if they would be my last.

The General nodded, resting on the front of the desk beside my armchair. I pulled on a chunk of my hair as I spoke up again. "I'm kind of afraid." I hugged myself, clicking quietly, "Really afraid, actually. I don't *want* to die." Ginger stared off; a knuckle raised to her lips pensively. She allowed what I'd said to sink in.

I was afraid she would restate what I'd already been told over and over again back home: sometimes death was a gift. *Don't you*

● ● ●

want to join Her forever? It's an honor, Guno. Don't be so ungrateful. My elders would say. There was some truth to it, but I couldn't help how I felt. I'd found a new value to life while being here. I felt, for once, that I could be made useful. Some people wanted me around, and at least to them, I could make a difference. Though it might have been selfish, it was true. I wanted to stay. Ginger finally picked up her head a little, regarding me patiently.

"It's okay to be afraid. True strength and bravery starts with understanding that your fear is valid and continuing nonetheless. Even I'm afraid sometimes, believe it or not." Ginger grinned, crossing her arms. "And if you truly think you need help, I will assist you. And I'm sure the prince would, too."

"But you both have your jobs here! What if something happens? Will the capital be overrun?" My voice quivered. Ginger listened, her gaze lowering to the ground as her smile faltered.

"Luckily, we have someone stubborn enough not to leave the capital for anything if worst comes to worst. But my offer still stands." She took in a deep breath. "I think we have some pretty well-trained people on our side who your witches may find to be at least worthy opponents." The General drove a hard bargain. I was sure with how patrolled Dark supporters were on ground level that they held at least a little bit of caution toward those who were particularly bright. At the very least, it left a mark on us villagers to see people getting pulled from seemingly nowhere, getting beaten and dragged to wherever the patrollers pleased. It had to be at least a tiny bit fearsome of an image to the people whose kind were being prosecuted. These criminals had been almost paraded around by authority. I would never remove that image from my mind. I could only imagine the impact it had on the Dark populus itself.

Plus, the capital guards were more than capable, I was sure. How else would you get into an exclusive circle working for royals and dignitaries? I guess it just didn't feel right bringing so many innocent people into something that, in the end, was *my* issue. At most, I would consider having Ginger help. She would be smart enough to flee the fight if she had to.

"Yeah, that's true. I'll let you know what I decide before I leave." I exhaled deeply, standing from my chair. "See you later, Ginger."

"Best of luck, Lamplight. May Light's fortune be with you." I resisted the urge to hug her again when I left the room. It was going to be a long day.

I knew I needed to tell Rengas one more thing. Even if it didn't end up affecting him directly, he had the right to know about any of my affairs. He was the reason I was here in the first place; In the capital and the physical plane.
Rengas was always there.

Maybe that's why he felt so alive. His presence never faltered.

I needed to tell him about Alice's command, and then I needed to tell him I was leaving. But when? I saw him once on his way to music lessons. I didn't pluck up the courage.

"Guno! Do you want to watch me practice? I'm sure Mr. Dhegai will let you sit in if you're quiet." He offered with a wink. He held a canister of water for class and his markings were alight with joy, visible through a loose sheer top. I couldn't bring myself to say no. As long as I told him before it was too late into the night, it should be fine- as long as I kept alert. I gave in, sighing through a grin.

"Sure, as long as I won't be distracting." I felt my smile spread, watching his face animate. With the way he took my hand then I wasn't sure if he would have let me say no anyways. Rengas pulled me up to the raised part of the room with the lounge. He sat me down on the platform's step to talk to an old man who I could only assume was Mr. Dhegai. Rengas gave a little curtsy and hurriedly sat on the edge of his settee, poorly hiding his excitement to have me there.

"Excuse me, sir, do you mind if Lamplight watches? He won't make any noise, promise." He pleaded, pressing his hands together. The weathered man's scrutinizing gaze turned to me. I showed my teeth and pushed some hair over my monster eye.

"Listen, if it's too much trouble, I'll go." I reasoned, putting my hands up.

"It's fine." Mr. Dhegai's articulated voice spoke, and I let myself exhale.

"Alright, Rengas, let's get your voice warmed up." He sat stooped over a well-decorated harpsichord which he used to sample Ren's notes to start on. As he began to rehearse the song he'd been memorizing, I leaned my head against the lounge and closed my eyes, listening to his voice condition and become more precise with each take.

Rengas had no clue what was going to happen. He was so blissfully unaware of my departure. It was just as his mood was seeming to improve, too. I didn't want to think about leaving, but my mind always found a way to circle back to it, even with the gentle lifts and turns of Rengas's voice accompanying my troubling thoughts.

● ● ●

As he began to work on the lute, I shifted away from the settee and stood, waiting until the two were relatively silent while Rengas made sure the lute was tuned.

"I have to go. I'll see you later, Rengas?" I questioned as I began to walk backward. I couldn't stay here like this. The guilt was excruciating.

"Oh, okay! Goodbye, Guno! Yes, definitely." The prince turned back to the instrument in his lap.

I shrugged off the bits of disappointment in his voice and wandered back to my room, where I began to write. A written statement of when and why I was leaving might be easier to quickly hand over. It left little room for slip-ups of rhetoric or accidentally setting the wrong tone if I could revise what I said. Plus, even if it were worse received in written form, I wouldn't have to watch the aftermath.

I opened my notebook to see Alice's command had been torn out. Just thinking about it sent waves of hunger shooting into my stomach. Pretty soon, the Dark-fueled cravings overpowered any reasoning I would've been able to put to use. I finished the letter, stretching out my sore hand, and went back to read:

Dear Rengas,

I hate to tell you like this, but there are a few important things I still haven't told you about. The first of which is a written command that the Dark witch wrote for me on the evening before we slept in your room. I can't repeat it now, since the note has been thrown away, but essentially she told me to kill you. It's crazy, because I would never, but now I'm wondering, have you always wanted me to? Sometimes I think you look at me all beckoning-like, and I think maybe you wish to become prey. You're simply curious, as anyone would be, to see what Dark really feels like. You know, I've dreamt about it, too. Maybe it's a sign

That's where I'd stopped. It isn't what I wanted to say at all. I stretched my back, then my hand again. I ripped up that note and tossed it into the trash. *Better try again,* I thought. I just wasn't thinking straight. I could do it this time.

It turns out I couldn't. I made three more futile attempts at forming complete rational sentences, but the more I tried, the more inaccurate they became in conveying such a simple message.

By the end, all I had on the page was,

Dear Rengas,
Alice wants me to kill you, and now I'm thinking about doing it for real

With an enraged growl, I tossed away that page as well. I was the sort that was hardly concerned for my posture, which meant my back ached as I rose unceremoniously from my seat to ring the bell again. Rocky, who I suppose had been the closest to my room's wing at the time, came in first after the guards. He hid his hand behind his hat, which he held to his chest and was sweating profusely. I shook my head, looking down at the little man.

"A-are you okay, Lamplight?" He squeaked, gazing up at me with hopeful eyes. *Hopeful for what,* I wondered. *Hopeful for me to tear him apart?*
His look soon turned more fearful; he gave one of his embarrassing, birdlike laughs that made me want to skin him like one. Maybe it wasn't Rengas who was appealing, after all. Maybe it was this guy who had been tagging along the whole time. He seemed the type to like pain.

"Lamplight! D'you hear me?" The newsboy's voice became higher, more urgently spoken. I fell back. *"What in Light's name is wrong with you?"*

He grabbed my wrist to yank away the hand that had been testing the sharpness of my teeth. As he did, he dropped his hat- he hid his other hand behind his back. I narrowed my eyes at him. I'd caught a flash of bandage wrapped around the hand that he hid.

"Rocky, what was-"

Rocky held out his arms to me, his face screwing up. *"Do it! Lamplight, you portal traitor! Kevik! DON'T BE A COWARD! DO IT! TAKE ME!"* He screamed and cursed in my face, sending me stumbling backward. I tripped over a cushioned seat and fell onto my back, grumbling gutturally under my breath. I craned my neck to squint at him, now just as scared of him as he seemed to be of me. What had gotten into him to provoke such an outburst? I'd never heard Rocky yell that loud before.

Rocky went stock still in the doorway, pale and trembling. He opened his mouth as if to say something else but couldn't manage a word. In one panicked burst, he grabbed his hat and ran. He was gone before I could recover from what I'd heard.

I lowered myself the rest of the way to the ground and let my sights drift to the ceiling. Rocky had a point.

What *was* wrong with me? I was honestly wondering the very same thing. *And why was Rocky hiding a cut?* I searched for some answer, but with the remaining rage in my body and whatever Dark influence was still pushing me around, there seemed to be no logical conclusion to any of my questions. That was, except the clearest one from what Rocky had screamed, literally, at me. There was no avoiding it.

He wanted me to kill him, didn't he? But why? My mind was cluttered with possibilities, none of which seemed better than the last. Was Rocky trying to convince me to kill *him* so I wouldn't hurt Ren? It seemed rash, but not out of the question.

I'd spent so much time dwelling that it was nearly sunset. The first moon was already well visible from my window. I was running out of time.

I searched the castle for over an hour, looking for Rengas, my head spinning. The hallways no longer made sense, even though I'd memorized most of the capital's floor plan by then. I became so disoriented that I feared Alice was back to steal my body.

"Rengas! Rengas, where are you?" I was tapped on the shoulder and jumped when Fyrnie greeted me. He smiled with concern, his mild-mannered visage looking me up and down shortly.

"You're swaying. Do you need anything?" He rubbed my arm. I resisted smacking it away. "Here, let's get you-"

"Rengas. I need to see him." I spoke firmly, looking the shorter man directly in the eyes. He pushed up his glasses with a scrunch of his nose.

"I haven't seen him this evening. You asked Ginger?" He asked amiably, his head tilting to the side.

"She didn't see him either." I growled, pulling on my hair. Fyrnie hummed, looking around.

"Well, I don't know. Let's see..." He tapped his chin with a knuckle. I had grown impatient, and though I realized it was rude, I started to walk away. Fyrnie didn't try and catch me, for which I was thankful. His head shot up in confusion, but he didn't say anything. I meandered around the palace near where his music class was, assuming he might've stayed in the area. The sun was setting still, and there was no one around in this part of the capital.

I was going to rot here; it was so empty. As I slowed to a stop, the sound of my footsteps echoed through an empty hall. I thought for a moment that it might be worth dying here, silently and without consequence, if no one else had to hurt for it. That's when I caught a glint through an archway: the balcony was just through a corridor, and a large figure was standing there, looking out into the scene outside. I began to jog toward it, which turned into a wobbly sprint.

"Rengas! Oh, Rengas, there you are." I'd found him at last. The balcony we stood on overlooked the royal garden. It was strangely beautiful out here, even when it was too dark and far away to see most of the flowers.

He was standing oddly still and didn't turn when I called. I huffed as unease built in my chest.

I approached him and leaned against the rail to see his face. He brought his hands to his chest, shying away. I blinked, stringing together my words. I couldn't risk misspeaking. I took a moment to let the dregs of Dark's influence leave my mind as the night air sharpened it.

"Rengas. Alice is contacting me more and more. She's trying to will me into killing you." I tugged on his sleeve. "I'm afraid if I ever lose control, I'll be forced to fight myself. There must be a way to limit communication, right?"

Rengas's attitude made me wonder, as well as dread, how often he came here to think and stare off like this. He was back to the way he'd been after the ball, yet he'd seemed so content just earlier. He didn't answer- however; he did tense at the mention of killing him. He must be frightened, I thought.

I clutched his shoulder and tugged to make him face me. His eyes averted to a distant point off the balcony. "Answer me," I ordered him. His soft frown deepened.

"You're the prince! You wanted more responsibility, so here it is! Tell me what I should do."

"Maybe you should listen to her." He mused, his chest rising and falling at a slow and steady pace.

"What?" I shook him. His eyelashes fluttered, but he didn't look up. I saw him swallow and shift uncomfortably but otherwise stand his ground for whatever it meant. "What do you mean, listen? You want me to kill you?"

"I just think maybe it would be best. For all of us."

I squinted at him. He couldn't be serious; after all he'd done to take me away from Dark? After all he'd discovered, all the progress we had made?

"No, actually, it wouldn't."

"Maybe if I were dead, then she would leave you alone. I'm no use anyway."

My eyebrows furrowed. I shook him harder; then, my hands gripped the front of his shirt. His lip was trembling, his eyes filled with a look of utter resignation.

"You have plenty of-"

He interrupted me with a broken and shaking voice.

"I don't do anything, Guno! I'm useless! If I were useful, I wouldn't be alone every day and night! I'd have friends! I'd make changes, Guno- I'd... be..." He broke down into pathetic heaves as he sobbed, and I released his shirt.

I watched him for a moment, sighing deeply.

"Do you want me to kill you because you think others would be better off, or because you think *you* would be better off?" The prince was staring off the balcony, a longing gleam to his eyes as tears continuously soaked his cheeks and peppered his eyelashes. His head turned to me, then. His expression showed something almost like disbelief. I was sure mine did, too.

"I don't know..." He creaked. *"I don't know-"* His tone grew more panicked, a hand going to cover his mouth. My eyes widened. I hadn't intended to cause this reaction from him. I bit my lip and moved closer, taking his wrist- then thinking that was too forceful, I gently took his hand. He was too weak to refuse as I guided him to a small sitting area nearby. I sat him down. His sobs were only becoming more pained, as were his breaths.

I shushed him comfortingly as one would a child. "Rengas, you have to calm down," I whispered, sitting next to him and lifting a hand to rub his arm while still holding his hand. He held it like a lifeline. Maybe it was. I couldn't be sure. "If you can't do all this work for anyone else, at least keep going for me, okay?"

He watched me blankly. Perhaps he didn't understand.

"I'm your project, right? I made it all this way because of you. That ought to mean something." I squeezed his hand a little. "Not to mention you becoming a beacon in your *twenties*. You've done so much."

I pressed a hand to his chest, tucking my fingers underneath the fabric of his robe to feel his pulse. The last thing I'd said looked to have stirred something in him. His breathing slowed, becoming increasingly less panicked.

He took my hand and moved it away from his chest before pulling me into an embrace. His large, warm arms enveloped me completely. I carefully found a way to hold him. It felt right. He smelled and felt like a soothing warmth. It was one I always relished when I was lucky enough to come across it.

His shaking soon subsided, his nose tucked into my neck. My hand found its way up his back and into his hair, which I ran my fingers through. It had always been a thing that relaxed me, so I hoped it would do the same for Ren.

• • •

"Promise me. Promise me you'll keep trying?" I whispered. It barely made a sound against his hair. I felt him nod against my neck. "Good." I held him closer. "It really is worth it."

Rengas was the one who made me realize life had value. That I had agency, that with enough effort, life can feel like your own, and most importantly, that it can feel *real*. For the first time in a year, my life started to feel like it was actually happening, instead of feeling like my existence being suspended in some sinister dream.

He let me go after a little while.

"But I'm not trying so hard because you're my project." He held my arms tightly, desperate to keep me there. "I'm doing it because..." His eyes started to grow hazy, his cheeks going pinker underneath his face paint. His hand found its way up my chest to cup my cheek, and I was surprised to feel my pace pick up. I was forced to look away; the magnitude of his watching me was too much.

"Because?" I breathed, still averting my gaze. His hand slipped away from my face.

"Never-mind. I should go to bed. Safe-night, Guno."

"Wait-" My breath hitched. I couldn't do this. I should've found a way to make this gentler on him, a way to soften the blow of my words, but I had nothing prepared. I'd spent hours trying to scrape together something to no avail. "I have another thing to tell you."

Two things came to mind now, not just my departure. There was something else, too.

"I came to tell you because, well, at first, I didn't want you to be concerned. I'd never, ever dream of hurting you." I inhaled through my teeth. "I've decided what I need to do that will solve this whole mess," I spoke tamely for him, lifting one of my calloused hands to brush away tears that were still forming in his guileless, pitiable eyes. I'd reassure him a million times if I had to. I'd be there through whatever it took for him to be okay again. It made my stomach ache to see him in such agony. Even so, the sweet Ren still managed to watch me attentively.

"I think I'm going to leave. I'm going to fight and hopefully get rid of the witches. Then they can't hurt us, or anyone, again." I patiently wiped away his tears as they came. Rengas's lip began to tremble. "Ren, it's okay. You did a very good job." This time I took him in, holding his head against my neck. I rubbed his back in small circles as he began to shake with sobs once more, letting out soft cries that were very much audible now. They were slow and subdued as if he were embarrassed to be upset. I clucked quietly in an attempt to soothe him.

• • •

"Listen, I want you to know one more thing before I leave. It's okay if you don't feel the same or anything. Just- it seems like there isn't going to be another time to tell you." I could hear my heartbeat as Ren lifted his face from the crook of my neck, gazing at me again with those eyes of his. I wiped away another tear.

He was so tangible—every move of his pulsed through my hands, into my heart. "I love you, Rengas. I really do. You're -*Light*- you mean so much to me." I shook my head. "You make me feel like I'm real. I want to stay here with you and make you feel the same, like-" My stomach leaped time and time again, pushing me to act.

"Like I have control. Like I have the power to change things and change myself. It's more than I can say."

Ren blinked, one last tear rolling down his cheek as he processed the statement. His cheeks became pinker again, and he was so soft, and I knew what his private looks and smiles meant now because he was smiling. *Everything made sense.* I couldn't believe how good it felt not to be confused anymore.

"I love you too." He beamed, and I looked down to see his beacon marks pick up their shine too. I ran a hand over one of his arms, then looked back to his face. *He loved me too. Rengas Averell loved me.*

I could think of nothing else as I leaned into him. I was guided by the grounding Light of his marks and the ever-present reminder that he was real, completely palpable, and so was I. Both of my hands found his face. I welcomed how he easily came undone, his lips flush and sweet like honeyed fruit. My fingers curled in his hair, each kiss bringing out another. I held a desire for him that ran deeper than Alice's commands. One I'd ignored for far too long until now. Now I ached to confess it to him with every affection.

Why have I turned away for so long? He was always here. I just pretended not to notice.

Rengas kissed me back so gently I thought I didn't need to leave the capital after all. Maybe tagging along with Ren would be enough. I knew I would be safe as long as I kept close to him.

I believed that while he softened against my hands, I would drive the Light from him into me. That the Darkness in my heart - though burdening and still present and as real as the rest of me- would then be banished by his Brightness.

After She-knows-how long, we parted, and I still held the prince's cheeks. He showed a little smile as I kept him there, our noses touching. I pressed my forehead against Ren's.

"*I don't want you to go.*" The prince whispered, his words slurred, "Take me with you. I can protect you." As I sat back onto my haunches, he found my hands, which I held comfortably. I thought back to when I would first watch him train. The pure ferocity in which he conducted himself only lent itself to a military persona. He fought like his life depended on it, then. Rengas was conditioned for war, and at first, I thought it was silly, maybe even sad. To have so much training and not even put it to use. But now I thought it might come to good use after all; it would all rest on the outcome of tonight. I'd been watching our hands as I considered.

"You're going to get in more trouble than you need. This is my issue."

"You said it yourself, Guno! I'm just as involved with this as you!" He pleaded, squeezing my hands. "If you really mean everything you've said, you'd let me come with you."

I met his eyes.

"Okay. But we're leaving *now*." I told him. There was a burning starting at the base of my spine that I couldn't shake. Even in the presence of a beacon, I was helpless. I was tired of being pushed around by some invisible devil. It was due time to take matters into my own hands. I helped pull him to his feet. He was wearing pants, which was good. We didn't need him tripping over any loose fabrics. "Come on, let's go to the armory. We don't have any time to waste."

I checked the sky once more. There was only a sliver of sun left over the horizon. We started to run and didn't stop until we'd scaled the staircase to the training arena. Rengas discarded his jewelry and scarf there, donning a belt and sheath for a massive golden Light blade which he held with ease. I myself was most practiced with staves and so took a Light spear- though as I took it in my hands, I still felt vastly unprepared. Vastly *small*.

We came back down, and then I remembered my promise.

"Ginger! Is she still in her office? I need her." I turned to Ren in a frenzy, shoving my spear between my knees so I could tie up my hair. I regained the weapon and started toward her office. The prince followed.

"I'm not sure. I thought you didn't want others tagging along! What happened to that?" He asked. I didn't turn around to address him, only picked up my pace into a jog. We came to a tower room with several doorways to other parts of the castle. It took me a second to remember which way to go. The tense, unmistakable feeling of Darkness was spreading up to the middle of my back. It would undoubtedly be felt in my fingers, too, if it weren't for the powerful weapon I held countering with its cooling energy.

"I promised her earlier that I would tell her when I left," I replied after I'd steadied my thoughts.

Finally, we had found her office. The general was hunched over her desk, staring at the papers with her head in her hands. She didn't seem to be reading- I don't think she'd done anything for a while since she'd been left to wait. Once she heard us, she picked up her head. She saw Rengas accompanying me, her posture straightening.

"Why's he here?" She stood, "You're bringing him with you?"

"Yes. I decided to bring you both. Just, don't get yourselves hurt." I cautioned, looking around. I knew I was safe in the capital. I just had to keep telling myself that. Something about the place just felt smaller, all of a sudden. Dashan itself was closing in around me. I was convinced the walls would cave in at any moment. I was convinced the stars would fall.

"You don't need to worry about that," Ginger grinned, holding the hilt of her own sword, which she always had on hand. In her case, there was nothing else to prepare, so I supposed we were ready.

I thought of Rocky again and his outburst. No one else seemed to hear or even catch the notice of his suspicious activity and his yelling. In fact, I hadn't seen him since he did that, I remembered. So where was he?

The three of us started to make our way to the front entrance, and my wonderings grew. Where could he be? He could easily hide, as small as he is. I just thought he should've stuck around a little longer if he wanted so badly to be taken.

Then, I saw him, just like I could "see" Ren without him even being in the room. He still had the bandage on his hand and was walking -no, running- toward us. He was right behind me.

I turned with unnatural swiftness, trusting out my spear. Ginger and Rengas froze.

"Where are you guys going?!" He demanded, not caring to hide the injury anymore. When I went to Ginger or Rengas for a response, they couldn't supply anything, which is when I remembered *they* were following *me*.

"I'm going to fight the witch. They're coming with."

"Y-you can't!" He sputtered, his wide eyes locked on Ren, "I won't let you!"

I narrowed my eyes at him. The front gates were so close. They were *open*. All I had to do was run.

"Why?" Ren asked gently. I got a spike of pain in my hand that almost made me drop my staff. I only held it tighter, fighting myself to lower it away from the elf. I was more than tempted to keep it pointed at his face, just to see him squirm. If it was a fight he wanted, it was a fight he would get.

He isn't who I held this weapon for; I had to remind myself. This wasn't for him. I turned, looking out through the entrance hall into the vast night sky, past the jagged peaks of mountains and hills obscuring one of Dashan's moons. The sky was the one thing in this damned dimension that remained constant, I thought. Everything else might change, but those stars were forever. Pinpoints of Her influence shining through the suffocating blackness of space. Glimmers of temperance, of good faith. Funny freckles in the expanse that, apparently, made Rengas a little tipsy looking at them too long.

I didn't know if I'd ever see them again after tonight. I made a break for the door, letting the air wash over me and ruffle the curls around my face. I could hear the others shouting indistinctly behind me, but I was already gone. I ran down the steps, almost hoping the night itself would claim me if I went fast enough, and when my vision went black, I thought it had for real.

    I didn't ever think I was "ready," like I told Ginger. I don't think there ever would be a time when I would truly be prepared to face Alice. If I stayed for another month, another year, the witches would just progress as I did. My power would always be a step behind. That's why I decided I needed to take that leap of faith and put myself in Light's hands. Only She knew what was right for me.

    The first thing I noticed when I came to was the breeze. It was a cool one, not dissimilar from Ninth at dusk, but free of any grit or debris. The type of air that wouldn't sting your eyes even if you faced it head on. I took a moment to straighten from my crouched-down position to survey where I'd been placed.

    We stood on a vast marbled stone platform with a clear edge, and beyond it were others similar. A thick cord even tethered some to the far corners of the platform I stood on, all suspended impossibly in the air. They were natural curving shapes of beautiful wood and granite that appeared all too artificial. The only thing I could see besides these were the stars, all the way across the sky. Stars and moons and even *planets* that felt far too close surrounded me, their rings seeming to reach into the atmosphere.

    There came no movement from any of my surroundings and very little noise. I turned slowly, grounding myself, trying not to bother the silence-

    I spotted her at the opposite edge of the floor. She stood there waiting as if I were the one who called her here. She was dressed in a simple red frock with childish puffy sleeves and equally adolescent-looking knee-high socks. Alice hadn't a care in the world; it looked like. Her flaxen bangs were clipped up, and as I walked closer with my staff, I didn't have to look hard to know what was there. Her six monster pupils, staring at me from inside her two sockets. She was unarmed.

I didn't make a move yet. I wanted to see what evil machinations she had planned for us. She stood there in silence for a while.

If the rest want to join me, they'll find a way, I thought.

"Are you proud of yourself, boy?" She asked, for the first time in months, in her own voice. A *real* voice made from vibrations in the same air as me. A voice that wasn't some delusion she'd manifested straight into my brain. Frankly, it was a relief to hear. Alice had managed to convince me she'd never been real at all.

"Where are we?" I asked, keeping a wide stance. She watched me prepare with passive amusement, her rouged lip curling.

"Yaskien, the dimension of solitude," She began. Our voices, though real, didn't do much to satiate the overwhelming feeling of stillness- and to hear that title made that feeling much more bearable. "Of course, "the" doesn't quite apply. There are hundreds of *dimensions* of solitude; I'd wager. Places of drab moral disbandment, but decent decor." She took a leisurely inspection of the scenery, but the utterly bored look in her eyes suggested she'd been here before and wasn't taking in anything new. I thought it funny for Alice, out of anyone, to complain about morals. "I asked you something, though. I'm trying not to pry in on your mind since we're in person, but denying me answers when politely asked for is just rude, Lamplight." She folded her hands in front of her.

I couldn't stand her waiting. After so much beating me down, to have the nerve just to sit there like she'd done nothing at all. It made my bones quiver with bright-hot anger.

"Yeah! I *am* proud. I'm *really* proud. That even though you made me a-a *damned portal traitor-* I still have two feet to walk on and a-a head that isn't all spent." I made my voice firm despite the fear that lingered in it, taking a step closer. We must've been ten feet apart now. Alice made it seem like it wouldn't take much to take her out with her getup and the precarious surroundings, but I was smarter than that. I knew there was more.

There were so many questions I had for her. Did she have other apprentices like me? How long had she been in Dark's service if He really provided you with eternal life in exchange for your servitude? Why had she stuck with me for so long? She probably had other options, right?

"You're so stubborn. No wonder He has taken such a liking to you." She shook her head, looking me dead in the eyes with those six pupils. She was one to talk about stubbornness. Look at *her,* holding out hope for my Darkness after a year of denying it—what a hypocrite.

• • •

I clutched the light staff harder, gritting my teeth.

"I HATE YOU SO KEVING MUCH!" I spat, running at her with all the fury I could muster. I could feel, for the first time, Light and Dark *both* coming to my aid. Dark loved the excuse to cause pain at whatever means, and Light was willing to make this sacrifice for the betterment of countless others like me. There would be no more apprentices that would suffer because of her if Alice was gone, and She herself understood this. A shocking chill started from my Light staff and coarsed up my forearms, all while He continued to burn with excitement in my belly. I thrust the spear straight at her-

-and she caught it easily in her hand, right over her heart.

The witch began to shake with little chuckles, which evolved into peals of psychotic laughter. Her eyes were focused on me still, elated in a sort of way that shook me to my core. I'd never seen that sort of look on her before- and I don't think I ever wanted to see it again. I'd never been able to get it out of my head.

"Don't you see what you've become? You're no holy warrior, Guno. You're destined for this. I've told you since the beginning, but you never seem to get it!" I pushed against her still, but my spear didn't budge. I followed her eyes down to my forearms. Between fissures of His thick substance were my veins, raised and glowing with Her influence. "Dark will always win. He will overcome regardless of how this fight ends, boy. I die; he wins. *You die; he* wins." She cackled again, throwing my spear out of the way. Since my grip on it was so strong, it made me sway a little before I stepped back and pointed it at her chest again from a safer distance. She stepped closer, and I backed up again. Alice had a twisted grin pulled across her face so tight it looked artificial. "He has a place in his ranks just for you. I chose you for a reason. At first, even I didn't know why exactly- but now I see it."

"See what?" My voice cracked.

"You're *destined* to become an Umbra, Guno. A level seven. *A god.*"

"*Shut up.*"

"You have control over the *very substance* Dark commands. You have it *quite literally,*" She giggled once more, "At your fingertips." I glanced down at them again.

"You mean-"

"Yes, Guno. Not even I have control of shadow fluid, and somehow *you* do. I have to admit; I'm jealous. Do you know how much time this will save?" More unrestrained giggles broke from her speech. "You will have unlimited power in no time at all, and unlimited control over your own destiny." Another step forward and another stumble back for me. "That *is* what you've wanted this whole time, right? I've given it to you." Her smile lessened down to one of charming normalcy. I began to lower my spear.

"It's never too late, you know." Calmly, her eyes lifted their focus from me.

"Your friends are here."

The devious look began to return as I heard a shout from behind me. I turned to see them: Ren and Ginger standing at attention, and Rocky shaking with rage. They could have been an illusion, I thought briefly, but that idea was quickly ruled out. I blocked out Alice's words as I took another swing at her, which she easily dodged. She planted a foot into my side, kicking me out of the way and sending me tumbling across the stone platform like a ragdoll. My light spear flew out of my reach. From my position on the ground, I could see Rocky run up and grab it.

"Hey!" I protested, getting onto my hands and knees. Ren made some exclamation of panic and motioned for Ginger to follow him closer to me. I coughed as I tried to regain my breath but held out a hand to keep them at a distance.

"We had an agreement, you nasty witch!" Rocky screamed, holding the weapon carelessly over his head, *"What in the Afterdull are you doing?"*

"Nasty witch. How cute." She drawled, drawing closer to him and seizing hold of the elf's head with one hand. He cried out, plunging the spear into her middle. She made a stifled noise, pressing her eyes shut as she proceeded to pull it out, not releasing his skull. "Cute, indeed. You're one of us now. You ought to act like it."

Rocky was still kicking and flailing, trying to land another hit. I finally pulled myself to my feet, clenched my fists, and ran at her unarmed- only to be thrown again. This time I was able to roll and get easily back to standing.

"NEVER! I'M HERS! I ONLY USED YOU FOR HER-" That seemed to truly enrage Alice. She dodged another attempted hit from Rocky. She was still strong, but I could clearly see the black mark on her stomach that stained her dress. She kicked Rocky straight in the chest, and he skidded a disproportionate length across the floor. Ginger and Ren froze.

In a moment of inspiration, I began to circle the platform and creep up behind her.

Before Rocky could even get up, she'd pushed him down again and clasped her hand firmly around his neck. I yelled, feeling Him and

Her cool and heat me back and forth at a dizzying speed as I attempted to tackle her while she kneeled. The Light spear was too far away.

"I used you. You'll never... win..." I could hear Rocky's voice beginning to dwindle. I threw all my weight into pulling Alice off him by the back of her collar. We tumbled painfully, and I evaded another stomp by quickly scrambling out of her way.

Rocky didn't move from the ground.

I saw Ren sheath his sword, running to take the boy into his arms. I sprinted to regain my Light spear. Ren was crying. Alice didn't run after me.

Why didn't she use her powers? She could easily pull me apart using mind tricks alone, I thought. Maybe her pride was getting in the way. Did ancient Dark beings have a sense of dignity, too?

"He's right," I told her, beginning to circle the arena just as she did. Calm, easy steps, one over the other. I ignored the stinging in my own chest and the part of Light that told me the easiest route right now would be to flee.

I heard Ren's cries intensify, and immediately I knew what it meant.

I took a steady breath outward and prayed to Her before the battle as Ginger told me.

May Alice hurt not another soul. May I get out of this alive. May my conscience and others' consciences be quieted because this agent of chaos is no longer there to instill it. May I fight with temperance and justice.

May Light win out.

I took a deep breath and tried to recall all the things I'd been told, letting the background noise blur out.

The witch tried to grab hold of the staff once more, in which I twisted it out of her hands, striking her in the back with the side of it. She rolled and regained her balance, advancing and landing a blow at the side of my head. I forced myself to recover quickly, tried a poorly coordinated counter-attack that obviously missed, and she tried to grab me by the neck from behind.

I flipped my staff, thrusting it back just beside my waist- and into her chest. She stifled a noise of pain as I twisted the spear and turned around to face her. Alice's grip loosened. She grabbed hold of the spear, but it had gone in too deep. She gave another psychotic laugh, weakened by pained fatigue.

"I knew you had it in you." She grinned as she buckled and fell off the spear point onto the cold stone floor. *"So fucking stubborn..."*

She shook her head, and suddenly I wanted to come closer. I knew I didn't have a choice in the matter.

All I could wonder was why she hadn't tried it earlier.

"As much as you hate to admit it, you know we're the same. I've told you again and again." She held her ribs. Strangely, the Dark ichor from her abdomen had turned to blood again. She raised a sticky hand to my forehead. I didn't have the will power to pull away as I kneeled over her and allowed it to happen.

The blood, still warm, touched my temple. "You can think you've won all you want, but," She wheezed and coughed. The blood that flew from her mouth didn't even phase me. I still looked her in the eyes, my face covered in her mess. "I know that even *you're* aware that isn't true. I'm going to show you what was in that damn diary, since you've never cared to listen. You love to turn a blind eye, don't you, Lamplight..." I furrowed my brow. I hated how she knew so much about me. So much more than Ginger or Rocky did, maybe even Rengas.

That's because she was right.

We were similar, and I hated her more than anything in Dashan.

I found myself in an unfamiliar room. The interior was unsettlingly clean and foreign. It seemed to be someone's quarters, judging by the bed tucked into the corner. I heard adults shouting, muffled by the bedroom door.

In the corner of the room, beside a bookshelf, was soft crying. I crept to see who it was.

A girl in her late teens held a book to her chest. It was a humongous, ancient thing. She held it so closely that I would have believed she was in love with it, her tears making dark mascara tracks down her cheeks.

I knew immediately who this was. It didn't take too much guesswork, given her golden curls and dainty features.

I sat on Alice's bed, watching her. I could see a second book now, lying on the ground beside her. One with a lacy plush cover, clean and unchanged. Because now, no time had passed. The diary was new.

"Are you there?" She rasped, her voice worn from sobs, "You can't just promise me a way out an' then not fill your side of the deal, ya know!" She scolded nothing, squinting up at the sky. It seemed that even in her youth, Alice had a fiery temper. "I did what you said! Bumped him off! I even did it in a real secret place, too. Those ritzy sonsabitches are really in for it now." She smiled bitterly, but it quickly weakened and turned into a scowl when she got no response. "I'll get my pal, Prue. She'll be on our side in no time, I know it." She nodded, sniffling and wiping her eyes with a sleeve. She didn't seem to mind that the mascara stained her clean white undershirt. I bet she would have torn apart her dress, too, just to spite whoever had given it to her.

Alice flipped open her notebook to a fresh page she'd bookmarked with a pen. She'd written down everything. Down on paper was a detailed recount of the murder she'd carried out at Dark's hand, from beginning to end, and a promise of what she would do next. Convince Prue to leave, find the "meeting spot," and be free for good. I'd paced around her to peek at what she was writing. I watched her eyes dart about the page with manic ferocity while her pen dug into the pages.

> *Goodwin Lighton is dead. His death marks the first of a pact which will get me out of Manhattan for good. I'm taking Prue with me, no matter what she says. I can't do this alone, and god knows she needs this as much as I do. Goodbye New York,*
> *And good riddance.*

Alice threw the book closed with passionate decisiveness, turning her mean glare to the sky again.

It unsettled me how easy this seemed to come for her; how she wasn't even that shaken about murder and willing to do it again if she could get out of the aforementioned "Manhattan." We were never that different, at least in circumstance. She'd been just like me. Small. Afraid. Trapped.

The context I got was enough to understand how she felt, as much as I hated to empathize with this wayward member of His army. It made sense, at the very least.

Alice stood from her spot in the corner, and then I was watching her bound across a field to a building that resembled a tiny castle. Kids her age walked about everywhere, and I was afraid to bump into any. I kept my arms at my sides, reserved even though none of them could interact with me. I was smart enough to understand at least that.

She ran up a set of stairs that circled the front entrance and came to a stop as she was just about to enter the building, crossing the front stoop to meet another teenage girl just out of the way of the doors.

This, of course, was the witch Prudence: untouched by Dark. Her familiarly pointed nose stuck out from the bridge of her little round (clear, this time) glasses. Her dark hair was pulled into an updo, and she wore a shirt under a dress identical to Alice's. All of the kids here wore a variation of this, actually. I narrowed my eyes once I noticed this detail before returning my attention to the two girls.

"I got us a way out, Prue! Look." She produced the old book from earlier that she'd held so dearly, showing her. "I've had a visit from a man. He might be an alien or a spector." She laughed, not dissimilar from the deranged look she'd given me earlier in Yaskien. Prue squinted with doubt at it, then up at her friend. "I know it sounds crazy, Prue, but I know it's real. Here, here." She pushed the book into Prue's chest. The young Prudence held it, growing tense with disgust.

I saw, then, that Alice had begun to cover her eyes with some hair that she'd brushed in front of her face, and she pulled it away to show Prue. There was her first monster eye, bloodshot and fresh. Prue screamed, dropping the book as she retreated toward the wall. A few students turned to watch.

"*What is that? What's wrong with it?*" She whimpered in horror as more kids started to gather. A boy picked up the book as Prue dropped it. Alice didn't hesitate to throw a punch straight into his face, making him crumple against the stairs as she snatched it back again.

"Don't touch my stuff unless you wanna regret it, Nelson! Now go chase yourself!" She spat in his face for good measure, and the boy scurried off. Kids gasped and ogled her monster eye still, which she quickly went to cover back up. She turned back to Prue as the crowd dissipated out of fear, though the kids continued to murmur and giggle amongst themselves. She exhaled.

"Listen, I didn't mean to scare ya." Her voice turned soft as she tucked the heavy tome under her arm to rub Prue's shoulder. The fear in the girl's face quieted.

"How'd that happen? Your eye?" Prue asked in a frantic whisper, her tired eyes darting around to check they weren't being snooped on anymore. I'd stepped beside them so I could make sure I didn't miss anything.

"It's part of my pact with Him." She grinned again in a much less concerning manner. Prue pushed up her glasses, pressing her eyes shut.

"You sound out of your mind, Alice. *I-I* mean, I believe you, but-" Prue stammered, trying to compensate after a sharp look from her friend. "Are you sure this will work?"

"I'm certain." Alice insisted, pressing a hand to her heart. She held out her hand. "Meet me back here after school, and we'll leave. You do trust me, right?" Alice raised her eyebrows. Even back then, her rhetoric was impeccable. It made me uneasy to think of her using the same sort of persuasion on her best friend. Prue nodded reluctantly, taking Alice's hand.

"I'll follow you anywhere," Prue told her earnestly and left Alice to go inside. I saw Alice bite her lip through a wide grin. The world began to close in.

When I returned to Yaskien Alice was already dead. My eyes widened as I shook her and tried to cover up the wound in her chest, besides myself with unnamable and unwarranted grief. She was just a child, my instincts told me. Sure, she was misguided, but I was too.

I thought most of Prudence. I saw the silent fondness and admiration in her eyes whenever Alice looked her way. I recognized how much Alice meant to her. I could only imagine just how long the two had been by one another's side, how much they had endured. I grieved *for* Prudence then, and part of me knew that she wouldn't come after me after this. I was safe.

Light, for once, I was safe.

I looked down at Alice again, steeling myself as I began to shake with forming tears. The witch's eyes were open, revealing two blue, completely typical irises. With further examination, I couldn't even find a trace of Dark's ichor. It had been washed away. She'd been slain with a tool of Her influence.

Something about that settled the unease enough for me to get up. I turned to see only Ginger remaining across the platform, standing with steady footing. I left the Light spear there, my gait quickening into a sprint as I ran into her arms. She caught me and held me tightly there, in her confident, consistent reality. I let my sobs intensify against her shoulder: cries of mourning, of time passed, of utter relief.

"You did it, Lamplight." She muttered into the lull of Yaskien's hushed sky. I could make out the quiet joy in her tone. "I'm so proud." My body ached and trembled with adrenaline and all else, but now I could be confident that my physical form was sure and true. What I did with it was my choice. It wouldn't blur out into some obscure thought, lost to memory. I was physical, just like Ginger. Just like Ren.

There would be no more surprises. I could rest. I could see Rengas again. I could see my friends on the ground.

Ginger held me up as she lifted a hand and activated the portal device in her monocle, and we stepped through. We were back in the capital, but Rocky was gone. My eyes swept across the room to see Ren on the steps beneath his throne, doubled over with sorrow. His face lifted from his hands when he heard the soft whirl of our portal opening, and his face twisted with emotion as he held out his arms. Though my body began to ache, I couldn't reserve myself and quickly returned to his side, throwing myself into his embrace so hard he had to support himself with an arm as not to fall over.

"*Guno.*" He sobbed, searching my face. I nodded tearfully, glancing at Ginger, who watched, her arms crossed as she shook her head with fond playfulness.

I returned my gaze to Ren and kissed him once more with a passion, smiling through my tears. To think I wasn't volatile anymore. I could do this whenever I pleased. I wasn't going anywhere.

Once I leaned back, his sobs had lessened, and he caught Ginger's look with embarrassment.

Ren's repose turned somber again as Ginger left us alone. "Rocky's passed. I think the witch turned him Dark or something..." He sobbed in a way that sounded painful, curling in on himself. I tried to soothe him, scooting closer to rub his back and rest my head against his shoulder. "He- he didn't deserve any of that, Guno! I-" His voice faltered again with more tears. The prince held me close. I rocked us gently back and forth, holding the back of his head. My own tears began to subside as I recovered from it all. "But, I'm so glad you're okay, and-"

"Shh, it's alright. I feel bad, too." I sighed, beginning to choke up again, "I can't help but feeling as if it's my fault."

"No, it's not. It's not." To my surprise, the prince pulled away from me, and I sat back, allowing him to fumble with his pockets. He produced a folded piece of paper, which he carefully opened. When he started to shake again with reinvigorated despair, he did quick work in stowing the memento away again.

"He- Rocky- he did this all for me. He made a Dark pact to ensure I wouldn't be hurt-" He wept, scrubbing at his watery eyes. "And I didn't do anything about it! Nothing! I was completely unaware. Stupid, so stupid." Ren pushed the heel of his hand into his forehead.

"You couldn't have known-"

"Even so! To know things could be- could be different." He ran a hand through his hair, distressed. "We're contacting his family now. We'll hold a grand memorial. It's what he deserves. He helped save

• • •

you." He sniffled, mustering a small smile as he pulled a strand of hair behind my ear.

"Of course." I took his free hand in mine and closed my eyes.

I hadn't known him that well, had I? Well, I knew a few things. I knew that Rocky was particular and loyal, a master at peg and chips. He had a large family. Eight siblings. He was loyal to Her and the capital and was willing to do anything to prove it. All in all, he was a good friend. I should have given him more recognition for it.

I hoped that even after all this, Light would recognize he did this for Her. He wouldn't have made that deal if he wasn't so loyal to Her in the first place. It proved just how much he cared for Ren and the capital. If loyalty was one of Her core principles, that should be forgivable.

He *belonged* in the Afterglow more than anyone. My head throbbed with a striking sharpness. It was probably just from getting hit, maybe stress too. Who knew how long it would take to recover.

I trudged back to Ren's quarters that evening once we each had our time alone to think and pray. My headache had worsened, making my eyes feel heavy inside my skull. I shook off the idea that it was Dark-related. Alice was dead. It couldn't possibly have gotten worse. I nudged the unlocked door open and easily found him at the foot of his bed, elbows on knees, head bowed low. I had been blinking to try and relieve the pain in my eyes and head. Despite my discomfort, I tried to regard Ren with temperance, smoothing back his hair to rouse him from his state slowly.

Once his head lifted, his distant look turned immediately to terror. Scrambling back from my hand, the prince gritted his teeth through sobs as if making a sorry attempt to weaponize his tears. In my dazed state of recovery, I couldn't tell why immediately.

My hand, left in the air, flexed. Something was writhing, angry and hot beneath my skin. I felt its power surge through me, as if my form were being overtaken, filled to the breaking point with unrestrained electricity. Ren shouted my name but didn't come closer. The blinking wasn't helping anymore. Maybe Alice really had won, just beyond the grave. The energy filled my lungs and stung down my cheeks. I held onto the bedpost. Anywhere I moved would result in some sharp, erratic motion unknown to either of us. There was nowhere left to go.

"*GUNO!* Guno- no, Guno." He had braced himself and was now holding my sides, lip trembling. "Guno, can you hear me-"

"It hurts. *What's happening...*" I rumbled, my vision blurring. Still, something about Ren's coolness relieved the painful fever that had struck me. What more would I have to do? I'd done everything I could. I had no options left. Carefully and gracelessly, I let myself back into Ren's embrace. He held me tightly there, rocking me as I had for him earlier.

His cries of pain sharpened my senses. His tears made my insides bristle. It was only when he became quiet that I began to see again and could bear to move. I brought my arms around his neck, keeping him close.

"Rengas, what am I doing wrong..."

"You're doing nothing wrong, oh sweet mouse, I'm so sorry-" Rengas paused, just as he'd assessed my face again. "Your- *oh, Light.*" Rengas shook his head, worrying his lip. The look of fear had returned.

He'd never looked at me like that. Even in the beginning, he'd never been *afraid* of me. Even when he knew I'd done wrong and what I was capable of, he treated me like he would anyone else in the capital. Something about me must have changed. I must not have been myself anymore.

I made a distant grumble as he delved into another fit of manic sobs.

"Tell me," I begged. It took a moment for him to answer.

"You have two eyes. You- you have two Dark eyes, *He took you, He-*"

I blinked, my breaths coming unevenly. I swallowed, shook my head, then shook it again-

"No." I pushed away from him, whirling to face the mirror.

He'd been right. Of course, he'd been right. Alice had been right, too.

Black ichor oozed from my tear ducts and nostrils, making ugly tracks down my face and mocking the places I'd been beaten during battle. I no longer saw either of my deep, earthen eyes anymore. All I saw was Him. I shook my head once more. *"No..."* I whipped my head toward Rengas. He laid there uselessly, face buried in his arms. He'd become utterly inconsolable, leaving me alone with this.

It wasn't *his* body being desecrated like an abandoned temple, I thought selfishly, barely feeling my own tears. They were watering down the thick Dark solvent that had done this to me—a futile bodily

• • •

attempt at returning me to some sort of normalcy after it all. I couldn't bear to say anything. I'd never been so disappointed.

That night I spent in his bed, saying nothing as I listened to him cry into the pillow beside mine. It wasn't to reassure myself that I stayed, nor to reassure him. I knew I didn't put his mind at ease, and neither did he for me. Neither of us slept one second. I dreaded having to wake in the morning.

The next day Rocky's family arrived at the capital. Torrid in particular was quite stern. They were a bit taller than Rocky, with their dark hair pulled back into a ponytail, dressed in Eighth sector's deep blue regalia. I noticed from a distance that they'd only brought some of his siblings. Maybe the others were too young to travel such a distance. The thought saddened me even more as I stood by Ren's side while he greeted the lot of them. Torrid gave a General's greeting to Ginger before walking up to the prince.
"What in Light's name happened to my brother, huh? I always questioned the stability of the Ninth sector, and this only backs it up. What happened to him?" Ren faltered. He'd dressed in his uniform for the occasion. He shakily handed over the note.
"I can explain more, but this is what he wanted to tell me in particular. Rocky was a- faithful and wonderful-" He started, and Torrid cut him off with a gasp, their ears pointing downward.
"This can't be." They reread the slip of paper as the rest of Rocky's family gathered around, his tiny mother promptly beginning to weep into his father's shoulder. We were barraged with questions and accusations after that:
"Traitor!"
"You're lying. Rocky would never do something like this!"
"Why you?"
"Did you know about this?"
I could see Rengas trying desperately to keep together despite his own sorrow and regrets surrounding the situation.
"Please. Please, all of you- follow me into the throne room. Please." He soaked up a tear with his handkerchief before it could mess up his paint. "I'll tell you everything."

He led the group back into the throne room, where staff members who had known Rocky were already gathered in front of his casket, a simple box wrapped in white linens. The throne had been moved to make room for it. Rengas made his way back in, crossing his arms and gripping the sashes on his uniform for stability. I took one of the cushion seats in the front. Torrid situated themself beside me. The murmuring in the crowd eventually died out, and Rengas began to speak.

"Yesterday, a terrible tragedy occurred, as you all know." He started softly, forcing himself to speak up more, "And you've all read his testimony to me. What you don't know is that before he passed, he fought valiantly and helped bring an end to a powerful Dark Supporter who had been wreaking havoc on our capital for nearly a year now." He had to swallow now and again to make sure he didn't choke up completely. I nodded in agreement, staring down at my knees.

"I truly believe his efforts were not in vain. He will be commended for his work and join Her for eternity. I can be certain of this." Rengas assured them, keeping his head down.

His family seemed to calm once they understood the context for his demise. We stayed in the throne room to share stories we had of him, fond memories, anecdotes. Torrid even lightened up, admitting they always wished they'd worked closer to him so they would have been able to see him more often than just Light festivals and celebrations during the Scarce Months. Ricky, who Ginger clearly showed hesitance in allowing here in the first place, shared an all too in-depth account of his and his twin brother's quarrels over the legality of the pocket dimension business. After fifteen minutes or so, Torrid grumbled and got him to sit back down.

The release ceremony would begin after. We led the procession down the front steps of the capital where a funeral driver was waiting for us, and we watched the sand drifter depart. It would take the casket where it would be left in the Farlands desert for Light to accept him, taking his soul to join the stars forever. If we were lucky and Light forgave him, it would be used to fuel portals too. I could only pray with Ren and the rest of the ceremony attendants that that was the case.

We left and went back inside after we saw the drifter disappear so his family wouldn't have to face the sight of the vehicle returning empty.

We served warm refreshments and talked long into the night with Rocky's family, and then they were gone, and I had truly fulfilled my purpose in the capital. There was an odd stillness throughout—a sense of "what's next" for a very long while.

● ● ●

I sat on the throne room steps as a couple of staff members moved Rengas's throne back into the room. Someone approached me that I hadn't expected to ever speak to again.

Rioh stopped in front of where I sat, and for once, his expression wasn't one of deep hatred. He held out a hand to me. Once I took it, he pulled me to standing. I looked around anxiously to see if any guards had followed him in, and seeing that they hadn't, I let my shoulders fall.

"Guno Lamplight." He addressed formally, raising an eyebrow, "You've slain the Dark witch."

I didn't know what to say. I didn't know what his point with this was. "Uh- yes, sir." I clucked politely, glancing at his cannon arm to make sure he wasn't going to do anything with it. He actually hid it behind his back as he caught me looking.

"I was wrong about you." He admitted. His eyebrows furrowed, creasing his face even further. I blinked at him incredulously. "You are," He paused, 'A man of decent morals. I can see that now, despite the fact that He marked you again." He squinted at the mark in question before shaking off whatever nefarious thought he'd been cooking up.

"I want to apologize for my," Rioh gritted his teeth, avoiding my eyes. I tilted my head to the side, grinning.

"Hostility? Your *hostility*, Rioh." I gently rebuked. The old man huffed, pinching the bridge of his nose with regret.

"Yes. Do you forgive me?" He said it as a statement with no inflection, moving his hand from his face to meet my eyes with his intense, deep-set gaze. I let him sit in suspense for a while before noting, decidedly,

"Yes, Rioh. I forgive you." The captain nodded.

"Good. That's all I wanted to tell you. I'm not sure if you will be a regular attendee of our capital, but either way, I wanted you to know-" He cleared his throat and stuck out his hand cordially. I shook it. He had a rough grip. I wasn't surprised.

"-You have my respect."

"*Oh.*" I wasn't sure if it was a good thing, since I needed to kill someone to earn his favor, and he seemed pretty clear about that part. I thanked him anyway, and he left me alone in the throne room. I went to find Rengas. Rioh had brought up something lingering on my mind for a while since my return: what *was* I going to do after this? I couldn't just stay in the capital for no reason, could I? Besides, the prince had been in an irreparable stupor only made worse by the appearance of my second monster eye. I felt as if I had a duty to protect him, or at least keep him out of trouble.

I knocked on the door to Ren's quarters, and heard a soft "Come in!" before I let myself in as told. Rengas had already lit the candles around the room and was sitting at his vanity scraping off his paint with a little paddle. He regarded me with a smirk that looked like it took a lot of effort to pull off before finishing his work on his face, wiping the used paint off on a cloth. He scooted aside on the bench in front of the vanity, and I sat down.

"Hey." I ran a hand across his shoulders, checking to see if he was still shaken up from earlier. From what I could tell, sharing stories and drinking tea after the funeral had allowed him to wind down enough to function properly again- or at least, so I hoped.

He turned sideways, tucking one leg onto the bench. "I'm glad you came. I've meant to speak to you." He picked up his hairbrush, then set it down again. Instead of using it he fumbled with the bevelings in the wooden handle. "Since you've completed your internship here, I've sort of realized I still don't really want you to leave. I do understand, however, if you need to go home. It's a reasonable thing to want, and we can find you a nice house of your own on the ground level. I can always send you letters." He kicked his foot, thinking aloud dreamily. He leaned on his palm, frowning distantly with half-lidded eyes.

"I wanted to ask you the same thing, actually." I wrung my hands, meeting his eyes. I felt tense and dirty doing it now. Did I still scare him? "I want to visit my village, of course, but I feel like I have more purpose here. I could help make a difference, you know? That is, if I'm allowed."

"Oh, for certain! Yes! I'm sure we can figure something out." Rengas insisted, pushing his hand through his fluff of hair, his hands twitching. He turned back to the desk, touching the marks on his wrists in a nervous habit. "I'm sure if the other officials know you're here for, uh- courtship, it won't be a problem at all." His eyes creased a little in a hint of a smile. The prince regarded me once more. I saw him bite the inside of his cheek before bending toward me and brushing the lightest kiss against my lips. I felt my entire face burst into flame, overwhelmed by it all, and he giggled a little as I blinked slowly in my attempt to recover.

"Uh, yeah. Courtship." I grumbled idiotically, thinking I might melt right there on the spot. Rengas took my hand, bringing me back

• • •

to earth. My smile faded as I recalled what had been on my mind that he had so easily made me forget.

Ren's fond look turned concerned- and, just a little bit, *fearful*. I pulled my hand away from his.

"I'm sorry." I blurted, "I'm sorry, I've failed you. I didn't think. Or maybe I didn't train hard enough. Something went wrong- I'm scaring you. I'm sorry-" I went back to pulling at my hair, trying desperately to hide my eyes for some thousandth time.

"Stop, Guno." He retook my hands forcefully, leading them away from my face. He brushed my hair back out of my eyes. I couldn't stand feeling so exposed and dirty. So inhuman. I'd been stripped of everything that I stood for. I'd trained endlessly, only having a few moments of Her assistance to show for it. "You don't scare me."

"Then, last night-"

"I was scared, yes. I was scared *for* you. Not *of* you, silly mouse!" He held my arms safely. "I'll never be scared of you. Besides, Prince Rengas Averell isn't scared of anything." He grinned. I laughed, shaking out my hair.

"Okay, 'Prince Rengas Averell,' I think we both know that isn't true."

"Not that I would tell."

There was a pause where the prince's look grew familiarly distant. I was about to ask what was wrong when he spoke. He took a deep breath, his worried gaze turning to his own reflection for a brief moment.

"You know, Guno, I've been through a lot. And I've still a long way to go before I can confidently say, without a doubt, that I'm fit and steady and good to rule. Especially after what happened in Yaskien." I held my breath at the sincerity of his words. How clearly broken he seemed about it all. I could tell he'd worked a long time to seem "decent" to the public, too. That alone deserved recognition. I was familiar with how someone leaving your life changes how one functions. I was familiar with how difficult that could be. Yet I knew he faced something entirely different from my own struggles; it didn't take a scholar to figure out that much. He took my hands in his and leaned close again.

"There is one thing, though, that I've found quiets my worries. You. Sure, it's no permanent fix, but there's no denying you have an effect on me." A small smile returned to him as he squeezed my hands. I blinked, opening my mouth to speak- yet I couldn't manage anything.

* * *

"I'm glad you've been so patient, and I'm glad you're around." Ren lightly searched my expression. I was, frankly, a little surprised. The sentiment was similar to what *I'd* been thinking to tell *him,* and how it went the other way around I couldn't fathom.

"I'd meant to tell you the same, actually-" Patience. Patience was it. That's what I'd needed and what he had needed as well. *"You're- thank you."* I shook my head, unable to process any of my own thoughts fully.

"Anything for you, sweet mouse. However thankful you are, I'm that tenfold." He gave a cheeky smirk, then softly came to rest his head on my shoulder. I allowed him time there. It was what we'd both needed at that time, I knew.

Maybe I would never quite understand the undercurrents of what made Rengas Averell work. What made him change his attitude on a cred or perform some ludicrous dance in front of a crowd of a hundred dignitaries... but then, I didn't need to know. I wasn't planning on leaving anytime soon.

I'd gotten a sort of reckless attitude since coming back from Yaskien in one piece. I'd gotten a taste of freedom, and I was ready to spend the rest of my life like this: with reckless abandon, by Rengas Averell's side. I felt like I could do anything. Light, I could build a garden in the Farlands if I tried.

    The next few days passed in a euphoric breeze: studying mythology in the library with Ren, play fighting with Ginger, staying up with the two until sunset to laugh as Rengas became increasingly star-drunk, insisting he was fine even as he began to tip out of his chair.

    But the best part, without a doubt, is that I was no longer living every moment on the edge of my seat. Even with my second eye, my choices seemed to be at my disposal. I felt that only if I consciously commanded it to would Dark come to my fingertips now.

    The capital staff began to spread and broadcast the news: A man once tainted with Dark successfully overcame and evaded his teacher and fell in love with the prince. I could only imagine how the story would start to morph and change in the villages below until it wasn't even recognizable as my story anymore. How many monsters or dragons would be thrown in to add a twist when it was deemed not interesting enough to retell.

    Six days after my return, I received a letter from Kalesse Limbernal herself, congratulating me on my success and notifying me that the capital was reconsidering giving Rengas more power over governmental decisions. I choked at seeing her wonderings of if the prince and I were to get *married-* In which I shook off the embarrassment and immediately ran to show Ren the news, and he burst into tears of joy and relief while clutching onto me for dear life.

    On the eighth day after my return, Ginger came to tell me she had a surprise. She led me downstairs into the temple chamber, a large ventilated place with silks that let in the wind from holes in the translucent wall slats.

    She smiled before turning and leaving me there. At the end of the long sunlit corridor, I could see an unfamiliar man- a beacon. I made careful steps toward him, across the length of the chamber's tapestried rug—herbs falling from plants far above decorated the floor around my bare feet. My eyes followed the line until I met him and gazed upon the object sitting on a raised platform he stood behind.

My father's staff.

I felt my eyes begin to sting as I touched the staff's worn loop, and I brought myself to address the beacon. His markings covered his neck and face and completely whited out one eye in a place of particularly concentrated marks. His white hair hung all the way down to his waist.

There could be only one thing I was here for- that the *staff* was here for.

"You've been waiting for a long time, yes?" The beacon asked, smoothing out his robes. I nodded pitiably, pushing my hair away from my eyes.

"A very long time, sir." My lip trembled as he thoughtfully walked to the back of the chamber, where shelves filled with various ingredients sat. He pulled down a small jar of shimmering gel and a brush, which he set down neatly on his side of the tabletop. He held out his weathered hands palm-up, and when I took them, he pressed my palms into the wood of the staff about shoulder-width apart.

The Light-layer opened the jar, and I saw his beacon marks flash even in the bright daylight. He brushed the shockingly cold material over my knuckles, tracing the staff's loop, and then had to reapply gel to the brush to circle back to its handle, running over my fingers once more. I began to shake with emotion then, attempting to hide my face in my shoulder.

"Hey, look here." The beacon spoke gently, getting my attention back to him. "It's okay to cry, but you must focus." I nodded, sniffling as I focused on the staff.

"State your name, boy."

"My name is Guno Lamplight." I watched as the gel began to ignite with a soft pearlescent glow that started at my hands, moving along the staff's length.

After all this time, She still responded to me. I could see my hair lifting a little, suspended as if it was as enamored as I was. I felt like I weighed barely anything. Light's chill soothed my body as one last tear rolled down my cheek.

"State your origin."

"Ninth sector Dashan, ground level. Son to Nezria and Tehr Lamplight." I recited. I'd practiced this ceremony as a child, daydreaming in my room. My mother would recite the Light-layer's part from the kitchen as she cooked, and I would practice my part. The words had become solidified in my mind, truer than anything.

※ ※ ※

"Repeat after me: With this device, I will bend portal fuel to my will. I pledge myself to Her, for as long as I am in Her service, so is this device to me." His hands hovered above mine.

"With this device, I will bend portal fuel to my will. I pledge myself to Her, for as long as I am in Her service, so is this device to me." I exhaled, then swallowed, preparing myself as the glow from the staff began to intensify.

"Once more please, Lamplight."

"With this device, I will bend portal fuel to my will! I pledge myself to Her, for as long as I am in Her service, so is this device to me!" And with that, everything in my vision was white.

It took a few moments for it to return as I grasped the staff tightly. I had seemed to lift off the ground for a brief moment, my senses lost to the enrapturement of Her holiness. My ears rang with the intensity of the flare. The Light-layer beacon was grinning.

When I gazed upon my father's staff again, the fissures in the wood grain had become stained white. Whenever I touched it, there was a faint glow where the wood felt my fingers.

My fingers.

Fingers, hands that once dripped with Dark's ichor, and definitely could again. Hands that made a mockery of Her very name, and yet-

Here was a little piece of Her, of Light itself, devoted to me. Entrusted in my soul. Bound to my family name.

I was in full control of my own fate with this device: any path, any dimension.

The sound of my joyful cries filled the temple as I held the portal staff close to my heart.

Epilogue

Yaskien, the dimension of solitude. A boring place, if you ask me, but I was never one for meditation.

I brought the boy with me. Alice had said it would be only a half-hour at most until her return, but by now, it had been several. The boy was growing restless. He complained that our apartment was too dark or that the water there tasted funny. The boy complained a lot, actually.

I had grown anxious and tired, and when having a cigarette or two wasn't enough, I found myself going to Yaskien to get Alice myself. A lot of the time I followed her orders without a second thought. I was Alice's shadow. Her accompanying side dish. In reality, I shouldn't have been. I had power as a level five. My potions and creams had immense capability. I could bend and change reality without alchemy, and soon I wouldn't need a binding agent for my power at all. It would be unprecedented and unhinged just like hers. I even took in my own apprentices, and *mine* actually stuck around.

You know, I'd been reluctant to join Dark too, and that's probably why my apprentices are so much more successful. Take Cypress, the boy I had with me now. He started by taking baby steps.

To think Alice starts with *Murder,* right out of the gate! A little intense, right? *I* taught Cypress how to be *smart* while working on his power. Setting up an invisible tripwire in the middle of the street to annoy hundreds of pedestrians. Replacing the sugar beside the teapot with salt. Just for starters.

Of course, nothing was wrong with murder. You had to work your way *up* to murder, though. Beginning an apprentice's training with murder will only make them detest you, as with the tragic case of one Guno Lamplight. He hated her more than he hated Dark Himself. It was a little sad to watch.

"Whoa! What's this place?" Cypress eyeballed the scenery, his head swiveling around.

"Nowhere, quite literally. We'll be out of here soon."

When I dismissed the kid was when I saw her lying prone on the ground. I left Cypress, nearly tripping on my heels as I painfully fell to my knees at her side.

"Alice?" I took off my glasses; my eyes must have been fooling me. "ALICE! Alice, you asshole, get up!" My breathing had quickened-without thinking, I threw out my hand, knocking Cypress back as he tried to pry in my business.

Of course, I knew Alice wasn't getting up. I'd seen enough bodies in her state to know Alice had been dead for hours. I looked at her wound, the culprit.

What the hell? Her blood was red again. Alice was a level six, and by then, it must have blackened. It must have.

I blinked my tears away, adamant not to show the boy how I felt for her. *Nobody* ought to know, especially not Cypress Cadler. I pulled her body into my arms, finally managing to look into her eyes.

I couldn't believe it. All her hard work was gone. Her eyes were blue again.

Part of me missed them being blue. I still remembered her looking at me with her original eyes, I thought. We were so young then, and that was over a century ago.

With a hand, I beckoned the boy closer. Hesitantly, he walked over, kneeling beside us.

"What happened?" He asked annoyingly, staying clear of the pool of blood gathering under my knees.

"I suspect Lamplight killed her," I noted feebly, glancing to the spear behind us. It was embarrassing. Thinking about him made me sick.

"Oh." I knew Cadler was familiar with Lamplight, yet not how familiar. I pulled Alice closer to my chest, lost in my own perplexion.

How had this happened? Guno was so weak. He rejected Dark time and time again. How come, then, had he still managed to strike her down?

I shook my head a few times, staring into her eyes. Something felt wrong. I was doing something wrong by being here, by carting Cypress around, by being *Dark* in the first place.

I met Cadler's eyes, furrowing my brow, yet I couldn't hold his gaze for long. My attention kept wandering back to Alice.

She gave up. *She gave in.*

Alice Walker had joined Light in death after a hundred years of hate.

I bit my lip and spoke.

"I've made a mistake."

Appendix i
Character Art

Guno

Rengas

Appendix ii
Terms and Definitions

Light Supporter	Someone with allegiance to Light. Everyone starts out with a Light allegiance, as Light's qualities are patience, honesty, temperance and kindness among others. Light supporters don't have any notable powers associated with Her unless they have practiced intensive worship or own a portal device.
Dark Supporter	Someone with allegiance to Dark. Dark's qualities are ambition, resilience, along with emotional and physical anguish. When practicing Dark qualities, you develop clear power as a token of His gratitude. Dark supporter ranks are divided into levels, where you gain a Dark pupil with each up until level seven. Dark eyes have a small pupil and a white iris with a thin black ring on the outside.
Beacon	The highest level of Light supporter. Beacons have met Light Herself and are decorated with skin marks as a denotation that they are a part of Her holy network. Since they are made of Her, beacons are known to perform miraculous feats.
Umbra	The highest level of Dark supporter. Umbras technically have seven pupils between both their eyes. However, the festering quality of Dark eyes makes them rot out at level seven. Though their eye cavities are empty, Umbras can still see as a

	result of them being part of, and made of, Dark Himself.
Afterglow	Where Light supporters go after death. The afterglow is comprised of a spiritual realm, but also a physical one where souls make up the fluid that powers portals.
Afterdull	Where Dark supporters go after death. Similarly to the afterglow, the Afterdull has a physical component in which souls are used as shadow fluid.
Portal Fluid	The physical manifestation of Light. Portal fluid is used to create portals as well as power Light weapons.
Shadow Fluid	The physical manifestation of Dark. Shadow fluid is used by Dark supporters to travel dimensions and retain increase their stamina.
Portal Device	An object that channels Light to open portals. Portal devices are not only obscenely expensive but require you to attune them to your soul in order to work. Portal devices can only be used by the person or people it was attuned to, but can be reattuned (e.g. a portal device that is passed down to a successor.)
Scarce Months	The coldest season in Dashan. At the end of the scarce months is the Scarcends Festival, in which villagers prepare for warmer weather and scare away Farlands beasts for the new year.
Standard Speech	The homogenized language and writing system used by dimensions familiar with portal and shadow travel.

Farlands	The empty, non-territorial regions of Dashan between villages. In the Farlands there is nothing protecting people from the desert creatures that live there.
Limber	The desert animal that Dashan is most famously known for, limbers grow to be roughly fifty feet tall and have equine features. They feed on sand-dwelling mammals and humanoids.
Fyrbex	A prey animal that defends itself by striking its hooves together to create sparks. These creatures can be eaten but are a hassle to farm raise due to the likelihood of them starting a fire.
Pygmy Beast	Sand-dwelling creatures with razor sharp teeth. They spend most of their time underground and only come up to hunt. Pygmy beasts travel in swarms.
Kevik	Dashan expletives.
Bright Saint Parkeyre	
Portal Traitor	

Made in the USA
Columbia, SC
20 October 2021